a time to live

novel by jim brogan

Equanimity Press
and

 **PUBLISHERS**   San Francisco

Published in the United States by
Equanimity Press and
GLB Publishers
P.O. Box 78212, San Francisco, CA 94107 USA

Cover by Curium Design

Publisher's Cataloging-in-Publication
(*Provided by Quality Books, Inc.*)

Brogan, Jim.
    A time to live: a novel / Jim Brogan.
    p.cm.
    ISBN: 1-879194-22-8

    1. Gay men--California--San Francisco--Fiction. 2. San Francisco (Calif.)--Fiction. I. Title.

PS3552.R628T56 1997   813'.54
                           QBI97-40211

First printing
10 9 8 7 6 5 4 3 2 1

ACKNOWLEDGEMENTS

I'm indebted to good friends Joel Dorius, Brian Smith, Terry Cavanaugh, Jeff Moran, and James Orlando for their inspiration.

I dedicate the book to Rob Olson, Michael Russell and Steve Colvin who were just as inspiring, but are no longer with us.

Thanks also to Janet Mattingly, Jasmin Clower, and Scott Littlefield for their insights; Joel Enos, Jim Welch, Dick Ludwig, Greg Marriner, Corinne Pettipas, Robert Drake, Norman Laurila, Brian Polk and Jack Post also helped out. Finally, thanks to Bill Warner for his top-notch editing.

"Heard anything from that retirement community? What was its name—St. Aidan's?" Brian bellowed out his question from Richard's kitchen, plunking down their take-out dinner on the kitchen table and mixing his cocktail so lickedy-split that Richard would not be tempted to get up from his couch.

"No, nothing at all." Brian quickly slipped back into the huge living room to hear his friend's answer, parking himself on the other couch, "his" couch, placed perpendicular to Richard's. "I'm very apprehensive about their decision, but I guess I have to wait another day or so. St. Aidan's Senior Residence—that's what it's called. I'm afraid they won't take me because of my back. I'd be up on the twentieth floor, the whole Bay Area shimmering beneath me." He propped himself on his elbows and shook his white mane from side to side, murmuring darkly. "But I must be able to get down to their dining room for every meal and they gave me a rigorous exam."

Richard rose and gazed out of his living room windows at the soothing blue mass of San Francisco Bay. It had been yet another sunny, almost warm winter's day, but ominous storm clouds had begun to darken the twilight. Even with the pronounced tendency of the glass to distort, Brian could not imagine either a more satisfying vista or Richard's living anywhere else. He was actively, if silently, rooting for St. Aidan's to reject him. For twenty years this retired classics professor had looked straight down on Alcatraz and Angel Island all the way east to Berkeley and north to San Pablo Bay. The flat was a treasure—immense rooms, low rent. But he was also aware of Richard's fears about a future when, his back worse, he might not be able to care for himself.

Despite unrelenting back problems, Richard, tall and thin, white hair swept back like a symphony conductor's, looked a full decade younger than his seventy-five years. His piercing blue eyes still sparkled with as much youthful curiosity as anxiety and pain, back pain which had been there since birth but then exacerbated early in the eighties by an automobile accident and an ill-advised operation.

Noticing the Siamese cat, Cleo, had fallen asleep on Brian's bright blue-and-green flannel shirt, he returned to his couch. "That's a beautiful shirt. Such bright colors. And I love your black T-shirt. It brings out the green in your eyes. And today your face seems to have a burnished, outdoor quality—so healthy-looking."

Brian's first impulse on receiving compliments was to deny the adequacy of his looks in regard to operating in the gay sub-culture. A generation younger than Richard, Brian had shaggy, graying hair which often crept over his collar. Since it was still thick and plentiful, he liked to show off its profusion rather than keep it super-neat and short as was the current fashion. He knew that his low forehead and prominent cheekbones often led people to inquire whether or not he had any Native American blood. He generally liked the way he looked, especially when he burst out into a smile which was not automatic by any means. His lips, whose latent sensuality emerged when he laughed, looked pinched and tight when he was worried, as he was at this moment about Richard's fate.

"If I have to stay here I fear I'll slip in the bathtub and not be discovered for days." Brian sat up abruptly, tempted to interrupt. Certainly Richard knew that Brian's daily call would eliminate such a horrible contingency, although there was always the possibility of an accident. "And how much longer will I be able to climb up all these stairs?" Richard rolled over and slowly lifted himself off the couch, eager as a young child to check out their dinner. Brian nodded in agreement, not knowing the answer but aware that he, himself, was still winded from having foolishly bolted up all fifty steps to the third-floor flat.

As Richard shuffled off to the kitchen, Brian felt an urge to argue for the status quo, but Richard, hard to interrupt once he had launched himself verbally, anticipated Brian's doubts by voicing his own when he returned. "But if I go to St. Aidan's will I like the people?" Brian remained quiet as Richard's forehead crinkled up. Richard's generous nature would draw new friends to him anywhere, but it was more a question of how many of his close friends—including himself—would get over to Oakland all that often. Brian hadn't been across the Bay Bridge for a couple of years, unlike the late sixties when Berkeley, especially, had been a regular part of his life. The very thought of either driving over the Bay Bridge or taking BART to Oakland struck him as unappealing, a sign that he had become voluntarily locked into his city-insulated life style.

"And then I'm afraid of losing what's left of my sexuality at St. Aidan's. It's almost eighty per cent women. Will I be reduced to attacking the janitors?" Brian knew what was coming as Richard paused, with a slightly stricken look. "Will anyone have porn? Wouldn't it be embarrassing if, while moving in, the tape of *Big, Bigger, Biggest* should accidentally fall onto the floor of the lobby?"

"Don't worry. I can always smuggle in some tapes for you." Laughing at Richard's bawdy paranoia, Brian was far from reassured by his own words. Richard returned to the living room and stared out at the Bay, seemingly not having heard Brian. "I get so wrought up just thinking about it."

"Just take it as it comes." Brian joined Richard in becoming mesmerized by the view. There was nothing more to be said so he changed the subject. "Had another of those interminable faculty meetings—some nasty wrangling about budget cuts and all." He pulled off his running shoes and, following Richard's lead, stretched out on "his" couch. This arrangement brought their heads within a couple feet of each other, perfect for easy conversing. Both the couches were protected from the ravages of Cleo's claws by white sheets which constantly slipped down, giving the place a down-home touch. Huge, yet intimate, the room struck Brian as anything but cavernous because of Richard's huge Steinway grand which doubled as a desk, piled as it was with books, magazines, tapes and heaps of miscellaneous personal papers.   Glass doors encased the room from an equally magnificent entryway which trapped the heat unmercifully on sunny days, providing a perfect greenhouse for Richard's monstrous potted cacti.

Even from his prone position on his couch, Richard's eyes lit up brightly at the mention of school, as if some long dormant fire had been stirred up enough to ignite once more.   "Oh, I remember all those meetings, hundreds of meetings, and I'd say to myself, oh, this is important, this is good talk and then, afterwards, I'd run off to somewhere, maybe a restroom, to cruise. Now *that* was infinitely more powerful, infinitely more meaningful."

Listening to the rich nasal of Richard's voice, Brian looked down at the cup holding his drink, the word "BRAVO" (and "BRAVA," too) emblazoned all over it, a gift from one of Richard's former students who had taken note of Richard's frequent use of the expression in class.   Brian found the expression just as appropriate now in the context of Richard's retirement because of his love of opera.

"We'd better eat. My back's beginning to act up—earlier and earlier each day."   Richard insisted on getting up to help serve the dinner, curious to check out the fine continental food from their local favorite, the Bistro Beaujolais, atop Russian Hill, where the Hyde Street cable car tracks crossed Union Street. Raised by an autocratic mother who demanded he become a perfect host, a woman who insisted he display a servility tantamount to "oriental deference," as he called it, Richard still felt the compulsion to respond to her training even while his poor back was insisting he stay put for his own good. After being shooed away from the kitchen by Brian, he still wandered aimlessly about the living room, and then pointed to the mantelpiece just as Brian finished setting up their dinner on the table which overlooked the Bay. "Take a look at this."

Brian got up to check out a modest retirement shingle engraved "Professor Emeritus of Education." "Just like them. So tardy and so messed up—not even the right department—I wouldn't dream of calling them up. I'll just leave it right there." Brian loved the touch of bitter derisiveness which seeped into Richard's tone as well as his rich sense of the absurd, his mastery of irony. "A classics professor in California! How absurd. All day long I've regressed to bewailing the futility of ever having tried to illuminate classical civilizations to students out here. But then I caught myself—I'm tensing up as usual because of. . ."

"George Youngblood's visit, I bet."

"I'm afraid so." Every year Richard's back worsened when his former colleague from the east coast ventured out for his regular visit. Virtually ignoring his food, Richard put down his fork and stared out in the direction of a huge cruise ship berthed at Pier 35. "He performs non-stop, you know, very theatrical, very brilliant, but very nervous. I like being stimulated but when he goes on a bit too much, I begin to feel we're in a rural outpost here, barely mustering a half-way adequate intellectual life."

Exasperated as usual by this constant theme of the intellectual inadequacy of the Bay Area, Brian put down his own fork to swallow a huge gulp of his cocktail. In the ensuing silence he started to list to himself other of Richard's traits which sometimes drove him crazy—his compulsive chatter, a need to control, no doubt, when he was nervous. And his dogged willingness to subject his back to lengthy waits for cabs to get useless advice from various specialists while he steadfastly refused, most of the time, to be chauffeured down to North Beach, to Greco's, say, for a cappuccino, for a quick hit of the outside world which he always enjoyed and appreciated so much afterwards.

Richard's grandfather clock struck six, jarring Brian out of his reverie. "Richard," he pled, "it's like that everywhere in academia. George admires you immensely but there's that element of his insecurity; he cannot stop himself from feeling competitive. Imagine surviving in that rat race. You know he's his own worst critic."

"Yes, you're right," Richard finally picked up his fork. "His depressions, his drinking, his writing blocks."

"C'mon now—it's almost as bad as that here, too." Brian's eyes switched their focus from the cruise ship to Richard's face, looking for a quick exchange of knowing glances—and got it. Then he relaxed and smiled, eager to make his point and enjoy the drama of catching Richard up on events at school. "Take David Grossman's memorial service out at school last week. Each speaker listed his totally intimidating accomplishments: five books, scores of articles, lecture notes so detailed and polished that they could be published intact as literary criticism."

Richard perked up, eager to leave his own plight for a foray into someone else's. "He's the one who died of AIDS, isn't he?" He remained curious about all matters pertaining to the faculty.

"Yeah, but what surprised me was the honesty of the dean's remarks." Brian stood up dramatically, attempting to mimic the dean's folksy, hearty style. "'David Grossman could never be satisfied with himself. He never had enough time, never would, no matter how long he lived.'" Brian sat back down. "I could have hugged her for saying that, trying to save us, maybe, from our collective self-destructiveness."

Richard remained morose, just picking at his food. "It's just that I'm so easily overwhelmed when someone rolls out his accomplishments. It's the very swiftness with which George speaks, the mental efficiency, like a bristling armadillo. That intellect emasculates me, leaves me shrivelled up. Oh, the intellect can lead to a terribly fierce isolation, such a separating force."

"But a binding force, too." Exasperated once again, Brian reached for his daypack on the floor beside his running shoes. "Look what I've got you." Brian tried to imitate Santa opening a big sack of toys. "Here's the CD of Kissin doing the Chopin Mazurkas, and that Harold Bloom book you wanted, the one where he talks about Mormonism, and here's that Bette Davis tape of *The Letter*." Brian continued to yank out the contents of his pack. "Let's not forget *Okoge*, that gay Japanese movie you wanted to check out, and look, here's a videotape of Glenn Gould, volume five of the series—remember it was George who brought you the third on last year's visit."

Knowing Richard could have no negative retort to this barrage of goodies, Brian slipped off to the kitchen, returning with a piece of cheese cake cut into two tiny slivers and two cups of Good Earth tea. The treat immediately lightened their mood. Dessert over, they both rose simultaneously, as if on cue. It was time for Richard to return to his inner sanctum, to lie on ice in his bedroom. It had taken years, but finally he had reached the point when, his mother's training notwithstanding, Richard knew he should not linger a second longer than necessary in polite conversation.

On the way out Brian noticed a pile of mail thrown over the table in the entryway. "Richard, have you seen all this mail out here?"

"I have not. I forgot about it when I got involved talking with that charming delivery boy from Home Drugs." A quick look on Brian's part revealed nothing but junk mail. But when Richard sorted through it, he declared, "The fateful missive has arrived." Once Richard had ripped it open, Brian saw it was a very brief message. "That's it. They rejected me. Just as I thought." Returning to the same dire tones as before, Richard drew a deep breath, threw his shoulders back, and attempted to send Brian off with a forced heartiness. "Well, cheers, Brian. We'll talk tomorrow."

But something important has been settled, Brian decided, as the two men hugged good-bye. They would remain neighbors; they would remain close. Relieved, on his way out a second time, Brian couldn't resist trying to pet Cleo, Richard's bosom companion, the ultra-feisty Siamese whose razor-sharp claws had already drawn more than a few drops of Brian's blood. When

Cleo, loyal only to Richard, lashed out and almost got him again, Brian exclaimed, "No Oriental deference there. You must be suppressing like anything today, Richard." Brian loved to tease Richard about how Cleo represented his id—it was she who got to act out every aggressive, self-indulgent, barbaric, primeval urge Richard had ever repressed.

"Cheers, Brian. Give my best to that dear, dear man, Will."

This was not the time to discuss Will's upcoming HIV test. Brian had trained himself to keep good-byes with Richard short and sweet. Instead, he said nothing, just waved back while descending the long staircase, using his own key to double-bolt the door. So Richard would be "stuck" in his flat for as long as he could take care of himself, maybe longer, with visiting nurses or whatever. Funny, how he had never before appreciated how the status quo so benefited their friendship.

Once outside, he decided to go home via Jones Street, amusing himself along the super-steep descent with fantasies of meter maids on their three-wheeled Cushmans losing their brakes while trying to issue $35 residential parking violations and plummeting all the way down to Fisherman's Wharf.

2

"Welcome to Jockstrap Night at the Endup. It's time for our world-famous Beautiful Buns Contest. Will the aspirants for this evening please come to the bar and sign in."

The slick, well-modulated voice over the public address system grated on an antsy Brian who hadn't been to this place in years. "You gonna do it?" He felt it to be almost a duty to encourage Will. "Are you a true ass-pirant?"

"I think so. I'm nervous, but excited, too." Will slugged down the rest of his beer, leaving traces of foam in his mustache. "Quite a few friends have made a point of telling me I have a real nice ass. It even made the cover of *The Advocate* in 1983." Will's nervous laugh grated on Brian who gave him a quick peck on the cheek.

"Good luck."

Even before Will disappeared into the crowd pressed up against the massive circular bar, Brian found himself feeling awkward standing alone on the spacious dance floor, observing his reflection on the mirrored walls, so he beat a retreat to the huge patio. Once outside he spotted a staircase which led him up to a deck from which he could study the infra-structure of the neighboring freeway. It was good to be outside away from the din. The club-of-the-day fad (Will mentioned sometimes going here to Club Uranus on Sunday night) hadn't been able to tempt him back. When he told his housemate, Liz, earlier in the day that he might go to the Endup, she just laughed. "What cute names you boys think up for your hangouts."

Brian checked his watch. Just about ten. He calculated they should at least have some time to themselves back at Will's place before Nevin got back. This wasn't so terrible, after all. Parking had been easy. And he wouldn't mind being the doorman tonight. There was a $4 cover charge, a tab not collected if you were in your twenties or willing to open up your pants to reveal a jockstrap, something Brian hadn't worn since ordering one for possible beach use years ago from the International Male catalog. It was a $5 purchase which had guaranteed him a lifetime of glossy catalogs of well-buffed, male bimbos.

This February had been nothing but a series of storms, although the most recent one had just cleared out. As a chill, damp breeze slapped his face and watered his eyes, he mused how easily he had become involved with Will six years ago. He supposed that Will's living with Nevin acted as a kind of reassurance for him in the sense that the limited nature of their relationship guaranteed he wouldn't have to endure another full-scale tragedy as when Marco had left him. It had been just after Brian had purchased his house on Telegraph Hill for the sole purpose of its becoming their love nest. But Will, unlike Marco, knew who he was and what he wanted. He had been the one to pursue Brian, all the while confessing fears of clinging to him like a puppy dog. Attracted primarily to older men, he was not put off then by Brian's being past forty or by his salt-and-pepper hair. From time to time over the years they had discussed elevating the part-time status of their relationship, but it had never been more than theoretical—Will hung on to his rocky relationship with Nevin with a dogged loyalty which Brian could only admire. In any case after absorbing the sudden shock of Marco's fleeing to Chicago with his former lover, maybe this kind of relationship hadn't been such a bad idea—it had been pretty much all pleasure and no pain.

Assaulted by the inevitable disco that signalled the start of the contest, Brian zipped down the stairs to get a good view of the proceedings. The emcee introduced the five contestants, all of whom had mustaches and all of whom, Brian guessed, were in their early to mid-thirties, although he found Will to be easily the most boyish, still exuding sex appeal, despite his receding hairline. Three inches shorter than Brian, about five foot ten or so, a Norwegian from Minnesota with a solid, natural build, dirty blond hair and a cute face which neither a beard nor mustache could ruin for Brian (Will periodically insisted on trying one or the other), Will obviously was relishing his moment in the spotlight, even waving to a fan, an elderly gentleman in a sports jacket and tie who had the good sense, in Brian's eyes, to take a fancy to him.

Slowly, simultaneously, each contestant stripped off an item of clothing while grinding to the hateful music. As Will stripped down to his jock with gusto and then wiggled his smooth, creamy ass from side to side, rotating every few seconds so that everyone could have a good view, Brian got smacked by an unwanted thought about Will's motive for coming here tonight. Was he so sure he'd test positive that he wanted to display himself publicly one final time before that fine, youthful body began deteriorating?

The music climaxed, the contestants took a final bow and Will appeared beside Brian a couple of minutes later. "You were great. I bet you win."

"Let's go. I'm high. No point in hanging around—they have my address if I've won anything." As they shoved their way through the crowd, several men shouted out rave reviews.

Will was glowing as they got into Brian's Toyota, but his mood dampened as they approached his Bernal Heights flat and his thoughts turned to Nevin. "He never pays any attention to me. Things are getting worse. And he completely refuses to talk about what he's feeling."

Brian grimaced at having to play, once again, Will's confidante, but he nevertheless persevered in a upbeat mode. "What about all those lovey-dovey notes you guys write each other on that little blackboard outside your bathroom?"

"But we rarely *see* each other." The whine in Will's voice rankled Brian. "He stays out drinking every night after he gets off work. He even admitted to me last week, 'It's the life-style I've always hated, but now I just sit there projecting attitude, doing all those things queers do which I used to hate.'"

Brian laughed, then lapsed into silence, wishing they could go back to his place and spend the whole night together, but that was only allowed when Nevin was out of town. Theoretically, they could have gone there tonight and not had to worry about Nevin's return, but tomorrow was a work day for both of them and Brian hated the moment when, sated with each other, dozing in each other's arms, he had to get up and drive Will all the way back to Bernal Heights. Only a sadist would suggest Will take Muni home at midnight.

Knowing this mode of thinking would only exasperate him, Brian returned to his role of comforter. "So Nevin's still in his 'blue-collar' phase, hanging out and drinking with the guys at work after driving a van to and from the airport?"

"It's more like one particular guy."

"Oh?"

Once inside Will's long and narrow flat, Brian peeked into the master bedroom, off limits to Will and him, although when Nevin was away, they had occasionally defiled the sanctity of the marriage bed. When they had first begun their affair, they had been like horny teenagers, making out in the car or in the bushes on Bernal Heights or savoring a private room during the final days of Finnilla's Finnish Sauna on Market Street. More recently they had made love on the tiny couch in the small, cluttered living room. (Will's tendency to accumulate stuff drove both Nevin and Brian crazy.) Teaching computer literacy to elementary school kids in the city, Will had amassed a mountain of resource material.

As Brian moved aside some junk just so he could sit down on the couch, he admitted to himself, once again, that, despite a monstrous problem with dyslexia, Will had been amazingly successful at breaking into the system. Soon after they first met, Brian had had a hunch about Will's problem which was immediately confirmed by the testing center at school. Finally, Will had been freed from the stigma of his step-father and teachers calling him lazy and stupid because he couldn't write a complete sentence, read more than ten pages an hour or spell as well as an eight-year-old.

Having made them drinks in the kitchen, Will sat down next to Brian and started giving him sweet little kisses. But when Brian began to embrace him, Will broke the spell. "I have a report due first thing in the morning—I need you to proofread it on the computer," his blue eyes pleading with sincerity. He always asks at the worst time, Brian fumed to himself, but he got up quickly, knowing Nevin could be back at any moment. He reversed himself on his earlier thought that this relationship had been mostly pleasure. More than likely he was apt to find himself with a Will who was dog-tired, drained, nervous, upset about some crisis at work, worried about some upcoming pressure, depressed about Nevin, bummed about one of his former lovers with AIDS—or any combination of the above.

But Brian performed the chore cheerfully, remembering how much easier this sort of thing—and the nuts and bolts of life in general—was for him than for Will. Despite it all, he would have put up with far worse. Will had given him so much love—more than anyone else, really. And afterwards, with Will's cat Ingrid, a Russian Blue, purring above them, they did make love, the usual safe sex rituals with lots of hugging, kissing and caressing with which Brian had no quarrel. He had given up anal sex long ago, back in the early seventies, a decision which was then a matter of personal inclination, but one which had probably saved his life.

Just as Brian was rising from the couch, a key turned in the front door. In strolled Nevin, a handsome guy, still in his twenties, taller than Will, with short dark-brown hair and a perennial five o'clock shadow. Speaking with a sardonic drawl, drenching every word in irony, Nevin greeted Brian casually as usual. "Nothing but cretins out there tonight." Brian laughed, knowing he did not need to stay to make polite conversation. He simply said good-bye and left.

As he drove home he realized that the evening had left him depressed. Although the bar action should have been enjoyable, he had felt left out, outdistanced by the youth surrounding him.

It was a feeling that was becoming more frequent for him these days, he admitted to himself.

3

Several days later, Brian rang the bell of Daniel's flat in Noe Valley with considerable trepidation. When they had first met at the AIDS walk a couple of weeks ago, they had retired here for a beer. Tonight, while driving past the huge, beautiful palms that mark the central island of Dolores Street, Brian felt quietly hopeful that they still might become good friends, no mean feat in the hectic nineties. Maybe Daniel would even become the equivalent of the bright, intellectually–stimulating younger colleague in the humanities who had never come along at the university.

And Daniel did welcome him warmly at the door. Once inside, Brian had made an immediate beeline for Daniel's bed where he flopped down and began chatting amicably while the harried Daniel returned to his computer. Swiveling his chair around to face Brian directly for a few minutes, his legs provocatively curled about those of the chair, Daniel simulated having sex with the chair, then paused for only a moment before popping up and jumping about the room, comically frantic.

"Have I told you about my breaking up with Allen, the Chinese weight-lifter?" Daniel's sweet smile projected an adolescent charm even while his bedroom eyes suggested a much less innocent approach to the game of love. "It took a year of flirting around the gym before he'd consent to a date."

Daniel's luxuriant, dark brown hair, beginning to creep down his neck, was enticing Brian to become reacquainted with that soft texture and sweet smell which had appealed to him so much when they had hugged good-bye on that first meeting. Yet the businessman's detached, mildly amused, worldly-wise tone of voice hinted at another, somewhat darker side. "Before we knew it, though, we'd slipped into a boring routine—eating out every Friday, returning to this very room for sex, I fucking him."

Daniel might be an actor, with that Roman nose and precise

manner of declamation. "Not that Allen isn't still appealing," he
backtracked toward his bed, "with those slightly haughty, regal
Asian lips, not to mention a belly that defines human perfection."
Instead of joining Brian on the bed, Daniel suddenly turned
around, as if conscience-stricken for having skipped out on his
chore at the Mac. "I *was* depressed yesterday, Saturday, the day
after our usual ritual, which struck me as not such an empty one
when the ritual fuck was no longer available. And Myron's foul-
smelling dinner didn't help, either." Daniel wheeled around on
his chair to face Brian again. "My roommate, Myron? You met
him last time, didn't you?" Brian nodded his assent. "I'm being
exploited for a mere $60,000 a year at Thunder-ware so I need a
flatmate to survive in this town—can you believe it?"

As Daniel's words rang out, clipped and precise, Brian
concluded he liked his voice, his wit, his whole take on things,
but he still had to challenge Daniel's disclosure. "Can't live
alone? C'mon, you make more than I do." Daniel hesitated,
then said nothing, a response Brian much preferred to the possible
alternative of having to listen to him expound on how he had
only temporarily overextended himself financially through his
various investments. He already knew from only a single
previous visit that Daniel was addicted to state-of-my-finances
raps. Yes, yet another millionaire in the making whose cash flow
had dwindled to a predictable trickle.

Relieved that, this time around, Daniel had chosen to pass on
the option of enumerating his financial concerns, Brian smiled
and relaxed, luxuriously stretching out his long limbs on the bed.
He stared at the handsome Victorian ceiling, then shifted his gaze
down to the highly-shellacked sliding doors which closed off, for
now, the adjacent room. When Daniel's attention predictably
returned to the console after only a few more moments of chatter,
Brian jumped off the bed and slid over the slippery hardwood
floor in his socks to the large front windows that peered out
directly onto narrow, tree-lined Chattanooga Street. It was a treat
to check out life in the dozen or so flats across the quiet, speed-

bumped alley. Most of these Noe Valley burghers used neither shades nor curtains to hide themselves from inquiring minds like Brian's. For a moment he wondered if he might be happier living out here. He liked this "if you show me yours I'll show you mine" attitude so different from the old Italian and Chinese ladies of North Beach who revealed only a warts-and-all nose peeking out from behind very thick curtains, their suspicious glares condemning the likes of Brian to disreputable marginality without due process.

"I've been so busy marketing this new product for Thunder-ware, writing and producing the brochures," Daniel wheeled about once more, this time yanking off his green sweatshirt and flipping it on top of the bed next to Brian. "And I still have to dream up a killer name in the next couple of days. You'd be amazed at how many have already been grabbed by our competition—Qwik-Scan, Easy-Scan, Apollo-Scan, Scan-Man. Maybe it'll be Lightning-Scan. At least I got a trip to Amsterdam out of it last month. Managed to sell about five hundred of these contraptions."

Daniel turned back to his usual roost and began typing commands so swiftly that Brian felt an utter novice to this techno-age. Having had his fill of the neighbors' lives, Brian returned to the bed, suddenly weary. "One last entry on my hard, hard disc and we can be on our sleepy way," Daniel reassured him.

Granting Daniel high marks for his immediate sensitivity to his depleted state, Brian let down his guard, allowing himself to anticipate their snuggling drowsily together. It had been Daniel who suggested that he sleep over, a sensible option since his host had no free time to see him until 10:30 PM. However, a moment later the phone rang. Daniel answered it immediately, launching into a long explanation to his sister about how he was just now completing her request for something or other. "Why don't you just leave it up to me? I'll put it on a floppy disc and drop it by sometime tomorrow." As they talked, Brian, losing patience, pulled off his T-shirt, yanked down his 501's, and burrowed under the comforter.

Daniel finally hung up and stripped down to his Calvin Klein briefs, flipping his clothes to the floor. He climbed into bed after slurping down the remainder of his nightcap. The two men lay on their backs, pressing together at the shoulders and hips. "So with no Allen on Friday, I found myself heartsick and lonely on Saturday night." Appeased and comforted by their physical contact, Brian found himself willing to be intrigued by Daniel's narrative. "I tried doing laundry, but nothing much was happening at the Wash 'n Fold. Fifty cents a pound and my, how those pounds add up, honey. So after lugging it home, I decided to go out for a drink, to the Stud, in fact. Why be a lonely, miserable gay man on a Saturday night in San Francisco?"

Brian winced at the thought of going to the Stud alone, at his age, on a Saturday night. All those poised, attractive young guys—was it worth all the energy, mustering one's courage just to start another futile conversation?

"On the way over I lingered at a stop sign, wondering if I should park and grab a piece of pizza at a little local place on that corner, when this well-dressed black guy rapped on my windshield. We gave each other the once-over, then he just got in on the passenger side, which I had left conveniently unlocked. When he said he was broke and asked me for money I got uneasy—I wanted him out! I pulled out my wallet, opened it up in front of him and took out all my cash, eight dollars." Sitting up and staring straight into Brian's eyes, Daniel paused, perhaps wanting deliberately to heighten the fear creeping into Brian's stomach. "He accepted my money, then offered to sell me some speed. I respectfully declined. He finally left when I gave him my phone number. The irony of it! I gave this guy my actual number even though I'm the typical gay man who's used to never, well, hardly ever, giving out his real number in a bar."

Brian found himself cringing, but he refused the temptation to be parental and tell Daniel how foolhardy he had been.

Not needing a verbal response, Daniel withdrew his intense stare and resumed the story of his weekend. "At the Stud I picked up this intriguing young guy with earrings and a nose ring. As soon as we got back here he asked me if I'm into meth! Weird coincidence. He didn't seem too upset when I said no. I was hoping we could forget that little quirk for at least this one night. Then, just after we had crawled into the very bed in which we're now ensconced, just as I was about to put my arm around him, there was this funny smell. I looked up to see flames leaping up in front of the bed."

"I thought there was a kind of acrid smell in here tonight. This bed was on fire?"

Daniel sat up abruptly. "A towel got too close to one of my romantic candles" Daniel had added a subdued exclamation point to his tone of voice by raising both eyebrows.

"So what did you do?"

"I jumped out of bed, put my shoes on my hands and stomped, stomped, stomped until it was all out. And this guy, Joe, he just stared at me, didn't even crack a smile, even though I must have looked ridiculous."

"Danger seemed to be in the air," Brian ventured.

"There's more." Daniel remained sitting up, peering right down at Brian's face. "Just as we were getting sexual, he let me know he wanted to lick my asshole. A fine old practice, but a moral dilemma. I've had the shots so I'm clean, immune to hepatitis, so why not? So he rimmed me and it felt great. After that, though, the sex just wasn't very good and the guy showed no signs whatsoever of having a distinct personality. Promising to call him next weekend, I dumped him on Market Street at nine this morning, minutes after we had gotten out of bed."

Amused, Brian still could not stop himself from labelling Daniel as a typical desperate-for-sex, no-longer-very-young gay male (not something out of the realm of his own experience by any means).

On his first visit here he had met a bitchy, manipulative man of about thirty, roughly Daniel's own age. Daniel had confessed to having been fuck-buddies with this unappealing mess for over two years. "He keeps pursuing me. I like that, I guess I need that," Daniel had explained. Not me, Brian had thought to himself. Who needs all that hassle just for sex?

Daniel rolled over on his bed, turning away from Brian, still keeping contact by shoving his buttocks into Brian's crotch. Brian had to admit to himself that he loved the feel of Daniel's skin which still retained the resilience of a slightly chubby Polynesian youth. The minutes ticked away, neither of them in a hurry to fall asleep. Brian allowed himself to stroke Daniel's body, but only to the point of his own incipient arousal which triggered his internal alarm. Okay, he knew he was not in a sexual situation. Why waste energy if this new friend obviously desired younger lovers and only just settled for contemporaries? And that was okay with Brian, really it was.

Daniel was not to be another Will, although, if pressed, Brian had to admit he might already be thinking ahead to life after Will's demise. Block those thoughts. A warm friendship—that was what he wanted from Daniel and he just might be able to get it. Brian *was* attracted, but he prided himself on not hassling people. He could read the cues and Daniel was just not interested in him as a prospective lover. But could that change with time? Despite himself, knowing it was a kind of masochism, he continued hoping. Context is all, context determines appropriate behavior.

Daniel had started playing with himself because he needed to let off steam tonight after his hectic day and that, too, was just fine with Brian. He hadn't been around this long for nothing. At fifty, if nothing else, he knew how *not* to cross boundaries.

"I like to touch people. I'm into giving massages. Sometimes I wonder if body work might not be my true calling." This time Brian feigned sleep as a way to avoid responding verbally. He, too, liked to touch people. Feeling Daniel's moving body against his, he rolled over on his side, pushed his own backside against Daniel, and followed suit, chiding himself for putting up with the frustration involved. This was, at least, a kind of bonding. He delayed his climax until he heard Daniel's deep breathing and then instantly he dropped off into a deep sleep.

4

"Goddam it." Brian pulled his hand out of the warm, soapy dishwater and let soothing cold water from the tap run over his cut finger for a minute or so. Deep, but not serious enough to show Liz—she was out anyway, at least her light wasn't on. He wished he had not bothered with the damn dishes, especially in his frazzled state after his Monday night class, but the chaos of his place was starting to get to him and he had to get up and teach early tomorrow. He slowly drained the hot, soapy water, exposing the shards of broken glass which had been lying there lurking like piranha. If he had just settled in with his nightcap and slowed down a bit at first, it never would have happened. All these years of living alone, he still hadn't mastered the Zen of it. But he wouldn't have it any other way, having finally surrendered to the fact that finding a "longtime companion" had now become a hopelessly long shot. Amazing that back in college and even grad school he had liked the constant company of roommates and didn't seem to need much privacy, even sharing a bedroom much of the time. No doubt his current need for so much privacy would complicate the "period of adjustment" for any new romance.

Band-aid in place, he collapsed on his sofa with his usual tequila and exotic juice, papaya tonight for his nervous stomach. It was quiet on the second floor of his Telegraph Hill house, set back so far from the rest of Union Street. Surrounded by bookcases, bolted to the wall, of course, in case of the next "big one," he promised himself he would pick up the dozen or so books lying on the floor around him. *New Yorkers*, *Christopher Streets*, and even a couple of *Steams* were also strewn about. When he snapped on his overhead reading light, the paintings (they were Timothy's, his colleague and friend in the art department) receded into the background. Over in the alcove, facing south towards the Transamerica Pyramid, his huge desk, freshly arranged this morning, held the stacks of books he would throw in his pack for school tomorrow.

Mulling over the day, he pictured this morning's breakfast with Daniel at Joe's, the great Noe Valley hangout on Church Street, at the end of the J-car line. Breakfast was a great social occasion, so short and sweet. Pumped up on syrup-doused pancakes and coffee, he had returned home to begin easing himself into the work week with the usual Monday morning rituals—paying bills, putting away the laundry, reviewing material for his night class. Nice of Daniel, really, to be open to their sleeping together; there's such a thing as skin hunger, after all. Brian liked his quick mind, he liked *him*. He hoped they'd click. They had made plans for the opera, *Il Trovatore*, later in the month.

Funny, Daniel reminded him a little of Marco. At the thought of Marco, all the usual garbage rushed back in: their four years as boyfriends, their plans to move into this house together (he never would have bought it otherwise), Marco's visit to his family in Chicago, from which he never returned, the subsequent news that he had found a good-paying corporate job there and had settled in with his previous lover from Northwestern. Those guys were still together, too, a fact which initially galled Brian.

But tempus had fugited for Brian. Those damn high-tech lighting fixtures in Daniel's bathroom this morning, lots of gray and white showed up in his beard—just a day's growth, too. (Generally he thought he looked okay for fifty in his own soft, forgiving bathroom lighting, but then he always missed places shaving, only to be shocked back into reality by those even harsher fluorescent fixtures in the bathrooms at school.) If he went two days without shaving, he looked like a street-person, a bum, a complete negative contrast to the sexy young models or baseball players who deliberately showed off a few days of enticing growth. Oh, that insidious, ever-creeping hoariness taking over his sideburns, descending even lower through the light fuzz on his chest. And his silhouette wasn't so sleek any more, either.

He sipped on his drink and pictured Gino, the seventy-two year old weight-lifter who had been a fellow volunteer at the Food Bank and had recently taken to auditing his classes. Must try to heed his advice. "You're a good teacher, but you frown, you scowl. Look at these lines above my nose, along my forehead. Relax, smile more—or else you'll have lines just like me."

The phone rang, Will confirming their usual Wednesday night date, maybe at Elisa's. Nevin was threatening to leave—yet again. Brian put down the receiver and guzzled down the remainder of his drink, wondering about Will's fate. All those transfusions in 1982 when he got knifed—it was reason enough to be positive. With Nevin out of the picture, they might be able to live together, but it might be more like Brian nursing him. Of course he would do it, without hesitation—he'd never let Will down.

It was an unseasonably warm night. Another sub-tropical storm had stalled. No rain yet, but the warm, southerly breeze fluttered the loose papers on his desk. Succumbing to a reverie of all the lonely summers of his youth, he kicked himself for not having avoided those boring jobs, commuting from his parents' place until he had graduated from college. Couldn't he have found a way to go to Europe or at least worked at a camp or resort up at Cape Cod or Vermont or something? Enough. He put down his empty glass, slipped on his jacket and headed out the door. At least he had made it here, to San Francisco, by his mid-twenties.

His next ritual, his constitutional to North Beach, jumping as usual, even on a Monday night. Mario's was crowded—he loved that place in late mornings—Mario's Bohemian Cigar Shop—best foccaccia sandwiches anywhere. The Savoy Tivoli had a sprightly crowd. Circling back, he picked up a bottle of Absolut Citron on sale, as always, at Coit Liquors. And then he trudged—he used to run—back up Union Street, noting that depression had started seeping into him. Stop it, he chided himself. You're going to be a curmudgeon. People are sick, people are dying, you have no reason to be grumpy. But another voice in him snapped back—*Fuck you.*

Depressed and grumpy, he allowed himself the rarity of a second drink upon his return. After all he was now in his decompression chamber after that three-hour class earlier tonight. He took a deep breath; the booze was kicking in. He threw back his arms and indulged in a long stretch. Fresh, eager-to-learn faces awaited him tomorrow. Afterwards, back home, he would feed the parrots and shuck the rest of that crate of peas he had picked up in Half Moon Bay, nibbling on the smallest, sweetest ones as he watched the tape of the next obscure Bette Davis film for Richard. And he'd also give him that new CD by Kissin, this time playing Schubert. How could that beautiful young genius, so protected from the world, know so much of pain, of sadness, of ecstasy? Brian put on the CD and lay down on his bed, feeling better. In spite of all his unsatisfied longings, there were so many new gay books to read, CD's to explore, films to check out—how lucky to be able to share them all with Richard. Life according to his personal whims. A quiet euphoria seeped through him as he lost himself in the beautiful music.

He woke up at 2 AM, took a pee, made sure the alarm was set and the door double-bolted, finessed brushing his teeth until morning, shut out the lights and passed out once again.

5

Five minutes after Brian arrived at the parking lot at Waddell Creek Beach, Robin's Datsun pulled in right between Brian's Toyota and a huge surfer van loaded with adolescents pulling on their wetsuits. Unfortunately, his car blocked the view of two of them momentarily poised in their naked glory. A good start–both of them right on time, although Brian wouldn't have minded, in this case, a bit of tardiness on Robin's part, at least until the surfers had finished suiting up.

"What a bummer. Fog." Robin shivered in the morning chill after he slid out of his car.

"The surfers love it. There's no wind to chop up the swell. Besides, where we're going, up in the mountains, it'll be sunny. Whose car first?"

"Let's take mine. I'll want to rest after our big hike. Throw your pack in the back seat." Brian locked his car and walked over to give Robin a timid hug.

They zipped down Route 1 through the little town of Davenport with its cement factory and tiny pastel shacks housing the Mexican laborers. Brian recalled to himself another era, the seventies, when he dubbed it The Heavenly City of Davenport because his heart would leap up when he beheld that huge smokestack in the sky, the landmark heralding his imminent arrival at his favorite nude beach. In those days, it sparkled with an unpredictable sensuality. "Maybe we could rest at one of these nude beaches along here after our hike," Brian suggested. "That is, if we have time, I mean."

"I haven't been to a nude beach for a long time. I need to think about it." Robin's admission was no surprise. "Let's see how I feel then." The younger man's prim response rankled Brian.

Looking over at Robin, Brian found himself still attracted to his dark swarthy beauty, a legacy of his Portuguese mother. His straight, jet-black hair tumbled down to his neck. In the last couple of years, he had taken to sweeping his hair back, forsaking the All-American boy image for a gypsy look, complete with a couple of gold earrings—very appealing. "How does your mom like those earrings?"

"My mom's still the same—at least she's not an alcoholic like all the men in the family. But, yes, she hates them, the earrings that is, because she's still ruled by appearances. Trying to be the perfect fifties' housewife, she'd stay up until three in the morning ironing our Sunday best so we'd look like little doll-kids at mass. And she *was* perfect too, that is until she had her big nervous breakdown. She got over that, but she never let me forget how much she disapproved of my dancing."

Although he danced much less often these days, Robin had retained his graceful, yet solid body. The huge biceps from his youthful weight-lifting no longer incongruously bulged. Brian had found them so out of character for this gentle, at times childlike, young man with the sweet dark eyes who was now approaching thirty.

"The last time I went to a nude beach, a couple of years ago at Devil's Slide, I chose a spot as far away as I could get from everyone else. But after only a few minutes in the sun, this totally beautiful man in jeans and mirror sunglasses glided by. He returned two minutes later nude, with a raging hard-on, playing with himself. He was gorgeous—tall, sleek, well-built. Admitting to myself I was turned on, I followed this dreamboat to a hidden cove and sat down beside him. But he just lay there like a bump on a log. When I started caressing his neck, stroking his stomach, the guy didn't even kiss me—didn't do anything. Forget this shit." Robin's voice took on a familiar tone of moral outrage. "I wasn't about to worship him. So I looked straight at him and said, 'I'm sorry. I've got to go. I just can't believe how impersonal this is.' And I got up and left."

Brian laughed heartily at Robin's self-righteous indignation. It was such a pointlessly austere approach—a phase that wouldn't last forever. Once upon a time, in his youth, he shared such views with Robin. Now, a couple of decades later, Brian had loosened up considerably about sex. Robin's story of a luscious-looking bimbo coming on to him made him envious. Robin still had the option, the opportunity to engage in such liaisons whenever he felt like it. Brian had no such luck. To Robin the worst case scenario was one-way sex, sucking the guy off–that struck Brian as not totally satisfying but hardly unbearable. And maybe, just maybe, the guy would have opened up when things got hot, maybe his better side would have emerged and it might have become fun, mutual even.

"I just seem to attract losers." Robin looked over at Brian who did not hesitate to return his gaze. "I've lost my innocence. I've had to become so tough to survive, emotionally that is, in this fucked-up world." That tone again, his voice modulating upward into a whine of self-righteous outrage.

Brian avoided a response this time by issuing directions for Robin to turn up the Bonny Doone road away from the coast. They sat mostly in silence for the next hour as they entered both the sunshine and the Santa Cruz mountains. Three thousand feet up, they entered Big Basin State Park and left Robin's car in the lot. The Sky-to-the-Sea Trail, fourteen miles, almost all downhill–finally!

Exuberant to be out of the city, Robin gushed about the bucolic splendors as he led their way through scores of magnificent stands of first-growth redwoods. Then he grew silent as they wound through the uphill section of the trail. Brian was content for Robin to walk a step or two ahead, happy to be alone with his thoughts. As they began descending, Brian pictured this place before the arrival of the white man; Native Americans had avoided Big Basin except to hunt because of their great respect for the grizzly which the white man had wiped out by 1880.

Soon they entered the actual "big basin" where the trail meandered alongside a bubbling stream. Brian was struck by his good fortune to have an occasional weekday off. Such serenity—they hadn't yet encountered a single person. They stopped at a bench for a picnic lunch where Brian, quickly and efficiently, ingested a puff or two of weed. None for Robin—no caffeine, no alcohol, no meat, no fish, no fowl, no sugar, and no drugs.

"How's your job at the Humane Society?" Brian found himself needing to converse. "I know how much you love animals. You don't have to put them to sleep, do you?"

"Actually, I prefer practicing euthanasia to dealing with the public. If you can distance yourself a little, it's not hard to see how putting animals to sleep can be a good thing. On the other hand, just the other day, this guy came in with his wife and a tiny, little girl." Robin's voice began modulating upwards. "They picked out this immense Doberman who knocked the kid over a couple of times with his huge paws. 'Do you people have any idea what's involved, the responsibilities of raising a dog like this? Don't you think he'd be too active, too hyper to be around your little girl?' Finally, I got the mother to suggest something gentler and this stupid macho slob got this childish pout on his face and stormed out of the office. Yes, I do prefer putting animals to death to dealing with such people. Not that it's easy. The young feral cats, they'll claw your arms to shreds if you don't hold them right. Give me the old dogs—they're resigned to their fate."

Brian was struck silent. The reference to old age and dying stirred a darkness within him that seemed to grow stronger each day. What was really involved to be resigned to one's fate. . . .

Luckily Robin changed the subject. "This place, the peace here, reminds me of the night of the earthquake. All the animals at the Humane Society were okay so Lisa, my co-worker and I, walked all the way home through the dark city, all the way through the Castro up to my house where it was so quiet, so beautiful, without traffic, without artificial lights. From the top of the hill on 21st Street the city lay out before us, gorgeous in nothing but starlight."

Brian liked Robin's description. At least he had found a responsive enough person with both a car and a free weekday who wanted to go on this hike. He had waited for years, but he had to wait no longer. He was here, the time was nigh. "Time to move on," he asked, not needing Robin's nod to know that it was.

Enjoying the crunch of every step on the soft, redwood bedding, Brian followed Robin down a slow, steady incline to the first waterfall, swollen by all the rains last winter, where, once again, they fell into silent appreciation for a few minutes. They decided to check out the second waterfall, a spontaneous addition to an already long hike. Fears of overextension welled up from Brian's manic youth when he would always end up exhausting himself and then get sick or have an accident. He decided if they didn't reach the second waterfall in twenty minutes or so that he would simply turn around and walk back to the first where he'd await Robin's return.

Robin walked so fast Brian could not keep up with him, but Brian granted him his solitude, happy to be enjoying this place after waiting so many years for an opportunity. Sure enough, in just about twenty minutes, he arrived at the second waterfall, after chasing Robin up a long stone staircase. They perched atop the tall, thin falls looking out at a magnificent vista of redwoods. As the stream fell freely onto the earth a hundred feet below them, silver and powerful, the loud roar of the falls rose up to soothe weary urban spirits.

Mature redwoods rooted far below branched out many feet above them. Brian found himself fixated on an extremely tall, thin redwood bursting skyward from just below the base of the waterfall. Two smaller trees, its progeny, clung on either side, all three joined as family at the roots. The tree to the right, an adolescent, maybe half as tall as the adult, maintained only a few branches, as if knowing it must propel its skinny trunk up into and then above the canopy for it to gather in its fair share of sunshine, not to mention that moist nighttime fog and morning dew. The baby on the left, maybe fifty feet tall, unbelievably thin, also knew that it had to grow a great deal more before he could produce the adult's luxuriously wide, feathery branches which swayed with a whooshing sound in the afternoon sea breeze. Brian saw his younger self in that sapling, so thin, so inexperienced, when he got his doctorate and came to San Francisco. Even now, so many years later, he was still trying to fill out, unfurl some of his branches, so slowly had he learned to drink in life's riches.

Leaving Robin behind in his own trance, Brian ventured down to the pool at the bottom of the falls, threw off his clothes and dove into the icy water. Awake.

"How is it?" Robin yelled down.

"Great." Tempted to grab for his shorts, Brian reassured himself that he had not gone naked to create a sexual situation with Robin. Not a tinge of attraction, anyway, not any more. Another voice was commanding him to act blasé, to not even try to relate to Robin who obviously savored the day as an escape—as much as possible—from *all* human beings. Was Robin so uptight that he couldn't let himself be physically gawked at by the average Joe—or Brian—the way most beautiful men could?

Brian admired Robin as he climbed down the steps—the solid, heftier-over-the-years body, the moderately hairy chest, the endearingly wayward small tufts of hair on his upper arms and back. (Timothy, his hirsute colleague, who anticipated the gay shaving mania by a decade, would never allow even his closest intimate to be privy to such a sight.) And that slight tummy, endearing because it suggested to Brian a healthy disdain for gym-induced vanity. Robin took off his shorts and dove into the pool, but, once out of the water, put them right back on, cuing Brian to follow suit.

A stellar jay chided them, but did not beg for food. Brian fixed his gaze on the perky bird, almost losing his sense of self in it. After a couple of minutes he could sense Robin doing exactly the same thing. They were all united as one until the jay snatched himself something to eat from the ground cover. A centipede. The spell was broken.

Robin jumped up and strode back toward the first waterfall. They had spoken their last words on the hike. Robin's pace once again outstripped Brian's. A sign—eight miles to go. Excellent exercise. He would rest if he needed to—he knew they would meet at the car. The picturesque trail became a fire road. The glories of the redwoods fell into the past. The bubbling stream became swampy Lower Waddell Creek. Its campground sported the sign: NON-POTABLE WATER—RECLAIMED SEWAGE. And Brian, suddenly, had had it with Robin.

As they descended ever closer to the ocean, the sea breeze evaporated all traces of perspiration generated by Robin's swift pace. Surfside the waves glistened in sunlight and the winds relentlessly howled. Scores of hunky wind-surfers in bright, day-glow wet suits and iridescent sail boards gloried in getting whipped by the raging, roiling surf. The fierce gale blasted sand into Brian's eyes, practically knocking him over as he fumbled with his key.

Robin climbed in, delighted with himself. "That was fun. Remember our first hikes, a few years ago? I could never keep up with your long legs. Bet I'll be sore as hell tomorrow."

"Rest your weary bones at Panther Beach. It's on the way, anyway. Just for an hour or so?"

Fifteen minutes later they descended the cliff to the beach and found themselves near a quartet of Latinos: two young men, a woman and an older man. One of the young men, the stud of the group, with a thin mustache and a well-defined chest, had passed out in the sand in his jockey briefs. The other younger man, the slimmer, darker one, a punk rocker, his brush cut shaved nearly bare around his ears, was making out with the busty woman. After a few minutes, he looked up and noticed Brian's frisbee. After pulling off his boxer shorts, he ran over to play. Encouraged, Brian finally tossed off his shorts. Robin, who had left on his pants, preferring the discreet nudity of the waterfall, declined to join. Brian tossed the disc with the young man whose gliding movements were easy to admire.

Back with Robin a few minutes later, Brian noticed that the dark-skinned young man was tenderly wiping off the face of his drunk friend. He followed up this tenderness with several kisses on the lips. Robin was watching, too, as the same young man put his shorts back on which, it turned out, were very ripped, thereby exhibiting his bare behind to the senior member of the group, a corpulent, mustachioed man who goaded his friend towards further exhibitionism. The punk rocker then grabbed his own crotch, pulled out his dick, and, while staring directly at Robin and Brian, took a long, leisurely piss. He then returned to the woman who leaned on his chest as he lay down in the sand. She kissed him and gently stroked first his hair, then his chest.

"Who *are* these people? What's going on with them?" Robin, exasperated, couldn't pigeonhole the roles within the group. Neither could Brian, except he was delighted, willing to grant them accolades he would never issue to any typically–dysfunctional American nuclear family. He could have enjoyed hanging around with them all day, but Robin apparently was impatient to leave.

They clambered back up the cliffs and continued their ride, this time Brian driving, back up to the mountains. He slipped Beethoven's Pastorale Symphony into his tape deck. Absolutely perfect. Robin was still comfortable with silence, a virtue for which Brian wanted to hug him, so thankful was he for being able to luxuriate in the music after that hike. Upon hearing the thunderstorm Beethoven unleashes in the third movement, a bolt of an idea struck Brian. Introduce Robin to Daniel. What was there to lose? They were both available and maybe he'd end up seeing more of them socially. They could walk to each other's place in five minutes.

Once he had had a crush on Robin and had hoped they might become lovers. Because Robin wasn't a typical bar-queen, maybe, Brian had hoped, he'd slowly come to appreciate his good qualities as a friend and then want to become lovers. But it had not happened. Robin professed to be a friend, but he had never broken through his passivity around Brian. The years had passed and nothing had happened. He had been willing to give it an honest try with both Robin and Daniel, willing to tolerate all their quirks. They had come to symbolize for him the futility of it all. Now he'd have his revenge–they'd have to put up with each other's peculiarities. And yet he had a hunch that there'd be chemistry between Robin and Daniel, probably a sizzling romance. After all, it did require a certain unselfishness to bring them together, to give them a fair chance with each other.

As he drove them back into the parking lot and to Robin's car, Brian realized he saw himself in both Robin and Daniel. Robin was his essence, his romantic younger self who put love above all. In recent years, however, he had taken on more of Daniel's worldly-wise, lusty paganism. Relieved to be letting go of any romantic illusions about either of them, Brian felt as if he were out from under a shadow. He jumped out of his car to exchange an abrupt, ritualistic hug with Robin and went off on his way.

6

"There they are, perched on their favorite acacia, waiting for us to finish our brunch so they can have theirs." Liz, who had rented the first floor of Brian's house for a decade, served their cappuccinos as they settled into their usual chairs on her deck to watch the antics of the flock of two dozen or so parrots who pretty much made Telegraph Hill their home base while swooping far and wide over the whole area to receive treats from their many other faithful admirers. "I gave them plenty of their favorite–sunflower seeds." Liz's keenly-attentive bright blue eyes sparkled with a particular intensity this sunny Saturday morning. Had she found a new romantic interest, Brian found himself wondering.

Saturday was Brian's favorite day of the week. He got up early to read the *Chronicle*, but since he also received the "dead" sections of Sunday's paper a day early, he got to comb through the alphabetical listings of films to be televised in the coming week. Hope sprang eternal each Saturday morning that he would unearth some long-forgotten treasure to share with Richard–no matter that such hopes usually proved futile. And then he'd start on next week's preparations for his classes or read some student papers until he heard Liz calling him down. Hating last minute pressure, he pretty much stayed ahead of the academic game, trying through industriousness to free up at least some of Sunday before his busy schedule resumed on Monday.

He always looked forward to this time with Liz whose well-appointed quarters contrasted with the "camping out" look of his half of the house, still waiting to be decorated in celebration of that lifetime companion's arrival–Marco's replacement, who had never materialized. Only then might he be inspired to utilize the potential of the place and turn it into a haven of domestic bliss. At least Liz had played that role in a practical sense for him. He modernized his own bathroom when he had to do so for her. He took her suggestion of painting the house white when he had to paint it—and he loved it. And he added decks to both floors when she convinced him how much use they'd get from the extra space.

He had now become totally accustomed to sipping tea outside, with or without her, appreciating the piers, the Bay, and the Bay Bridge which loomed up as the centerpiece of the scene. Facing east and south brought them a great deal of sun, which often rose behind Mt. Diablo at dawn just beneath the layer of fog which had blanketed the city during the night. But one could not walk east very far from his old "blue collar" house—only forty yards from his deck, his garden abruptly ended; Telegraph Hill, in fact, abruptly ended. The cliff was utterly sheer—straight down to the Icehouse of the egregiously-tasteful Levi Plaza, that constant reminder to Brian that this was the San Francisco of the 1990s. At least this location kept him in shape. No matter in what direction he walked, returning home meant a climb up either a steep hill or a seemingly endless staircase.

Saturday mornings with Liz gave them a chance to mull over the week, to share observations, to sympathize and encourage. This particular morning, a lovely, warm day in May, he needed sympathy. The reality of Will's finally submitting to being tested had hit him the last couple of evenings at home by himself. "The honeymoon of denial is over. I think he already has it because he's been so down about teaching (which he loves) this semester. Very little energy. I wouldn't be surprised if his T-cell count had already dipped really low."

"Don't write him off yet," Liz had just brought out omelets, scones and fruit salad. "Even if he's positive he could be around for a long time. And he'll need you to be there for him." Upbeat to a fault, Liz rarely allowed herself a prolonged bad mood, usually able to exorcise her demons by means of either a quick outburst or a long workout on her Tunturi exer-cycle.

An attractive blonde in her mid-forties, Liz had still managed, despite her successful and very busy career with a downtown publisher, to cultivate a lively social life. The daughter of Hungarian Jewish intellectuals who also had managed to remain more or less optimistic after fleeing the Nazis, she had remained philosophical about her own romantic ups and downs—with both sexes. Currently, she was involved in a frustrating relationship with a considerably younger man, but it had been mostly women over the past decade and, judging from that glint in her eye this morning, Brian was guessing that a new romantic interest, probably a woman, had popped up on the scene.

Not perked up by Liz's encouragement, Brian merely stared out at the bridge, wondering what he'd be like if he had had such parents—accepting, compassionate, "enlightened." "You're right," he finally responded, "day by day—let's wait and see." Their friendship had become especially close after the '89 earthquake when they pooled their supply of candles and booze and threw a party for the neighbors up on Brian's deck. Brian had also become a kind of uncle to Liz's daughter, Stacy, by an early and disastrous marriage. Stacy, a militant lesbian who lived in the Outer Mission, often chided her mother for her bisexuality, giving her an especially hard time about her current beau, Sean, a red-headed student in his late twenties.

"I have good romantic news—at least Stacy will think so, probably you, too. I've broken up with Sean and there's new hope, a woman, almost my age." Liz smiled wryly as she heaped some marmalade on her scone. "She had just joined the San Francisco Bach Choir when I moved right in on her. It was easy, natural—we're both altos. I can just hear Stacy." Liz assumed an obnoxious know-it-all tone. "'It's about time. You know, mother, we dykes avoid women like you because we're afraid we'll be left with a broken heart when you suddenly, impetuously, inevitably go back to a man.'"

She refilled their cappuccino cups, still thoughtful. "But this time I think she's wrong. I've had it with men, especially young men who drone on endlessly, making pronouncements about the local music scene, not in the least bit interested in anything I might have to say on the subject. Oh, he was cute, charming even. But too self-involved, just not mature enough."

Wired from the caffeine, Brian was more than eager to divert himself with the various details of Liz's life. "You sound like *me* talking about younger men—except Will, of course. But remember not to take Stacy's complaints too seriously. She's using sexual politics as the theme of her inevitable rebellion against her mother, her typical Jewish mother who constantly worries that her daughter's various piercings will become infected."

"Wouldn't you worry?" Liz temporarily lost her cool. "And ruining her looks with that nose ring and crew cut."

"Sure, but so far nose, ears and navel have held up well, haven't they?" Brian, amused by the inevitability of it all, strongly suspected that mother and daughter would become good friends in a few years. "I sure know what you mean about the self-absorption of the young, though. Even Daniel, whom I like and who's over thirty. I've gone out to a couple of concerts with him and I like listening to him talk but only up to a point. It's especially annoying when he keeps revealing his ambivalence about such issues as piercing, anal sex, even S & M. If I suggest one thing, he has to come back with the opposite. So what can I say except, 'Find out what you like and do it.' Anyway, did I tell you, I'm going to introduce Daniel to Robin. I've got nothing to lose—neither of them is turned on to me. And I might be doing them a big favor."

Liz guffawed, then smiled wryly again, with just a touch of mock-condescension. "Don't worry your little head over them. If I didn't know you better, I'd think it some Machiavellian plot so you can sit back and watch them self-destruct. High-powered Daniel finds his perfect complement in sweet, passive Robin. Sounds like heterosexual marriage in the fifties."

Surprised at her cynicism, Brian took a final stab at playing the helpful matchmaker. "I think they'll really go for each other. And just maybe we'll all end up spending more time together."

"Ha. Innocents abroad. Never lose that charming naivete, Brian. Maybe you'll see something of them, probably you won't. Meanwhile, enjoy the single life. Indulge your every whim and let yourself emit stinking farts even when serving dinner. As for today, grab your pack and go to the beach—it's such a beautiful day."

"You're right about my current life, of course, but doesn't anyone care about affection in this town? Self-absorbed young men and jaded old queens—is that all there is? I can hardly think of a single, long-term gay relationship in this town that could tempt me to be envious. I doubt if most men have the time, the stamina, the courage for working something out. We're all damaged goods in this demented culture." On a roll, Brian poured himself the dregs from their second cappuccino. "The worst thing is that even though I know this is all true, I still feel like a loser, obsessively testing myself as a prospective lover. Am I still resilient enough to share my living quarters? Has my worth in the gay market place dropped so low that I should simply give up and become the gay equivalent of the chaste, stodgy bachelor or, worse maybe, the dirty old man who encounters tiresome versions of himself at every gay bar, bath or beach in the entire world?"

"Hey, I'm obsessive about that kind of self-testing, too, already going through it in my mind thinking of my new love, Lynn. Look!" Liz jumped up, the air suddenly filled with chaotic squawking. "The parrots are arriving!" They both moved to the railing to watch. "Have you seen that little blue parakeet that has just joined the flock? There he is, over on the eucalyptus, waiting his turn. Probably just escaped his cage." Liz put her arm around Brian. "Remember, my friend, this is an intelligent, sensual, sensitive man standing next to me. If I were a gay man who wanted a romantic relationship, I'd beat a path to your door."

Frustrated, and not good at taking compliments anyway, Brian let her words roll off him like water off a duck's back. He might have been encouraged if he were a heterosexual man or a lesbian (younger women often seemed to desire the middle-aged), but he wasn't, so he resisted her words, first lowering his eyes to the floor, then looking right into hers. "But my qualities have no *practical* value given the nature of this sub-culture. Here and now, though, I vow to pursue only men over forty! Now tell me about this 'sensible' new choice you've made, this Lynn."

"Well, she's down to earth, maybe a bit heavy, but so solid as a person, so much fun to be with."

Brian laughed. "You remind me of Edmund's fatuous comment about lesbians. 'It's so refreshing that two fat, homely dykes can just walk around looking starry-eyed at each other for years on end.'"

Liz laughed, too, but only briefly. "So far everything is suspiciously easy, probably because we both want and need time alone. I knew I was attracted when she told me, 'I'm not one of those dykes who demand total attention and want to discuss the relationship all the time, especially at two in the morning when you should be either asleep or making love.' No hints about wanting to move in either—at least not yet."

"Sounds great. I'm going to find a Lynn—mature Brian wants a mature lover."

"Give yourself a break. You're open to love—just stay alert—it'll come along, although you never know from where. Meanwhile, I reiterate: you have it good—enjoy yourself." Liz left the parrots to their feasting and moved towards the table which held their brunch. "I still want you to meet Jeremy, this nephew of mine when he comes out to visit—at least as a potential friend. After college he tried to make it as an actor in New York, but he got involved with a fast crowd, and then with a couple of boyfriends who treated him badly and, finally, with drugs. After a complete emotional collapse he ended up a chronic introvert. After he pulled out of that, and with my parents' strong encouragement, he took off to Europe—lived first in Prague, then Berlin, finally Amsterdam. Now he's back in the country, living temporarily with them. He says he wants to give America another try, but I know Philadelphia's not for him and he'll never break out of that shell if he hangs around all the time with my folks."

"He was a fool to come back. Not now. This whole country's under a shadow—I realize it every time I get out of it." Brian took a deep breath and put his arm around Liz for a moment. "And it's you whom I have to thank for that, getting me off my duff to go not only to Europe, but then to Thailand, Nepal and, of course, Indonesia."

She gracefully released herself from his arm to start cleaning up the deck. "Remember, though," she insisted, "Jeremy is an American; he needs to be reconciled with that part of himself. You could be very helpful in that process when he visits, just by being yourself, just by going to the symphony together or touring the coast."

Brian hugged her good-bye, half-ashamed of his needy state this morning, but determined that the next time he would steer the conversation towards her. Meanwhile, he was more than inclined to follow her sage advice to spend the afternoon at the beach.

7

The fog, that old gray aunt who insisted on prolonging her gloomy summer visit, had little effect on Brian throughout the week. Thanks to his usual ritual with Liz, several appearances by the parrots, and the surprise appearance of the sun (some of the best anti-depressants he had ever known), he cruised through Saturday nicely. Sunday's fog got to him, though. Throughout the day he remained homebound, parrots nowhere in sight, Liz off to see Stacy, and the fog, instead of breaking, gave way to a gloomy, gothic drizzle.

He called Richard. Because he moved slowly and his answering machine switched on after only two rings, Richard's recorded voice came through first. ". . . Thank you very much for calling." At this point Brian managed to discern Richard's "live" voice groping about in the audio fog, "Hello, hello," as desperate as Brian to make contact with another human being. "Just a sec, Brian, I'll turn this damn thing off."

"Richard, are you as depressed as I am?"

"I'm at least that depressed." Richard's voice sounded particularly resonant this afternoon. "I was listening to that late Mozart Quintet, the one in a minor key. Talk about gloom. It takes you right to the bottom and, just as you think you might manage there for a bit, he opens a trap door and one sinks even lower, to an unfathomable abyss. Good to hear your voice, Brian. So far it's just me and Cleo."

"How's the back?"

"It's been a miserable couple of weeks. The back's been worse and the medication has almost done me in. Nausea, dizziness, constipation, insomnia, forgetfulness, temporary insanity—I just don't see any way out."

"Hang on. I'll bring by some dinner in an hour or so."

Brian found himself in the mood for an old cassette, the Mormon Tabernacle Choir, the very organization Richard hated so much when he sang in it as a teenager in Salt Lake City. Four hundred middle-aged people sitting on their big butts made a beautiful, if subdued, sound. He began to soar to the strains of "Jerusalem," but it was the sweetness of Bach's "Jesu, Joy of Man's Desiring" that did him in. He grew sad over the pain of his own lost youth, for Richard's agony and immobility, and for Will who faced a tragic early death. Brian's *mater dolorosa* mood confronting the sadness of the human condition.

Feeling better as he climbed the green carpet of Richard's staircase a bit later, he recoiled at the sight of the ashen-faced Richard, bags under his eyes, swathed in a ratty bathrobe, looking like the Old Man on the Mountain. "I've brought you an excellent tape of Mozart's *Idomeneo.*"

"Good," replied Richard. "I'll have plenty of chances to listen to whole operas once I'm completely bedridden."

Not quite ready to eat, they took their usual places on their respective couches. "This country's becoming so fascist," Richard fumed. "And they're still cutting funding for AIDS research," he stammered, eyes intense.

"You saw that orthopedic surgeon this week, didn't you? Did he hold out any hope?"

"I suppose it's good news, but my reaction has been severe depression. He recommended no more operations—the damage is in the nerves. He thinks the first one probably worsened things. And then I made the mistake of asking him about his own bad back and he used up the rest of our time talking non-stop about it."

"You didn't need a specialist to tell you that." Brian squirmed about until he found the right tone with which to attempt to be upbeat. "Hey, no more operations. Your body won't have to submit to being opened up. You won't have to endure that terribly long recuperation."

Richard remained silent and Brian resisted charging into the gap. "It's not that simple," Richard moaned. "I have this passive side which yearns for fulfillment by heroically submitting to the knife and then waking up all fixed. That passive side is disappointed. Oh, for the good life of an orthopedic specialist. Their patients never die, but they never get better. Guaranteed income. . . . How have you been?"

"I'm just relieved not to have to deal with school for a few days. We're firing hundreds, decimating whole programs. The wailing and gnashing of teeth of rejected students, the exhaustion from teaching overcrowded classes. Sometimes retirement strikes me as appealing. And then there's Will—he's being tested next week and I have no hope whatsoever. I guess I'm not very good company these days." Perhaps it wasn't such a good idea to get together with Richard when they were both depressed. "Enough of this—let's eat."

Richard insisted on getting up to help Brian with the preparations. "Poor Will, that dear, sweet man. Oh, this terrible plague. How it makes us all confront death. But no one, you or anyone else, can live in this state for very long. We seek out a kind of normalcy, however absurd. I myself wish I could find it. Despite how bad things have been lately, I've decided I prefer pain to a clouded mind—and all that bowel upset."

"So the morphine didn't work?"

"No, but I do have a bit of good news. I've started therapy again, but this time it's different. I like my therapist. I admire him. I adore him. He's gay, very supportive. All those others—I think I have the expression—'broadcasting into space.'"

Brian laughed as he began bringing their dinner into the living room. "Richard, could they have all been that bad?"

"The rest of them were all dildos. This one's intelligent, stimulating, knows what's going on. Unfortunately, so far raking over the past with him has only increased my depression. I've always contended that nothing good could ever come from trying to deal with that incident with the law, that restroom in Boston. That kind of thing has permanently scarred my entire generation." They settled around the table. Alcatraz barely peeped out from under the fog and drizzle. "I've also just recently learned that not only stress but enjoyable escapes, such as thrillers, murder mysteries, can tense up my back, increasing the pain."

"You need to adopt an evening ritual—maybe something like mine. Start out with a thriller early in the evening. Then switch to something more soothing—maybe some pretty boys, then some Mozart or Schubert."

"I wish I could. I told you on the phone what that quintet did to me today—and that was in the afternoon. I'm still afraid of the intensity of my response to my most beloved compositions."

Brian was frustrated by Richard's resistance. Long moments passed before he made an attempt to break through it. "But now that you have that good therapist maybe your responses will become cathartic. I had such a good release, listening to Bach this afternoon." Brian neglected to mention the Mormon Tabernacle Choir.

Richard shifted his position slowly, swivelling awkwardly to make eye contact, looking right at Brian, his eyes filled with sadness. "Thanks to you, to my good friends. Only they stop me from falling to the very bottom, to a place from which one's afraid one can't bounce back."

This time Brian could not respond. Gloom hung in the air for many more moments. They fell into mutual resignation, a place where they dared not harbor any hopes lest they all be instantly dashed. Then Richard struggled up out of his lounge chair. "Don't mind me. I just can't seem to get out of this funk . . . and I need to go to the john. Please excuse me for a couple of minutes."

Left alone, Brian wondered if he, still so active, could handle so much immobility and pain without extreme bitterness.

"Come quickly! To my bedroom!" Startled by Richard's call, Brian leapt up, ran through the kitchen and down the long hallway to Richard's bedroom which faced out onto the street. "It's Cleo. I must have left the window open. She's fallen out." Brian stuck his head out the window. Cleo lay immobile on the concrete thirty feet below. A neighbor was approaching her with a towel to cover her up, but was she alive?

"I'm calling the emergency vet. I've got the number right here." Richard started dialing immediately.

"Okay. I'll go down and wait with her." Brian raced down the long stairway, his heart filled with anguish for the feisty Siamese, who, like her master, was fated to an indoor existence. She had leaned too far towards that forbidden outside world.

But when he got to her, he saw she was alive, meowing piteously. He spent a very long fifteen minutes waiting there for the vet, first shouting up encouraging words to Richard, then trying to comfort him after he had made his way down.

After the vet carried Cleo off, they returned to Richard's flat, trying to kill time watching television while waiting for the vet to call. Two hours later the phone finally rang. Good news. Cleo had broken a leg and sustained minor liver damage, but she was going to live.

As Brian gave a him a long hug good-bye, Richard thanked him profusely for his help throughout the crisis. "Almost losing Cleo has brought me to my senses. Life's too short to avoid the things you love. You know, Brian, I'm going to follow your advice. I've avoided all my beloved masterpieces over the years because they evoke too intense, too painful, a response. I'm going to start listening to them tonight, let the tears fall where they may."

8

"People are in such a hurry these days they don't even say good-bye." High-strung, her gray hair pulled back into a tight bun, Elisa was wrapping up the paper work from her previous clients, looking up occasionally to smile at Will and Brian who were waiting patiently. "Now, what can I do for you gentlemen today?"

"We'd like a private hot tub." More than half a century old and Brian still had to battle his shyness. He wagered to himself that Elisa had presided over thousands of such trysts.

"Fine. Room Number Two's available. You get an hour. I'll give you a ten-minute warning knock on your door."

The room struck Brian as pleasant enough, with cut flowers and potted plants in every corner. The simple white walls and stained natural beams softened the artificiality of the plastic hot tub. Will looked less anxious than usual, despite having to face his test early in the morning. As they slowly undressed, sitting on a bench right next to each other, Will leaned over and unbuckled Brian's belt, then reached in and grabbed his cock. Brian took a deep breath and relaxed, confident in Will's attraction for him, knowing neither his age nor the couple of pounds he had recently gained would put him off. On the other hand, Will looked as good as ever—he never exercised, except for carrying bags of groceries up Bernal Heights from the Mission Street Safeway. Maybe he was so high-strung he burned everything off.

They lowered themselves cautiously into the hot, swirling waters of the turquoise tub and stretched out in quiet luxury, guzzling some of the vodka-and-juice-cocktail they had smuggled in. Will enjoyed the buoyancy of the water in the tank, languidly floating, his smooth chest etched just above the water line. He intertwined his legs with Brian's, then squeezed one of his nipples. They were in a safe cocoon, immersed in chlorinated water; neither germs nor the outside world could get them here.

After some more playing around, Will motioned Brian to sit on the edge of the tank so he could suck him. Brian took in as much pleasure as he could before jumping back into the water and attacking Will with kisses. Will wrestled back and so they slipped and slid in and out of each other's grasp. Brian loved this kind of exchange, loved being able to sit back and let it happen. Will was working them up into a sexual frenzy, into their somehow not-yet-tired porn star routine. "Suck that dick," he commanded. Silly, clichéd words but how healing to Brian's bruised, middle-aged ego.

After more precious minutes of pleasure, Will turned up the emotional heat. "You are a beautiful man. I love you," he whispered. His words did not scare Brian. It was one of the great gifts of life that Will found him to be beautiful. And after six years there was no denying his love. The frustrations inherent in their situation had only made it easier for Brian to feel deserving of every bit of love that Will dished out. He, too, loved Will and had no trouble expressing that love, except for a twinge of melancholy about the limitations of their part-time affair. That's irrelevant now, he chided himself. Enjoy the moment—even this might not last.

Someone knocking on the door—Elisa's warning. Already the end of the hour was approaching. They beat each other off to a much-needed release, lay there in each other's arms for a minute or two, then casually dressed.

Back in the lobby Brian tried to release some of the waves of love engulfing him by being particularly nice to Elisa. Then carefully observing the PLEASE CLOSE DOOR SLOWLY injunction, they scampered down the narrow staircase out onto 24th Street, the main drag of Noe Valley, what Liz delighted in calling the Dyke Capital of the World.

Driving back to Bernal Heights through the fog and drizzle, mostly in silence, Brian noticed Will becoming more and more uneasy. Finally the dreaded subject. "I've put off this test too long, anyway. The other night Nevin and I were both confessing our sexual mistakes. He could be positive, too, but he's totally opposed to being tested."

Brian agonized about how to respond. Personally, he agreed with Nevin's strategy, but Nevin hadn't had all those blood transfusions back in 1982. He knew of several guys who had had unsafe sex and got away with it. But pointing that out to Will wouldn't help. "Enough of that Catholic guilt about sex," he exhorted. "You've been careful enough. Let's just keep our fingers crossed."

Pitifully inadequate words. The tragic irony of it all. Will, stabbed in the heart by a man robbing him on Gough Street and rushed to surgery, forgave his assailant as he went under the knife. He claimed he left his body, looked down on the operating table, then floated through a dark tunnel into a White Light which bathed him in Love, even let him know it was fine to love men, then sent him back just in time to hear the surgeon saying, "It'll be all right. He's young, he's strong, he'll make it."

Brian declined, for somewhat cowardly reasons, perhaps, to accept Will's invitation to come in for awhile. Instead, he got out of his car and gave him a long, long embrace. The last thing he heard from Will as he drove off was that nervous laugh which he associated with Will's insecurity, his desire to please everyone. But, in his own twentieth century urban way, the guy was a saint–so sensitive, so loyal, not just to Brian but to all his friends, especially those with the plague. Meeting Will in his mid-forties had initiated the most sexually satisfying phase of Brian's life. Satisfying mini-affairs with others soon followed as well as encounters at the beach as if knowing Will had somehow changed his luck. Sexual luck, that is. Brian didn't want to think too much about his luck on the subject of romance.

And yet as he drove home, Brian refused to be sentimental. Yes, he admitted to himself, their once-or-twice-a-week policy had worked out very well. It would remain a moot point as to whether they would have been happy living together–Brian certainly had his doubts. *The Wizard of Oz*, Disneyland, Dynasty, Palm Springs, posh hotels—all those passions of Will's bored him. Will loved Sondheim the way Brian loved Schubert. And all Will's apartment clutter would drive him crazy.

Cruising the northern end of Polk Street, Brian noticed a shocking-pink neon sign lit up in a third-floor apartment window—BOYS. Where the hell did they get that? The silly sign picked up his spirits as he negotiated up steep, curvy Francisco Street onto Larkin, past that balcony where he had spotted the parrots feeding a few days ago. And then Filbert to Hyde to Union, on the tail-end of what, since 1989, had become his regular route from school since the destruction of the Embarcadero Freeway, his old route out of North Beach. Instead he now followed the city's northern and western shoreline allowing him to stop off at the beach on his way home. All those years he could have been having fun at the beach after school. But then he remembered how, as a young teacher, he'd leave school, head spinning, needing a knock-out nap to recover both his equilibrium and his capacity for physical pleasure. In some ways, Brian had to admit to himself, his middle age was a refinement, an actual improvement over his youth.

9

When the sun finally broke through the overcast above the infamous meadow on the banks of the Russian River, Edmund wisely positioned himself under his umbrella—he was not supposed to get any sun at all. Solidly built, an imposing six feet four inches tall, Edmund has been cursed with a ruddy complexion, the typically "bad" Irish skin he loved to joke about, even though skin cancer had inevitably developed, requiring repeated minor surgeries over the years.

"Not surprisingly, really. All we had during the forties was the pathetic 100% alcohol Skol. We hailed the coming of Coppertone as a miracle drug." Having just turned sixty, Edmund sported a bushy, silvery head of hair, clear plastic glasses, and an extremely hirsute frame.

"You remind me of my hairy colleague at school, Timothy," Brian put in. "Same white, freckled Irish skin. Except he likes to shave all his body hair. Some days he's Mr. Stubble."

The meadow at the Russian River's Wohler Bridge, now so underused compared to its busy past, glistened in the sunlight. What a relief to escape from the summer's unrelenting fog in the city. A strong urge to cruise hit Brian. "Not many people around today," observed Edmund. "My favorite spot. I call it 'the killing fields.' This was where it was all happening. So many have passed on." Edmund slithered through the tall, lush grass, then set up his creamsicle-orange-and-white plastic beach chair in an area that had been somewhat beaten down. "Got to get above the snakes." He unbuttoned his red-flannel shirt, wearing it like a shawl so that it partially covered his handsome Nordstrom blue-and-white vertical striped shirt. With his white cap and aqua tennies, he looked quite the affluent pensioner.

Stroking the copious hair on his arms, he feigned seriousness, leaning close as if to impart something ultra-confidential. "I've dropped more $35 Remington shavers on the floor trying to get at that damn hair on my shoulders. Or I'd put hot wax over my arms, then strip it off. When I looked at myself in the mirror, I'd always see a little line of hair that I had missed. How I'd wince when my trick started caressing the stubble on my shoulders." Edmund paused with a silly grin and then peered over his glasses at Brian whose expression urged him on. "All this hair on my chest, too. Sometimes I still find a young guy curious to try it with a 'hairy one.' But it's all turned white—that's something I could have easily done without." Brian laughed, starting to relax, even though he had recently contemplated some discreet shaving to offset the steady descent of mutant white hairs on his own chest.

Wohler Bridge, Edmund's old stomping grounds. Brian hadn't been here for a long time. He had forgotten how beautiful the area was, even the drive along River Road with its splendid redwood groves and long-established wineries. Edmund, who loved to drive, had volunteered his VW Fox, a treat for Brian who rarely got to be a passenger. Half an hour earlier, avoiding a barricaded lot, Edmund had parked along the road. "Funny thing," Edmund had observed offhandedly. "That parking lot—all those demolished cars in there. So many men these days, too lazy to walk all the way to the river, cruise right there in the parking lot, ducking around all those abandoned wrecks. Love Among the Ruins, that's what I call it."

On the way in, past the huge dam and the Sonoma County storage facility for heavy equipment, they had tramped across the little gay beaches, still pretty much as they had been a decade ago. Then a short, steep path to the infamous meadow, now choked with thistles, poison oak and ten-foot high grass. There were ominous NO TRESPASSING signs everywhere. "Don't worry about those," Edmund had explained. "The deputies haven't busted anyone in years."

"The river doesn't look clean." Spreading out his towel next to Edmund's chair, Brian sat down on it, having decided to hang around a bit before taking his walk. "Is Santa Rosa still dumping untreated sewage into the river?"

"Oh, I wouldn't dunk your head in that water. You gotta be careful these days. You know my friend who has a place up here—he got parasites. It took him the longest time to figure out what it was so he could get rid of it. Also, watch out for ticks—Lyme disease. Tetracycline the first week does it—early diagnosis. Otherwise it's like third-stage syphilis. Thirty cases in Sonoma County already this year."

Brian noted how Edmund had made himself a lay expert on so many diseases and ailments—not just AIDS. "Isn't it worst in the East? Old Lyme's not far from your family's place in Fairfield."

"Seven hundred cases in Fairfield County last year." Edmund divulged his facts in a silly, childish whisper, like an obnoxious nine-year old girl who knows she's the smartest in the class. Brian laughed again. Then silence, just the light sea breeze rustling the grass and surrounding bushes.

"I had the most exhausting day yesterday." Edmund had abruptly changed his tone. "Those doctors. You go in and there's a whole roomful of people. Had to wait two hours. After the doc saw me, I left feeling much worse than when I went in. I hope there aren't too many more days like that ahead."

Brian had known Edmund socially for years, but it was only after the older man tested positive that he pursued an active friendship. Initially he felt put off by Edmund's decidedly unromantic view of things, especially his obsessive cruising, a needed release, in Edmund's opinion, for having to act so "straight," nine to five, when he was personnel director of a high-tech firm in Palo Alto.

They had become good buddies once Edmund began battling the virus. He seemed to become more human, more accessible, once he was forced to confront his mortality. And Brian found him very likeable once he stopped moralizing about the older man's approach to sex and love. He soon found himself cultivating a fantasy about their friendship; he had known

Edmund in a medieval monastery (those glasses of his still reminded Brian of authoritarian Catholic priests he had known in his youth). Edmund had been the head monk, Brian the young novice. Now, this time around, because of so much sexual repression in previous lifetimes, Edmund had tried to make up for lost time. Fine, except Brian didn't like the karmic implications of his stupid myth, what with Edmund contracting AIDS and all. "You're looking good, though. Feeling okay?"

"A thousand times better. Switching doctors made all the difference. No more diarrhea after six terrifying weeks—it was just a matter of switching medications. And no more pneumonia—neither was plague-related." Brian sighed with relief for Edmund. He had regained control—life still promised some joys. "For a while I was in a tailspin, deeply depressed, thinking about death all the time. (They're flying my body back to Connecticut, by the way.) But, with the AZT, the T-cells are up. I did get some ddI, for $3500, from a friend off the black market in New York. Like everything else it's politics. You have to know somebody." He peered over at Brian and they exchanged a look of complicity about East Coast politics. "But I'm scared of using it—can't anyway. It has to be mixed into a formula and they didn't tell me how to do it. It's available now anyway. I'm being tested to get into an experiment with it."

Relieved that Edmund could still maintain the illusion of an indefinite life span, Brian got up to take his walk but Edmund hadn't finished talking. "So the other day I'm up here," Edmund said, "and I meet this young guy who claims, 'I'm not gay—there are some things I do, though.' He showed me these pictures of him in bondage, most of them not showing his face. He gave me one—without a face—then let me beat him off."

"You've cruised so much around here over the years, Edmund, you must know all the ropes."

"When you cruise there are three basic categories." Edmund had reverted to his silly, know-it-all tone. Brian resumed sitting on his towel, curious. "First, men you want more of, but they're tired of you. Then there are those who want more of you, but you are not interested."

"Yeah, and what's the third category?"

"Men you want to shoot. There's this guy up here. As soon as I approach someone, he slinks right in, all heavy breathing and slobber. And it's all over, ruined. Last year I'm in Hawaii, at the showers at the Queen's Surf. In comes this Asian with an erection—you know how I am about Asians. He's looking at me, I move closer, we're right next to each other. And what happens? The slobberer! He's even in Hawaii! He comes over and stands about three feet away, instantly shrivelling up our wee-wees. Those kill-joys are everywhere. Here they perch on rocks, obnoxiously in view, making sure no one else gets any. And the smirkers, like my 'friends' here who later run into you at a bar. 'Oh, Edmund, we were just talking about your exploits yesterday.'" Edmund assumed an even sissier tone, breaking Brian up.

"In some ways it might be better today. In the old days it was rare to pull off a trick without someone getting screwed—even if you weren't in the mood. And we missed out on all the tit-action the kids are into today. I get such a kick seeing those guys tweaking their nipples in the porn films. I never missed out on armpits, though. Used to drive my Filipino boy friend, Carlos, crazy. He'd always get ticklish when I'd dig my face into his pits."

"So the good old days were a myth?"

"It's just different. Hell, I go back to the days when gay doctors had it made. They'd just shoot up the penicillin and then, with a little wag of the finger and a twinkle of the eye, would tell you 'to be a little more careful next time.' And we'd go out, have more fun and be back for another shot in a couple of months."

"It was also the golden age of poppers, wasn't it?"

"Hey, up until three years ago, it was three times a week. If you were having trouble with a shy Asian, just shove it up his nose. It was hard on the white cells, though, hard on getting up early for the commute."

"Have you ever actually gone to Asia?"

"No, but there was the time my friend Bob and I gave about thirty blow jobs to the kids at the baths in Mexico City. Too bad they were those light-skinned, kind of ugly, middle- class ones. I came back from that trip with parasites, the clap, even syphilis. And the baths in Harlem thirty years ago! My friend and I were very popular there, the only whites. I was probably fucked by twenty of them in a night. I came back to California on a prop plane, itching like crazy, my hairy body covered with crabs." Switching into his Hints from Heloise voice, Edmund assured Brian, "If you take your vitamins, though, they won't bother you."

Brian finally slipped on some shorts for his walk. "Watch out for all those ticks," Edmund added in his nelliest voice as Brian, determined not to be delayed further, stalked off along the path to the woods.

10

It felt good to be alone. Brian hiked back towards the riverbank where a huge tree had fallen, its thick trunk the only path through the dense undergrowth. Halfway down the trunk he came upon a little house, a lean-to in which someone had recently camped. After finding the hideout deserted, he fought his way through the underbrush and emerged back on the main path.

A man marched by, then another a few minutes later. Neither struck him as interesting. He veered away from the riverbank to a much more defined trail, the route to the cistern. He expected nothing, of course, yet each time a man appeared and then passed by, pangs of loneliness permeated him, that sad sense of having missed out on so many possibilities. He had yet to transcend the curse of a sexually-inactive adolescence.

Deeper in the woods, though, he yielded to the beauty, the serenity of the place. He quieted his mind to take in the singing of the birds. The aspens along the river quivered in the afternoon breeze, their leaves glinting gray-green in the sunlight. Stately redwoods began to dominate, with a variety of ferns popping up alongside the small stream that led to the river. At the cistern he chucked his shorts and immersed himself in its clear, cold water. Once out, as he absorbed the bracing coolness of the lush shade, he admitted to himself that he was happier than on any previous visit here although he couldn't say exactly why. How many times, more than a decade ago, had he wandered aimlessly about here, overheated, bored and frustrated?

On his way back he reached an elevated overlook where the river broadened to fifty yards or so. On the other side a well-built man stood near a canoe. Squinting intensely for a bit, Brian guessed him to be about forty, then revised it upward to as high as fifty-five. But he was solid, hardy, Nordic even. And he was naked. Was he beating off? Yes, he was playing with

himself, looking up expectantly. Brian dropped his shorts and
placed a tentative hand over his crotch, knowing he was
silhouetted on his high vantage point. Give him a chance, he
urged himself. You've told people you're getting interested in
older men. And in this beautiful, romantic setting.

The man began swimming across the river towards him.
Suppressing an urge to bolt, Brian found a sunny spot closer to
the shore and started beating off in earnest, feeling a little like a
maiden in a fairy tale waiting for her prince to rescue her and
carry her off. The platinum-haired, senior viking, once out of the
water, walked right up and immediately starting playing with
Brian who then reached out to him. But disappointment came
quickly. No amount of fondling aroused the Norseman. Okay,
Brian understood that *he* was the lovely young thing in this
pairing. But in this mood the one-way limitation was too
restricted for him, rendered the whole thing pointless. Didn't he
deserve interaction? Reciprocity? He decided to take off just
before coming. The maiden, again, demurely pulling up her
panties. But the older gent instantly granted him leave with a
jolly farewell–he had had a good time for a while.

Back on his towel alongside Edmund in his aluminum chair,
Brian recounted the episode, curious if Edmund knew the guy in
the canoe. "No, but it all helps keep you young, doesn't it? Last
week I met this Brazilian under the trees at Land's End and we
went off together to have sex. He's one of those passionate types
drawn to a daddy. He even serenaded me going up the hill. But
damn those young, athletic ones. My leg was just healing from
that clot, the one I got last month cruising there. I'm okay now,
but, I'll tell you, every time I see a lame person trying to drag
himself around, I have plenty of compassion. Anyway he zipped
up the hill so quickly–you know how steep it is there. So I'm
huffing and puffing trying to keep up. And then, at the top, I
start having these spasms."

"'Spasms?' What do you mean 'spasms'?"

"Like my heart. I'm scared to death. I think I'm going to go right there."

"Edmund, you've got to pace yourself." Brian, however, smiled to himself, thinking it wouldn't have been such a bad death.

"The guy was worth it. He wanted to come over a couple of days later, but I couldn't handle him then. I never thought I'd send away someone like that, but it felt great to be wanted. Anyway here I am dying at the top of the hill at Land's End and all I can do is fixate on all those soiled Kleenex strewn all over the trail."

Brian laughed, but noted his own ambivalence about the concept of a "daddy." Why didn't any younger men seek him out as a daddy? Maybe he didn't want them to?

"I've had enough of the meadow today." Edmund stood up to stretch. "I'll treat you to an early dinner at this great place, the Russian River Inn—straight out of the fifties with prices to match. Lots of mashed potatoes and gravy. I want to keep putting on weight."

They packed up and once more took to the trail. At the exit to the meadow, Brian paused to give Edmund a breather. "I bet you reached this spot many times, looked back, saw something interesting and went back in."

"Many times, believe me," Edmund readily confessed. "But not today. Let's get something to eat. I'm famished."

They drove west along the river, almost to Guerneville. The Russian River Inn delighted Brian, with its ersatz Alpine decor so popular to the south in the Santa Cruz Mountains. They both ordered a beer and five-course dinners for $5.95. Their friendly, grandmotherly waitress brought Edmund his turkey and Brian his filet of sole, which was fine.

"Sounds like Hawaii's still a possibility for you." Brian was trying to be reassuring.

"The doctor says I can go in a couple of weeks." Ravenously hungry, Edmund wiped off traces of mashed potato and gravy on his mouth with his napkin. "Last time was great. Stayed up on the twenty-first floor of this luxury hotel. I met this Viet Namese kid, eight inches, pretty good for an Asian, except he would not visit me in my air-conditioned room and I couldn't bear the stuffiness of his place. Even so we had a few good days. Then I hung around with these Japanese men, all about my age. And I still caught lots of various activities going on in surrounding hotels with my binoculars."

"And the slobberer didn't follow you on this trip?"

"No, but there was this fat, blond German who began to hassle this Polynesian kid who got hard next to me in the showers. This time, though, I was ready—I detached the shower head and doused him with freezing cold water—that did the trick."

Brian laughed heartily. "Sounds like retirement agrees with you." Despite his better judgment he ended up joining Edmund for a huge dessert.

"I tell you retirement is the best thing that ever happened to me. I don't miss the grind at all—getting up at 6 AM and commuting all the way to Palo Alto. Too many headaches as a personnel director. I prefer my current problem. Why does Superstar video open so late? The Castro is already so crowded by 11 AM it's hard to find a parking place." Edmund grinned like a silly little girl. "And I'm completely retired—I'm saying 'no' when the big wigs try to pick my brain or the office ladies invite me to luncheons."

The waitress brought the modest check which Edmund immediately grabbed. "I still owe you for all your help with my move. Funny thing, you know. That long commute, all those hassles at work—no boy friend would have put up with it. I was married to my job, didn't have time for anyone else. Maybe it worked out for the best."

Brian, feeling good, plunked down an absurdly big tip, wanting to delight the waitress. Side by side they walked down the long dining room, out into the early evening sunlight. Edmund flipped up the lock on the passenger side of his VW Fox to let Brian in. "This thing spends half its time at Werner's

Repair Shop, although, God knows, I never tire of seeing Werner, such a beauty, even under such trying circumstances. 'Not good news, Edmund. $900.'" Edmund's German accent was perfect. "'The Bosch fuel injectors—not so good that year.'"

"Indulge yourself, go out and get yourself something nice." Brian couldn't understand it; if he had plenty of money like Edmund and maybe a year or so to live, wouldn't he break down and splurge on something at least comfortable, if not luxurious? An Altima, an Acura—even a Toyota Camry?

On the road Brian took over the driving at Santa Rosa after Edmund indicated that he was feeling queasy. He asked Edmund about his brother, knowing that with the recent death of both parents, they had inherited a small fortune. Brian figured that never having closely connected to anyone out here, Edmund had resorted to "family values," even though he still resented his brother for bullying him, for calling him a sissy when they were growing up.

"My brother? He's just the same—families never change. He's still the eight-year old tying to grab the biggest pork chop on the plate. He has one last payment to send me from our parents' money, so I'll suck up to him just a bit longer and then you can bet I'll send him one snide letter."

"Forget him. Enjoy your retirement. You're your own boss now."

Edmund slipped into a nap for the rest of the drive down 101, waking up only as they crossed the Golden Gate. As they drove across Polk Street, Edmund suddenly perked up. "It's windy as hell down on Polk Street the other day. I see this car, completely covered with balloons, with this guy inside. Actually I should say 'lady'—it's this year's Empress. I've seen her picture in one of the local rags, so, one of her big fans, I try to get her attention. But then a big burst of wind blasts some of those balloons right into my face and, of course, she can't hear a word I'm saying. Such a dottering old fool. But, AIDS or not, it's the same old Polk Street—it could have been 1965."

"So still cruising Polk Street?"

"I'd go crazy if I didn't get out of my place at least once a day. So it's Land's End when it's nice, Polk Street when it's not."

Brian, who had driven the Fox up to Edmund's garage, got out to open the door. Edmund also got out and waited for him to lock everything up. Then, as they walked around the corner to Edmund's front entrance, Edmund's lips tightened as if he had sucked on a lemon. "The other day these old friends wanted me to be in their group—you know, all HIV positive men. I couldn't do it. What would I get from it? Just depression."

"Don't even think about them," Brian assured Edmund, escorting him inside where he would, as usual, spend the night by himself. "I'll see you in a couple of days for breakfast."

11

"I was feeling neglected. Our relationship always lacked a certain amount of intimacy." Will stared out of his living room window, distracted, upset. It had already been quite a day.

"You've always felt that way." Brian had settled down in Will's tiny, cluttered living room, having just painfully bumped his shins on a lurking magazine rack.

"Yes, but he used to hang around sometimes. Now it's disintegrated to nothing at all." Will's nervous laugh was particularly irritating tonight. "That trip to Atlanta was the last straw. After years of our planning a big trip, he just disappeared with his new boy friend for a couple of weeks. So we've agreed that I would keep this flat. As you can tell, he's already started moving out his stuff. And he's been spending every night with his new boyfriend."

Will looked forlorn, not that Brian could blame him. "Let's have a drink," he suggested. "Look, you have your career. Even if Nevin won't be there for you, you know I will." Although sudden break-ups often characterized gay romances, Brian was still a bit put off by the unnerving efficiency of Nevin's disappearance.

"It's just like a divorce." Will persisted in moping. "Nevin gets the TV, the VCR, the Black and Decker mixer, the coffee maker, the Gumbys and most of the teddy bears. I get to keep about fifty of the other stuffed animals."

"A bit chilling, to have to divide up all the warm fuzzies," Brian uncrossed his legs and barked his shin on the coffee table.

"That monster piano—he's promised to have it taken away, but it's still here. And he owes me $620, charged on my Visa when he went to Atlanta. Also half a month's rent." Will's complaining tone was beginning to grate on Brian's nerves. "We've had such a bad time lately. I'm not a fighter like him. He knows how to hurt me, expose my greatest vulnerabilities. Hostile cracks about my taste in books, my laugh, even my clothes." Brian shrugged his shoulders, unable to comment, but Will seemed to settle down. "At first with Nevin leaving, I thought I'd never be sexual again. But just the other night I went out to a bar, the Powerhouse, on Folsom Street. I got very stoned and, I don't know, I just felt so comfortable there. Everyone—all the men in leather—looked right at me. I had my leather jacket on. I looked back at everyone; they weren't at all intimidating. Everything radiated with electric energy. And then it passed and it became just another bar. But I left feeling great."

Brian was surprised by this change in Will's tastes, but was saved from having to react by a knock on the door. It was Jacky, Nevin's mother, who had come up from Menlo Park for the day to go to a funeral with them—Keith's, one of Will's former lovers, the one who had put him up after he got stabbed. Still dressed in an appropriately dark suit, Jacky's long, thin face reflected the stress of the day. "A beautiful service, wasn't it? I told Nevin I'd pick up some of his things and store them at our place."

Will got up to hug his surrogate parent, but the hug was prolonged by his sobs. Jacky seemed flustered. After a long, awkward pause, she stammered, "I know this doctor at Stanford—some of his clients have been living for seven or eight years so far—with the virus."

"It's been a rough week for Will." Brian felt awkward sitting by himself on the couch. Indeed it had. First he had tested positive and then Nevin left. What a mess. Something about Jacky's dogged loyalty to Will touched Brian deeply.

"I know you and Nevin will talk things out and do what's best for the both of you." Good for Jacky—she was refusing to blame either party, refusing to hold out phony hopes of a reconciliation. Tragedy definitely brought out the best in some people. "I haven't seen or talked to Nevin for a while. Just tell him if he needs anything—except wanting to borrow either money or my car—he can have it."

Brian was sniffling when he hugged Jacky good-bye. Will put an arm around Brian, trying to comfort him. The appalling irony of it. "I'm fine, Will. It's good to cry at funerals—or a little bit later. You don't have to comfort everyone else all the time, you know."

Brian had found the funeral offensive. A Catholic Church in the Excelsior district. Keith had been one of the most militant gay activists, but the words "gay" and "homosexual" were never uttered. The usual tasteless propaganda for the Church from the priest, plus a banal rendition of "The Impossible Dream."

But Will, who had perhaps wisely popped a Percodan, seemed to be taking everything in stride. As they returned to sitting side by side on the couch, he attempted to be philosophical. "My T-cell count has dipped pretty low, but my doctor thinks AZT can raise it, so I'm already on it. I suppose I should quit smoking and start practicing relaxation techniques. Not now, but soon."

AZT. Low T-cell count. Brian could hear Daniel's clipped, cut-and-dried objectivity—"an average of thirteen months from diagnosis."

Will turned around and once again stared out the window at nothing in particular. "How much I wanted to give Nevin a gift, to tell him, 'I'm clean, I'm negative. You have nothing to worry about.'"

Was Will serious? No resentment towards Nevin for leaving him at this juncture? Brian sat up and fixed Will's gaze. "Don't be silly. You've told me that he's shot up speed, that he's had unsafe sex." Perhaps it was cruel to insist on reality, so he relented. He shrugged and shifted to the lightly philosophical. "Worry about yourself, not Nevin. I know he's been, like you, putting off being tested as long as possible. Maybe that's not such a bad strategy—that's probably what I'd do. But sooner or later. . . ."

Sitting there, shirt carelessly opened, one nipple exposed, a bit of baby fat near his waist, the top button of his pants opened enticingly, Will suddenly was very appealing and Brian quickly responded. We can use that damn forbidden bedroom, thought Brian, who was still computing the implications of all these changes. Finally they could stretch out deliciously, even fall asleep together.

Will picked up on the chemistry of the moment and reached over and pulled down Brian's zipper, allowing his cock to spring up. When Will started to wrestle Brian down into a clinch, Brian cried out, "The bedroom, the bedroom," willing to sacrifice the heat of the moment for greater long-term comfort.

But after they reached the bed, Will had to jump up because of indigestion. He lit a cigarette whose smoke drove Brian crazy. "There's no ventilation in here—my throat's getting scratchy," he complained. "No wonder—look! You've lit two different cigarettes."

"I'm kind of spaced out tonight." Will crushed one out while taking a long drag on the other. "I still need these—can't take all the fun out of life. After all, it was seven years with Nevin, you know. I guess I sowed the seeds of a destructive relationship with him by always being so accommodating."

"Well, I could have pointed that out to you a million times, but I held back." He couldn't resist the temptation; he was glad he had the chance to say it.

"I know, I know. I had to find out for myself. But hey, I'm still learning and life goes on. A new phase. Sometimes I sleep twelve hours—no guilt! I have a gay doctor I can trust, a good medical plan from work and I'm even thinking about seeing this new guy, Doug."

Brian was shocked, overwhelmed. Already a new possibility? What about their relationship? His questions tumbled out. "How did you meet? How did it happen so fast?"

"At a party a few days ago. We hit it off right away. He's HIV positive, too. I'm curious to see what happens."

Gay men, thought Brian, we move so quickly. A part of him felt a guilty sense of relief that AIDS-stricken Will might not be his responsibility after all.

"Did I tell you about those recent phone calls I got for Nevin?" Will was quick to change to subject.

"Nope."

"I think men were paying him for sex, probably because he needed cash to buy drugs. When I told this one guy that Nevin didn't live here anymore, he asked if I was available." Will suddenly lunged for Brian on the huge double bed. A willing victim, Brian submitted to being stripped, throwing his head back, ready for a blow-job. Instead he heard clanging. He opened his eyes just as Will placed his wrists into a pair of handcuffs which he locked, leaving the key in full view on a table beside the bed. Then he draped a chain, loosely, over Brian's balls. When he pulled his own pants down, Brian noticed he was wearing a cock ring. "It helps me stay hard," he explained. "My pubic hair has almost grown back from when Nevin tied me to a chair and shaved me. We were attempting to re-ignite the old fire, but it didn't work." Will's cock engorged a bit after he put on a condom. "I just can't take any chances with people now."

Brian didn't mind the handcuffs because he totally trusted Will, but, resenting Will's sudden paranoia, he couldn't stomach the chemical taste of the condom. Luckily, he allowed Brian to pull off the condom to jerk him off–the joy of real flesh. Then, just as Will started sucking him off, they heard a key turning in the front door, barely ten feet away. They froze in place.

"I just needed to pick up a few things to go on a little trip tomorrow." Nevin stuck his nose into the bedroom, then quickly withdrew after assessing the situation. "I'll be gone in two minutes."

Handcuffed, cock erect, Brian felt an urge to make some kind of defensive comment like, "Did you teach Will all this stuff?" but what did it matter? Nevin was already out of the picture anyway–they weren't doing anything "wrong."

Once Nevin was out the door, they resumed their sex, not the best for Brian. He had a strangely delayed ejaculation, plus an unpleasant sensation with it, mildly painful. He then attempted to bring Will to a climax, but Will needed to take charge of himself. At least they could share the afterglow. "That chain did something funny to me," Brian explained as Will unlocked the handcuffs.

"Look," he picked up the chain. "There's no big deal. It was just lying lightly on you."

Brian acknowledged to Will that he probably had some unconscious resistance to the idea of bondage. He then wondered to himself whether Will might be going in a direction that did not work for him. Maybe Will just wasn't up to it anymore—the warm love and hot sex they used to have. They snuggled for a while, then moved apart—Will, unlike Brian, did not like much physical contact while he slept.

At 3 AM they were jarred awake by Will's alarm—time for his AZT. He had sweated so much that they had to change the sheets. Brian fell back asleep only to wake up again shortly, fleeing a horrible nightmare. In his dream he had contaminated blood and had to stay in the hospital. What a wretched, rotten feeling—intense, bleak pessimism. Restlessly he wondered if they would ever live together. He was willing. Would their love intensify? But what about the neurotic lovers syndrome—would Nevin come to his senses, would they reconcile? No, that was what heterosexuals would do. After seven years a straight couple would make-up, break-up, make-up ad nauseam. Brian could conclude nothing, merely advising himself to keep his expectations low.

When they got up for breakfast, Will moved more slowly than Brian, blasting all-news AM radio while he showered, then watching a talk show on the black and white set in the kitchen as they drank their coffee. In the bathroom Brian had to put up with an ongoing torture at this place, an empty toilet paper dispenser. (Nevin's sisters would send them a case of it, just so there would be some for their visits.) Brian had to smile to himself as he wiped himself with the tissues Will brought him.

He would be happy to return home, where his life seemed to be under better control despite its loneliness.

After another half cup of coffee, Brian kissed Will good-bye, happy to have some time to himself. The first thing he was going to do when he got home was feed the parrots.

12

"I think your lights are flickering, Daniel." Brian had just settled down in Jorge's living room on Potrero Hill where, despite some dread about hanging around the new lovebirds, he had accepted Daniel's invitation to have a hot tub with Robin and himself after having managed to avoid them both for a few weeks. The Saturday night blues—Brian was trying hard not to see himself as the pathetic old bachelor rescued from his morbid isolation by this younger couple. He particularly dreaded the eruption of any sexual sparks between them. As it was, after a promising start to his friendship with Daniel—concerts, operas, films, occasionally sleeping over at each other's place as buddies, Brian had seen precious little of Daniel and virtually nothing of Robin in recent weeks.

"I'll call PG&E right now. Something in the wiring—maybe the circuit breakers aren't kicking in. I don't think Chad and Jorge cared at all about long-term maintenance around here. And who could blame them? Chad's already gone, leaving Jorge behind, but at least he got six months out of the hot tub. They had to lift the thing over the house with a crane! Then he went and used an everyday extension cord buried three inches deep in the ground to carry power to the hot tub." Daniel raised his eyebrows to indicate his own mild shock at the situation, then got up to call the power company.

"They can't come for a couple of hours. Let's take Jorge out—he needs stuff from the health food store anyway. Shouldn't take us long. Robin called to say he'd be late, but he's got a key."

"So Jorge's not doing so well?"

"Jorge started going downhill quickly once Chad died. As Chad's best friend at work, I kind of inherited Jorge—and what a volatile relationship it was, too! I tried visiting everyday, sometimes twice. But he'd still call me practically every hour, leaving these mournful messages on my answering machine, castigating me for abandoning him, begging me to come over."

Once out and about, things went pleasantly enough on their little expedition until Jorge, inside the Rainbow Grocery, spotted a cute boy in front of the bins with all the nuts. Eyes popping, veins bulging on his very high forehead, Jorge called out to the winsome young thing, "Baby Blossom."

"What an expression," sighed Daniel, after trying to calm down his friend. "He must have picked it up from Chad, something from his adolescence in Utah."

Jorge then spotted another young man and stood transfixed, staring at him while he ate cashews straight from the bin, refusing to stop even after a clerk intervened. Instead he started yelling, "I have AIDS!" at the top of his lungs.

"It's all so unmistakenly San Francisco here," Brian mused. "Nobody's uptight. Everyone's so cool about it."

"If the end is near, why not live it up?" explained Daniel. "At first I loved his devil-may-care attitude, but now it's beginning to get to me. The dementia's getting worse. I had to lock him up in the loony bin for a few days—he needed the structure, the stability of it. Since then he's been more or less okay until tonight."

He shepherded Jorge through the check-out line and the trio moved on to the old drugstore atop Potrero Hill. Brian was delighted. "It looks like something right out of the forties."

While they waited for a couple of prescriptions for Jorge, Daniel gave Brian the dreaded state-of-the-romance report on Robin. "It's going well. It's quite passionate, actually. We've spent a few nights together although its hard to find enough time, what with my job and Jorge and all."

Back at the house, Daniel flipped the new prescriptions to Jorge, indicating that he might want to start taking them, but Jorge would have none of it. "What good are they?" he exploded. Glowering with indignation, he ripped off the childproof caps and scattered the expensive capsules all over the floor. Then he ran to the medicine cabinet in the bathroom, flung open the door and threw scores of other containers across the living room rug. "Look! Look at all those pills! Chad's pills! They didn't do him a damn bit of good and they won't do me any good either, not with my T-cell count at twelve!" His eyes rolled frighteningly.

"Jorge, Jorge, do you want anything for dinner?" Brian was impressed by Daniel's patient tone.

"Make me a shake. Make it thick. Very thick."

Brian picked up all the containers, searching out and finally finding every one of those loose capsules. Then the phone rang–Daniel disappeared for a couple of minutes. "It was a boyfriend of Jorge's from Amsterdam, someone who's sending him a painting," he reported. So Jorge was still leading an interesting life so close to death. Brian was impressed. "He's gotten rid of the amoeba he picked up in Budapest but he had to take Flagyl–the stuff strips your intestines bare. That's why I put so much acidophilus yogurt in his shakes."

After feeding Jorge, Daniel ushered him to his bedroom. "At least he goes to bed early. I need some peace and quiet. It's been a big week for lawyers and bankers. Jorge has signed over the deed of the house to me. I just have to put out $25,000 cash to buy his mother a house on the coast of Bahia. I'll have to liquidate all my cash and take a second on this house; there's still a mortgage on it."

"But do you want to leave Noe Valley–it's so lovely there." Brian felt isolated on Potrero Hill, nervous even, with the projects lurking just two blocks away.

"Don't you see? This is my chance at some equity. I'm practically married to my job but I need a divorce. I don't think the company's going to make it." Daniel raised his eyebrows dramatically to impart the shocking news. "These new products are a desperate attempt to stay competitive, but they've just laid four engineers off, two in my department, plus half the regular staff. The owners don't care any more and I'm sick of being subjected to their patriarchal whims. Last week, even though I'm working ten hours a day, this nosy woman, who makes half my salary, caught me not deducting an hour or two for dinner. Now she checks on me everyday. I'm desperate to change careers, but right now I'm paralyzed, afraid to make a decision. I figure I'll try living in this house for a while on a wait-and-see basis."

The door bell rang—the PG&E man—maybe they'd have a hot tub after all. Brian wandered about, noticing a clipping on the refrigerator door which detailed the plight of some poor guy who had shot up coke through his penis. "The gangrenous member fell off while he was in the bathtub one day." For some reason he found it utterly hilarious.

After the power was restored by connecting a new heavy-duty wire to the hot tub, Daniel ushered out the P. G. & E. man and returned, eager to make his point. "You bought your house just before prices in the city skyrocketed—all we damn faggots upgrading everything and then selling for huge profits. Maybe I can do it too. $60,000 a year and no deductions. A crummy '82 Honda. High rent, high commute costs. What's holding me here anyway? I subscribe to Theater Rhinoceros, I'm in the Bicycling Club, take Tai Chi lessons, but have no social contacts. Everything's a fizzle. Imagine this place with a second story deck out front, coffee in the morning sun, just like yours. A new kitchen, a laundry room down in the basement, with a small guest room. And then I'll sell it."

"What then? How about Robin?" Brian wondered aloud.

Just then the doorbell rang again. Daniel jumped up. "He's not that keen on staying in the city either. Actually, I've got my eye on this place up in Oregon—the Portland area. A couple of friends live there now. They're HIV positive and afraid the current owner's going to throw them out."

Just as Brian began to warn Daniel about overextending himself financially, Robin entered, eager for a hot tub. So they stripped in the kitchen, donned the white terry cloth robes hanging at the top of the staircase, padded down the rickety stairs, hauled off the water-logged top, and gently eased themselves into the turgid water.

Brian, who brought up the rear, wondered at first why he had dreaded this situation. That old adolescent feeling of being left out. Surely that was not relevant here. He'd have his own chances for romance some day. He took a deep breath and attempted to settle into the tub casually, enjoying the garden lit by floodlights above an Italianate fountain in the middle of the yard. A huge apricot tree, a date palm, and several Norfolk pines loomed over them. There was a nip of autumn in the air, just right for a hot tub. He allowed his thoughts to roam free, and found himself anticipating the beginning of the school year with enthusiasm.

After a few minutes, he figured out, by the way Robin squirmed, that Daniel "had his hands all over him," to use that hateful phrase of his mother's. (Another one—"she can't keep her hands out of his pants" was so nasty that it struck him as sexy.)

Robin, seemingly embarrassed by this semi-public display of affection, looked over at Brian for a distraction. "Did Daniel tell you what happened that time a couple of weeks ago, after I picked him up at the airport?"

"No."

"Right after we unlocked the door of his place, he dragged me into the bedroom. After a few minutes, we heard a sudden thump on the porch. He jumped up and darted out to the porch. 'Fuck. It's gone. My briefcase is gone.'"

"What did you have in it?" Brian was envious of their gay abandon.

"First, the briefcase itself was a graduation present from my sister," Daniel explained. "Also lots of business stuff, my bank statements, my goddam journal, too."

"You let your lust get to you," Robin teased.

"Why do I always have to take all the responsibility?" Daniel complained. "It's my fault, right. I was supposed to drag everything in myself."

Silence. Brian decided to help out, just to avoid further sex talk. "Robin, how's your new job? You're at UC Med Center now, right?"

"I don't like it. They're exploiting me, got me driving this huge truck around the city, shuttling the experimental dogs back and forth between the lab at Parnassus Heights and the kennels at Hunter's Point. At least I don't have to put up with that damn new supervisor at the Humane Society any more. She drove me crazy."

Daniel jumped right in, sounding like a patriarch. "I keep telling him to keep it for six months, then check out the job board and move around in the UC system to a better job–hold onto those great fringe benefits." Daniel swivelled about to look directly at Brian. "He's got this neurosis about money, anyway. He's saved thousands with no use for it. He's stuck. He should work on his acting career, maybe spend some money on therapy. He's so careful, so prudent."

"All my family's totally irresponsible about money. Maybe I've overreacted a little. But at least I don't have to juggle the books every month like you." Robin, pissed at first, decided to take advantage of Brian's affable presence. "I'll admit my family's as messed up as anyone's, but I wasn't always this stable, you know." Robin shifted away from Daniel to look more directly at Brian. "Before I went to AA I'd come to the city every weekend to party, driving back totally drunk on that scary San Pedro Dam Road. Even worse, I used to go on speed-crystal binges. I got so high that when I came down I was close to suicide. One time, flying high, we went to the Trocadero Transfer and danced all night. For the first time I felt this great sexual power over men. They had mirrors all over the place and I had been working out. I looked in the mirror–at my body–it looked incredibly stunning. 'You are gorgeous,' I said to myself. I had never seen myself that way. Tons of stares. Tons of offers. I embraced it. I accepted it."

"You were turned onto yourself. Those men saw someone

appreciating himself. They love that," Daniel chimed in.

"Once at the Russian River I got so depressed on speed it was so painful I just wanted to jump through the window, just crash through and kill myself. When you shoot off like a rocket, you come down like a ton of bricks." (Hearing about this side of Robin made him more appealing to Brian, perverse creature that he was, especially with that slightly naughty gleam back in his eyes.) "So then I got rid of all the bad influences in my life and went back to basics, became a vegetarian. And I started meditating. That's speeding up my evolution—you can learn a lot about yourself meditating, you know. And I learned that being physically beautiful does not ensure that you get love, only attention—and I had confused the two."

"Still," added Daniel, "I see in you issues hanging ripe on a tree, waiting to be plucked."

"At least I can sit still for an hour, not like you, with all those ants in your pants," Robin retaliated, irked by Daniel's air of superiority.

"Remember," Daniel forged on, ignoring the remark, "if we move out of the city, to Oregon, say, I won't know any therapists you could use. It's a delicate art, like a doctor's or a priest's. I know what's going on with them, been using them on and off for a decade, know the best ones."

"I respect your experience and appreciate the fact that you want to share that with me," Robin answered in a slightly clipped, formal tone, "but I don't feel that way. I've delved into a treasure trove of spiritual masters and now I've got a key to unlock the door. With meditation there's a huge door opening, huge horizons, expansive vistas. Change is happening, coming from within."

"Okay, okay," Daniel backed down, but Brian could see his eyes light up mischievously for one more prod. "Just let me know when you're ready for a good therapist."

"It will be a while, I assure you. I think I'm on the right track for now."

"And I think I'm turning into a prune. I've had enough, how about you guys?" Brian really meant that he had had enough of them for the night. He was not proud of the feeling that revenge had been sweet. Still it hadn't been that rough an evening, finding out that these guys weren't quite ready to settle in together, happily ever after.

They put the cover back on the hot tub and carefully made their way up the creaky steps to dress. Beating a hasty retreat to his car before they could start making out again, Brian, remembering that he had admitted to himself that he would have had a tough time living with Will, wondered just what it would take to make a romance work these days. Could he do it? Could he possibly put up with all the bullshit?

13

Some weeks later, Brian called on Richard on his way home from school and stumbled into a tense moment between Richard and his younger brother, Peter.

"There's the bell–that'll be the shuttle to the airport." Peter, obviously relieved, stood up to give Richard a quick hug before picking up his bag.

"Nice meeting you, Peter." Brian, who had just arrived, shook Peter's hand as he began to stride out. "Oh, I wouldn't do that if I were you– "

Too late. Having leaned down to pet Cleo, Peter's hand was viciously assaulted by the Siamese's teeth and claws. Even though he instantly pulled his hand away, it still became a bloody mess. Brian escorted Peter into the kitchen where they quickly cleaned up his wounds so he could be on his way.

Back in the living room, alone with Richard on their respective couches, Brian couldn't help teasing his friend about the feisty feline. "So the visit didn't go well with Peter?"

"How did you know?"

"How did I know! First, I felt all that tension between you two. And then because I know you get Cleo to act out all your dark motives–your shadow has struck once again."

"It was most disappointing." Richard looked sour, not appreciating Brian's humor. "Peter was here under promising circumstances, for an architect's conference without his wife, but he always brought over a colleague–no chances at all for intimate chats. His usual avoidance. He did say a remarkable thing, though, something I've never heard him admit. 'I don't remember ever being happy as a child.' That touched me very much." Richard reached for his tea. He had said all he wished to say about his brother, and changed the subject.

"Welcome back, Brian. How was your own visit with that wildly expressive mother of yours, who lives out her feelings so directly that even Stanislavski would be proud of her? Is her health improving?"

"Yes, but I think it's only temporary. Her mind's still as sharp as a tack and she survived this last stay in the hospital, but we've had to put the house up for sale and she's going to live with her younger sister who, luckily, still lives in the same town. But the cancer's getting worse. I keep saying to myself that she's eighty-five after all. But I can tell you I'm freaked–the idea of this strong-willed woman dying leaves me feeling exposed, vulnerable." Unnerved, Brian jumped up to pour them some wine.

"Did you get along okay with her? Sometimes the nearness of death can prompt improved communication."

"Not really." Brian's immature scowl returned with a surprisingly bitter tone. He could barely muster any optimism. "That's what I'm hoping will happen with her sister. They've fought all their lives, but maybe this time, their last chance, will be different." Brian returned with their drinks and collapsed on the couch. "As for myself, I lacked my usual patience and forbearance. Even though she was in the hospital for just about the whole visit, she still gave me a hard time about my life style, but I insisted on defending myself, even though she's at death's door."

Richard sipped his wine and looked up. "The same old issues, I suppose?"

"What can I say? Here I am, in my fifties, still scratching and clawing away, trying to forge my adult identity in her eyes. You reach a certain age and it gets so ludicrous. I'm already her parent, supporting her somewhat financially and I've always been her father-confessor. But yet?"

"But yet you get depressed that she, and the past itself, still exert so much power."

"Exactly." After first smelling and then lying on his jacket, Cleo, amazingly, slowly crawled onto Brian's lap. "She more or less accepts that I'm gay, but she tries to impose heterosexual standards on me. 'Why can't you, a college professor, find someone to settle down with—I don't want you sleeping around and coming down with AIDS.' I seethed as she went into a moralistic paean to the virtues of celibacy and monogamy. I've told her many times how the virus gets transmitted, but she can't, she won't, absorb the concept of safe sex. And it's not like I haven't been trying to find that 'special someone.'"

"How exasperating."

"Another time I mentioned visiting someone from our home town with AIDS, a son of one of her best friends. And even though she knew better, she went into a long harangue about how I'm endangering myself, that I must never accept clothing or bedding from such people after they die. A totally irrational prejudice, but she just can't stop herself."

"Yes, it's a lifelong battle." Richard sighed, slipping into his persona of the Old Man on the Mountain who has been through it all, the baggy-eyed Sage, in his long johns and gray sweat suit. "Still, you're lucky. Because she's still alive you can work some of this out."

"I guess." Brian reconsidered Richard's point and then perked up. "You're right. I've been feeling guilty about this confrontation I had with her right in the hospital. It was triggered by my own perception that she had not asked me a single question about myself or my life the whole visit. So I told her about teaching some new courses with gay themes. I didn't exactly expect credit or recognition, but boy was I pissed when she came out with, 'You mean they actually let you teach classes like that?'"

"And you exploded?"

"Boy, did I explode. I didn't care who heard—doctors, nurses, patients, whatever. I just yelled and screamed. 'Tell your friends anything you want to—or need to—about me. Say I'm divorced if you must. But when you're with me, I don't want to hear anything negative about my life. I'm in excellent health, with a fine career, and make competent, adult decisions.'" Startled by

Brian's fierce tone, Cleo suddenly bolted from Brian's lap. "I guess I was insisting on her respect. I think the outburst did some good because she was extremely pleasant for the rest of the visit. She even mentioned that because the lady in the next room had hearing problems, probably no one had heard anything."

"Brian, a trip like that—you'll need months to recover."

"I honestly don't think she has months left. It must have been so scary for you when your own indomitable mother passed away at ninety." Brian offered to fill up Richard's wine glass, having guzzled down his own.

"Yes, it most certainly was. She was such a cold, stony, creature. I sometimes think you were lucky that your father died just as you were about to enter puberty. That way you could choose to become your own man. I think my mother was just desperate for a husband. An unmarried Mormon woman—talk about a stigma. Already in her thirties, she latched onto my misfit father. But so mismatched were my parents that I've spent all my adult life trying to unify myself, yoking together their violently antagonistic and mutually repellant halves."

It had begun to rain outside. Brian got up and lit a Dur-a-flame in Richard's handsome fireplace. "Are you still haunted by not having connected much at all with your father?"

"Indeed. He was a travelling salesman, having been convinced by my macho mother that teaching rated as too unmasculine a profession, so most of the time he was away—my mother learned of his philandering only much later. I guess I'm still subject occasionally to those wide mood swings of his. He was far more intense, had a far more volatile nature than my mother's, so ugly when he lost control." Cleo jumped up on Richard's chest. "Mother warned us to stay cool, never to go the way of excess, so I adopted a very narrow aperture of emotion within which to operate. In the role of the eldest sibling, I became ever more the diplomat by trying to prevent quarrels from starting, always expecting disaster, throwing oil on troubled waters. If we kids had stayed as cold as she, we would have become ice-houses on the surface, but trembling volcanoes within."

"So he was more like my mother?"

"Exactly, capable of acutely embarrassing us in public. Oh, those Mormon gatherings when he tried to get everyone involved in a sing-along. He'd put his arm around friend and stranger alike, an aggressive bid for control which struck me as a form of invasion. So incapable of drawing boundaries, he would spill over into our territory, so possessive of us, so clawing that I never wanted *anyone* to touch me. I hated his body and his smell—that made it extremely difficult for me to be intimate. Had a beautiful boy touched me, I probably would have fainted dead away."

That shockingly loud doorbell. Brian got up and paid the beautiful brown-skinned boy for their Thai dinner.

"I'd certainly faint if *that* creature touched me." Richard shooed Cleo off so he could move to the table. "I'm convinced that restaurant is only a cover for a big drug cartel. The K-1 Corporation—that's what it says on my Visa bill."

Brian set the table and served them their dinner. "So it was probably better your father was gone most of the time?"

"I always felt relieved when he took off. I preferred life without his constant judgments, his arbitrary exercise of male authority. But with my father gone, my mother gave us endless chores, holding us to an almost impossible standard of cleanliness. I took some consolation in her love, but what a cold, stony love. My mother could not cry, for to do so would reveal their similarities." Richard picked up his fork, but hesitated to start eating. "Repelled by my father, however, I hungered for love from her, always terrorized, though, by trying to keep that dormant volcano controlled. Later in life, with her bad back, she became very feisty, feisty and scrappy. You have to fight for everything when you're an invalid."

Brian wondered, as they began eating, if Richard were referring to himself as well as his mother. "Sounds as if you really sympathized with her plight."

"That universal identification of gay men with our mothers, antennae all over our bodies. We had an intense intimacy, the heart of which was sharing books and movies. We would come out of a film exhausted, laughing or weeping, having left our daily selves behind, often feeling transformed."

"Good training for a classics professor!"

"Sometimes I'd be so moved teaching poetry I could barely mouth the words in class. When teaching a play, I frequently could barely go on. Yet I took great pains to hide my feelings, not wanting to be embarrassing like my father. At a performance I'd identify so totally I'd have no separate being. I'd come out of it as though stunned and shattered by reality. All my nerves, open and bleeding, exposed conduits. Friends would say, 'My goodness. You were really mesmerized in there. You weren't in this world.'"

"Nothing wrong with that really. It's that empathy with the mother that scares me, though, repulses me even."

"Yes, I've come to see the neurotic element in trying, as a boy, to fuse with her, to become her, a fateful desire in the male, of course. Back then I feared I'd never find more satisfying intimacy for the rest of my life and I probably never have. I peaked too early, sharing all those worries and fears, and I gave up part of my autonomy waiting on her when she was so demanding, bedridden with a bad back."

"Yuck, Richard. That's so horrible I have to assume you're exaggerating. Such inappropriate bonding."

"And remember, too, that strong mother who suffered with so much pain never let herself cry. No wonder I needed art as a catharsis. But now I'm just trying to connect up more circuits. That's the glory of life, tolerating a wider range of emotions. All I saw in my family was hysteria verging on madness."

"Sounds as if that doc of yours is really helping."

"Yes, yes. Last week he dared to bring up the concept of psychological incest between mother and son."

Richard's comment excited Brian. He had never seen this perplexing issue from that perspective before. "Yes, the violation of a child's boundaries. Yes, I see it's *not* the mother's latent sexuality. That's not the taboo that poisons the son. It's the possessiveness, the refusal to let the son lead his own life. That's why I exploded on my trip."

It seemed that their conversation had had its climax. Exhausted, they stared into space for a few moments until Richard tried, a bit self-consciously, to wrap it up, as he returned to his couch for Good Earth tea and their modest dessert of a couple of Apple Newtons. "Families—families tend to become more and more themselves," he philosophized.

Brian found the comment hilarious. "Families? I just don't know. So many friends have recently had kids just to extract *some* meaning out of their going-nowhere lives. They survive all right, but both parents have to work like crazy and end up exhausted, with no time to see anyone except in-laws. The irony of it all. Trapped in the very model of the nuclear family against which we all once so vehemently rebelled twenty years ago."

"Consumed by life."

"That's it. A great expression. 'Consumed by life.'"

Richard rolled over, chasing Cleo off, once again preparing to retire to his bedroom. "They need an object of love to live by, something with vitality because people just aren't so self-generating—we're consumed by life. The child can open the door, seemingly, to meaning, vitality, curiosity, challenge, accomplishments."

"Okay, okay." Brian too got up, delighted by Richard's sonorous voice pushing things to mellifluous, extravagant extremes.

"Only later in life did I see that my father was 'consumed by life,' by his wife, his children, his business, the Mormon authorities and, at times, his own childish and uncontrollable nature. Years later I would weep for his life, but in youth, I hated him and wanted to be the opposite of him in every way."

Richard shuffled into the kitchen and opened the refrigerator to get ice for his back.   "Well, cheers, Brian, and a very fine evening to you. We must discuss these matters again very soon."

14

"I'm writing a book using the persona of a woman artist, the woman I know all about, my anima, the woman who knows what it's like to be a sexual object." Timothy, Brian's colleague from the art department, handsome and charming as ever despite having just turned forty, granted a warm smile to Brian, one of his many admirers. Brian responded by moving his eyes down from Timothy's slightly receding hairline to fixate on his full, luscious lips. Every Thursday they got together for lunch at Martha's Mexican Restaurant, one of the few halfway decent places to eat within walking distance of their campus. "Interested in checking it out?"

"I'd love to. After all the subject does fascinate me." Brian took a sip from his cheap, lightweight margarita, a libation which had become an integral part of their ritual celebrating the end of another week of teaching.

"Me, too. After all, as an only child who lost his father to divorce at the age of two and who was brought up by a mother obsessed by her own body, how could I not be interested in the objectification of women?" Brian noted how Timothy gulped down his drink while he tried to nurse his own. "By the time she was forty she already had her breasts perked and her tummy tucked. No huge extra pieces of flesh for her. She's ever the *femme fatale*."

"You're not just kidding—she's your role model all right," Brian was often sarcastic with Timothy. Images of the female nudes with their intriguing faces at Timothy's last exhibition flashed across his mind.

"Of course, I used to have somewhat the same problem she had, people drawn to me as a kind of *objet d'art*. Funny, though, despite my feverish protestations of bisexuality during my early twenties, only men, never women, told me I rated a 'gorgeous.' Maybe men are just more frank about it, women more shy."

Timothy concluded his provocative statement raising his eyes in assured anticipation of his friend's total attention.

Brian winced, shifting further back in his wicker chair, annoyed by Timothy's inevitable return to his obsession about the aesthetics of the human form. He had just seen one of those network news magazine's reports on how virtually every human being, every species, even, on the planet favored the classically beautiful, one researcher even suggesting that the trait to favor the beautiful was genetic. "Well, everyone admires beauty. Isn't the issue how well one integrates the concept within one's whole life, with a balanced, humanistic existence?" From time to time he had resented Timothy, about a decade younger than he, as one of those charming beauties who got special treatment, all the breaks. But for how much longer? That super-short haircut didn't hide the retreating hairline, and already there was some gray in that jet-black Irish hair. Furthermore, those facial features would accelerate their drooping if he didn't cut down on his drinking.

"It's funny the way people use beauty," Timothy rambled on, seemingly not having heard Brian's statement on these matters. "I'm excited. I mean I think I have a decent idea of how difficult it is to be a beautiful woman these days." He smiled at Brian who tried to register absolutely nothing. "Another drink?"

"Let's stick to our usual routine and switch to coffee. I feel guilty enough as it is, having one so early." Timothy, the archetypal Irish lush with the hollow leg who could consume scads of booze and still handle himself impeccably (but then regret it come the morning hangover), knew better than to make such a request, but it was understood that Brian would be the restraining force.

"True, true," Timothy submitted to the voice of reason. "By the way, dear Brian, returning to our previous theme, do you know anyone about sixty, about my height, who's just as hairy as I am, maybe gray, just a bit paunchy, too? I want to do a new painting, a self-portrait, me at sixty!"

Edmund immediately popped into Brian's mind—the same

height and build, the same white skin and dark Irish eyes and hair. "I know a guy, but you'd better hurry—he's not going to be around for long." Brian pushed back his chair, uncrossed his legs and using a tough-guy tone, issued a challenge. "Is this your attempt at self-acceptance? Some way to placate your fears about aging?" Then he quickly switched back to his usual sincerity. "Actually, I like the idea."

"How can anyone who has to extract nose hairs once a month feel beautiful?" Timothy tried to stick the tines of his fork up his nostrils.

"Don't forget those millions, could it be billions, of hairs you shave all over your body every few days." Between his many visits to the gym and what must be an incredibly time-consuming shaving ritual, Brian wondered how Timothy had any time for his art or writing. Still, he remembered those lovely alabaster arms from when they first met a decade ago—it wasn't until months later that he realized Timothy had shaved them. And his chest and his back. Of course he left just enough tufted pubic hair for aesthetic display at the beach. "Anyway I'll tell my friend, Edmund, about your painting—he might go for it."

Timothy smiled wanly, then continued, ignoring Brian's news. "I remember asking myself as a senior in high school—just before I enlisted in the navy and got turned on to men—only to get kicked out—why should I be interested in another hairy man with a dick? *I'm* a hairy man with a dick. I want tits and pussy. C'mon, Brian. Isn't there a part of a you that wants to grab tits and lick pussy?"

"Are you kidding? Unlike you, Mr. Enlightened Bisexual, I've never had sex with a woman. I can't even remember the last time anyone asked." His brow furrowed. "Well, my mother, of course."

"Isn't it strange," Timothy pressed on, "how the drag queens led the way, shaving their chests. And then so many gay men followed. And now even such straight icons of masculinity as Andre Agassiz and Lorenzo Lamas."

"Meaning that the masculine ideal has become much more androgynous these days?" Brian finished up his coffee. "Or is it just a way to look younger? I notice the only hairy-chested men in ads are daddies vacationing with their families in Bermuda."

"Traditional masculinity dies hard in this culture," injected Timothy, also finishing up his coffee and accepting a refill from the "blonde" Mexican waitress. "One of my first lovers, Jack, came to despise me because I refused to embody his ideal, masculine Ivy League image."

"Jack—was this back when you first became addicted to compulsive serial monogamy?" Brian still envied Timothy's (and now Daniel's) apparent great success at the game of serial monogamy—repeated romantic affairs, none lasting much more than six months, although Timothy had slowed down considerably lately.

"I'd grow my hair super-long or shave it all off just to infuriate Jack." Timothy smiled, revealing rows of even, ultra-white teeth, but refused to acknowledge Brian's satiric thrust about monogamy. "Or I'd strut in front of him in ballet tights. Coincidentally we ran into each other near my flat in the Castro the other day. He's back from Paris where he has lived for many years. It's good he left me because I never would have left him."

Eyebrows raised in skepticism, Brian didn't believe that statement for a moment. "Well, I guess your art is your life," he bantered back.

Timothy looked up bemused, unperturbed. "You know, the worst thing Jack ever said to me was, 'Don't laugh. Laughing makes you look ugly.' I was devastated." He smiled, those beautiful lips still had not lost their appeal for Brian, but Timothy had never, ever shown the least interest. "Oh well, time to get back to my painting. Free time for you. What's in the works for the afternoon?"

"Maybe the beach. It's beautiful out. Why does our best weather always come in October, when we're so busy with school?" They both stood up. "Or maybe I'll drop in on Richard."

"Have fun under that gorgeous bridge and I'll see you next week."

15

They reached Half Moon Bay at noon, still in the fog, but the drizzle had slackened off. Storm after November storm had transformed the coastal hills to a bright green, soothing the arid atmosphere that had persisted during an usually dry October. This time Brian was at the wheel since Edmund now pretty much limited himself to driving in the city. In the intervening weeks since their last visit, Edmund had rarely called him. Of course Brian knew he spoke to his old cronies for hours at a time on the phone, but he rarely saw them either.

A few minutes earlier, back in the heavy drizzle of the Pacifica seascape, on the other side of the hill from Devil's Slide, Edmund had startled Brian out of his foggy reverie. "Yeah, the nephews, nieces, even the cousins, are getting the money. But I wanted to ask you about my furniture. Do you need it? Will you do me a favor and take it?"

Brian figured his half of the house could use some of Edmund's stuff. Hell, why make this a complicated moment, just say yes. "Sure. Why not?"

That decided, they continued rolling along towards Tunitas Creek on their way to Santa Cruz when Brian had an idea. "Do you want to stop at San Gregorio? There's no sun to damage that Irish skin. And it's only a short way from the parking lot to the beach, an easy climb back up."

"I don't know. My heart will break if Carlos is working the parking lot." Edmund claimed to have been in love with the sad-eyed Filipino, but the relationship, like all his others, did not last very long. "I guess I just got too possessive, tried to smother him."

What was the best tack to take? "C'mon, Edmund, you admitted you were 'married' to your career, right? Anyway, he might not even be there. Here's the driveway. There's nothing to lose."

They drove up the rocky, rutted dirt road, past the duck ponds and the meadow sprinkled with sheep. As they approached the tollgatherer, Brian could see it *was* Carlos. He registered some surprise when the Toyota pulled up with Edmund in the passenger seat. Was it surprise at how terrible Edmund looked? No, Brian decided that Edmund still looked pretty good.

Carlos immediately walked over to Edmund's side. "How're you doing, Ed?"

"Good enough. Just thought we'd come down for a quick visit, for old time's sake."

"Not many here today," Carlos moaned. "All these storms have been killing us lately."

"It hasn't been that bad," Brian injected. "Lots of sun last month." He didn't want Edmund thinking his final year was a dud.

"Just go right in." Carlos waived the usual fee, but after a few more pleasantries, he moved on to greet the next car. They parked on the bluff, right above the beach and started to meander down the path towards the ocean when they came upon a sign: WARNING: NO SEXUAL ACTIVITY ALLOWED. SAN MATEO COUNTY PLAINCLOTHESMEN MAY BE PATROLLING THE BEACH. SEXUAL MISCONDUCT IS A SERIOUS OFFENSE.

"Poor Carlos," mused Edmund. "It took so much out of him, getting sued by those horrible people who built that garish house on top of the cliffs, about halfway down the beach. They claimed their teen-age daughter had been traumatized by seeing men having sex below, but she must have had a strong pair of binoculars. Look down there, you tell me if you can figure out who's a boy and who's a girl this far away."

"You can't."

"So they settled out of court. I'm happy for Carlos, but he's become paranoid, just like the rest of society." As they carefully wended their way down the trail, Brian noticed that the damp fog somehow exaggerated the pink, flaky texture of the skin on

Edmund's face. "What changes," Edmund continued. "Twenty-five years ago I'd see carloads of dizzy queens pulling up here at ten in the morning to spend the whole day, every day. I was sorely tempted, but I prayed for the discipline to keep at my career. However, looking back at it, where's the harm? It's not such a bad life in the fresh air, lots of exercise—not to mention the sex." Brian laughed, secretly grateful he could maneuver his own schedule to get out for an hour or two many weekday afternoons.

Once down on the beautiful beach he led Edmund to a "condo," one of the many elaborate driftwood shelters crafted by primarily the gay clientele, not only to avoid the usually cold breeze, but also hide—as well as strategically display—their endowments. Peeking here and there through the holes in the driftwood struck Brian as both demeaning and sexy. And, of course, the condo provided a place for a rendezvous. For some reason, however, he had never done well over the years with the kind of men who had typically frequented this place.

"Years ago," Edmund waxed nostalgic, "I'd eagerly trot the mile or so to the cave up at the north end. This huge, gorgeous beach, those magnificent cliffs, especially up at that end where they're so steep, with those wonderful rounded shapes." He paused for a moment, then chuckled. "I can still see myself stranded on the ledge of that cliff below the cave, the tide coming in, trying like hell to hoist myself up, then being swamped by a huge wave, holding on for dear life. I'd finally drag myself onto the ledge, half-drowned, but still more than ready for any action in the cave."

The image of Edmund—and himself—flailing about helplessly on the ledge as wave after wave crashed atop them tickled Brian's fancy. The reckless courage of older gay men on their wonderfully absurd, sexual chase. "Last week, Edmund, I climbed down that scary cliff at low tide to that remote beach at the Marin headlands on a cold, windy day. Whom did I find? A half dozen men all like myself, all of us at least fifty! And with 'attitude,' too. Men over fifty with 'attitude,' probably only in Marin County!"

Edmund chuckled, then yawned, once, twice, then a few minutes later many times in succession. "I'd like to say it's the sea air, but it's the goddam medication, the stuff I take for gaining weight—it can cause blood clots so I'm taking anti-clotting stuff and *that* makes me sleepy. But such benefits. I usually nap at three, go to bed at nine, and wake up feeling nice and hungry."

"Sounds like you've been doing fine."

"I think the ddI's working. I've gone back to the Y for both exercise and yoga, although when I lie on my stomach I can barely reach back and touch my feet, much less grab them. But they say those natural interferon studies are coming out here soon."

Brian marvelled at Edmund's capacity to believe in organized medicine. How predisposed he was to let his doctors help him.

As if reading his mind, Edmund bragged about his doctor's compliment after a painful test. "'Most other patients—I'd be chasing them around the room.'" He gave one of his rare, outright smiles. "And I've even outlasted this competitor up at the River who used to take so much pride in his negative status. He's gone—a heart attack."

Brian saw the point. Edmund had made it to the age where almost anything could "get you"—heart attack, cancer, stroke, not just AIDS. And he refused to give up. "You couldn't even get an issue of last week's B.A.R.—that report on how fish oil can help keep weight on. It repeats on me, that awful aftertaste." Something was doing him good, Brian figured. The guy hardly huffed and puffed up the path, back to the car.

Driving further south they passed the classic lighthouse at Pigeon Point, then burst into the sunshine just north of Ano Neuvo. In an upbeat mood Edmund launched into an account of a party a couple of nights earlier where "I had a few vodkas, a great time. Met my old friend, Al, there. Still sniffing amyl every night and having sex at the sleazy Locker Room on Polk Street. And what does he say right in front of a bunch of our old friends at this party? 'So what does Edmund do with his money? He doesn't drive it, he doesn't live in it.' I could have killed the guy," Edmund simmered with rage. "After all the times I treated him to dinner and drove him around anywhere he wanted because he never learned to drive."

Something struck Brian, some kind of realization. Edmund had told him the exact same story on the phone last night. Another piece of the puzzle he couldn't solve this morning had fallen into place. Now he understood why Edmund very uncharacteristically failed to show up for their breakfast date at his favorite haunt, the U. S. Restaurant, early that morning. Not finding Edmund in his usual booth, he had asked Lena, the huge blonde waitress who liked to tie her hair back in a severe bun, if she had seen him. "He no here yet." So Brian had stalled for time by visiting the U. S. Restaurant's severely truncated unisex bathroom, six feet high at the entrance but only four feet above the john. A tall person like him had to do the limbo to take a piss, but it was fine as a dark, cool respite to enjoy a satisfying dump.

Still no Edmund. Then, when he had called him up at his flat, the older man had complained, "Where are you? Weren't you supposed to come by here first?" Perplexed then, now it made sense to Brian—the next stage, dementia.

He had then picked Edmund up and brought him to his usual "healthy" breakfast of poached (not fried) eggs, mashed (not french fried) potatoes and fresh French bread with endless pats of butter. Lena, who knew him from two decades of early morning visits before his commute to Palo Alto, had waddled over to his favorite red vinyl booth often this morning with coffee refills, much friendlier than usual, no doubt picking up on his fragility.

Edmund was wide awake by the time they reached Santa Cruz, but, easily fatigued, contented himself with a short walk on the boardwalk. "I've always liked this place. Feels kind of like

an East Coast amusement park back in the fifties, doesn't it?"
The comment, wonderfully predictable, made Brian's day,
sending tingles down his spine. They had both gone to Playland
at Rye Beach in their youths. So funky, so downscale, the same
classic old rollercoaster. It was so fine to interconnect with
Edmund, sharing the past.

After Edmund treated them to a sandwich, they sat on a
bench outside the Surfer Museum at Lighthouse Point observing
the myriads of surfers, skateboarders, and bikers.

On the drive north Edmund fell asleep as soon as they
re-entered the fog at Pescadero. Brian felt a little like a guardian
angel, almost in communion with this man whom he had once
judged to be so different from himself. Soon they crossed the
city limits of San Francisco, the city that had become Edmund's
geographical womb where he would remain for the rest of his
life.

16

"Stacy! Come down here. I want you to meet Dante." Brian stood under the acacia tree, Dante perched on his finger.

"He's so pretty, such a bright blue." Stacy descended the steps quickly from her mother's porch to meet the parakeet.

"The parrots, those wild-cherry-headed conures, are too shrewd to let anyone near them. But Dante must have had a good home. He's comfortable perched on my finger but, of course, I've never made even the slightest move to grab him." Not trusting Stacy to leave well enough alone, Brian flicked his finger upward, encouraging Dante to resume a perch high up in the acacia with the parrots. As he had feared, she made a futile grab for his tail feathers just after his little friend had made good his escape.

She looked good to him today, without her nose ring, her hair a brush cut just slightly longer than the average marine's, her skin exceptionally white against her usual all-black outfit. "I'm so glad Mom dumped that slimeball, Sean."

"He was so cute."

"She should definitely stick to women. That Lynn is okay, kind of square, but I like her."

"Wasn't Sean a friend of your cousin? What's his name—Liz told me a little about him."

"Jeremy. You'll like him, I think. He's supposed to visit some day. Grandma said he's slowly breaking out of his self-imposed exile from the rest of the human race."

They ambled back up to Liz's porch. Brian, a bit irritable today, had sought out the soothing companionship of Liz who at that moment was kissing her daughter good-bye, admonishing her, as usual, to take care late at night in her neighborhood.

Since the fog, escorted by a cold wind, was rolling back on that chilly evening in early December, they decided to take their coffee inside, at the table which directly faced the graceful span at the west end of the Bay Bridge. "I'm grumpy. Not particularly good company."

"Is anything the matter with Will?"

"He's holding his own, but his new boyfriend, Doug, has pneumonia—he's at Mt. Zion and Will's so busy running back and forth that we finally had no choice but to arrange to meet at the hospital in a couple of days. Trouble is, whenever I think about Will's life I get this incredible guilt for complaining. Then I start obsessing on what a steadying force he's been the past few years. When I shared a hot tub with Daniel and Robin the other night, for example, I felt much more like an elderly outcast because I know I won't have Will for long. With them I'm caught in the role of the unap-preciated daddy who's there to listen to all their problems. And, of course, the scorching chemistry between them doesn't help, although they have started bitching about one another."

"Already?" Liz beamed one of her cool, gracious smiles which simultaneously mocked the new lovers, Brian's foolish concerns and herself as well. She looked so fine in her lavender sweats, her firm, full breasts asserting themselves pointedly, her golden hair almost making up for the lack of sun. "Just sit back and watch the show, partner. It won't be a long one. Opposites may attract, but only for so long."

Brian heaved a sigh and looked around her place. What a beautiful decorating job she had done. By comparison his place exuded tackiness, even though the second floor had virtually the same layout. He decided, once again, that he must throw away a lot of old papers, buy a new desk and dining room table, and hire someone to come in and clean once a week. "So what?" he finally responded. He wanted to resist her lightness. "Even if they break up I still have a sense that I won't see much of either of them. Robin and I just don't have much in common. And Daniel's just too busy—and I expect he'll stay that way. But even more irksome to me these days—Timothy."

Liz's eyes lit up. "Here, I expect, is the culprit for your bum mood, not Timothy himself, but your insistence on comparing your life with his."

He ignored her advice. "I've grown to love this house, I love being close to you, but sometimes I envy his living in the Castro, what with their being no places any more for gay people to meet in this part of town. Here the remaining gays are older, usually retired. And then, immature as this may sound, I envy Timothy's body and the bodies of all his lovely boyfriends. I envy serial monogamy—it's all so romantic and thrilling for a few months. Then, at the first sign of trouble, you throw in the towel, flee the coop. No fuss, no muss."

"Brian!" Liz pretended shock. "Blasphemy. After all, Timothy is a man who once proclaimed he didn't like to date because it led to mixing sex and friendship! Which then led to someone's having too many expectations. And then, of course, to someone's wanting out. No wonder nothing lasts for him. Do you think he really wants love?"

Brian sheepishly shook his head, but, in his present mood, he wasn't convinced.

"That's not you. Timothy plays around, that's fun, but he also 'plays around' with people's feelings. I don't think he's consciously cruel—he just ain't ready yet for a long-term connection."

"I suppose you're implying that I am." Brian watched the parrots, Dante too, take off on their rounds. "And what good does it do me? No, I'm changing for the worse. I want a body like Timothy's, I want to experience those hot boy-friends."

"My dear friend," Liz arched her eyebrows during a pregnant pause, "we *all* must deal somehow with middle age."

"Fifty or not, I'm still so tortured by my imperfections that, for the first time I'm seriously considering shaving my graying chest and working out in a gym. To hell with expanding my sense of attraction to men over forty. I repudiate Maslow—he used to be my Bible."

"Oh, yes. The more mature we become, the more we want an equally mature person. Isn't that what he says?"

"Yes, and the more mature we are, the less we're attracted by looks and physical development—and the less we're put off by body hair or a bit of a belly. You're right. I am a heretic. I'm becoming a slave to youthful beauty like the rest of the sub-culture."

"Just put the ideas together. Enjoy every last bit of beauty, it's a fact of life, anyway. Young, beautiful people will always get the breaks. I understand where you're coming from, the frustrations of the closet when you were younger, but I know you too well, know that you're still honing in on your true priorities."

Brian shrugged off her encouragement. His lips tightened, bringing his cheek bones into prominence and momentarily giving his face the air of the distinguished professor. "Our culture is *not* mature. Maybe someday we'll all get collectively bored with this superficial crap and grow up. Remember our trip to Bali, the time I spent the afternoon swimming in the river with the locals in that town that hardly ever sees a tourist? Men and boys of all ages frolicking in the delightfully warm current, soaping themselves so sensually. Young slippery boys getting thrown around by teenagers while daddies and grandads sat by smiling." Brian paused and looked down, deciding the right phrasing for what followed. "Quite a few erections, too, sometimes on the heterosexual pretext of watching the young women downstream, sometimes just showing off to each other. Quite an important event in my life, a kind of delayed adolescent initiation, being accepted by them like that."

"Yes," Liz readily agreed, "think about it—old and young enjoying that bonding virtually every day of their lives."

"One guy—I was so embarrassed—even checked out my own erection and declared, 'Bagus. It's good.'" Brian sighed and unveiled his eyes. "And every face so beautiful, every body so naturally athletic, every individual with a sense he belonged. Oh, of course they acknowledge and appreciate those men and women with truly classic beauty. But it's no big deal. They aren't nearly so conscious about it, not nearly as insecure when assessing themselves. That wonderful innocence—or is it maturity? Their sense of beauty's so naturally integrated with the rest of their lives, as you might put it."

"Yes. And if they're sexual with each other, in their pre-marital phases I mean, there's always affection. I think it's so beautiful when those men walk around town holding hands." Liz paused to nibble on her croissant—Brian had already wolfed his down. "And I loved the way the young men who worked at our resort all cuddle up with each other every night, even the married ones. In fact remember that hunk, Ketut, who had just gotten married, he was the ringleader. He's the one who shouted 'bagus' when you said you weren't married and were attracted only to boys."

"Somehow women," Brian observed, "especially women attracted to women, have been spared this curse of putting beauty first. You keep zeroing in on what we all want— affection, expressed by lots of touching."

"Yes, Lynn's perfect in that way for me." She paused and then continued, a touch of defensiveness evident in her voice. "Stacy kids me about her weight, but, honestly, even with a few extra pounds, there's nothing *not* to like—just good warm, firm flesh. You're right. That's what I crave."

"Sounds like it's going well." Brian could not resist another croissant.

"Actually we've hit a snag; her ex-husband's visiting for a couple of weeks. She married him a long time ago, when she didn't know herself very well." Liz looked up and shrugged off her doubts. "It's not really a snag, just a bit of a test. They need the time to work stuff out, to become friends."

"That's the way you did it with her, right? First becoming pals in the Bach Chorus before you started going out?"

"Yes, but even so, things are still happening too fast. We're talking about her moving in with me. And she wants to get pregnant—she's never had kids—and she's even thinking of having her ex act as the biological father. Of course, since he's committed to his career back in Hartford, you could become one very active uncle."

Brian was intellectually fascinated by the possibility of a child in his life, but also slightly freaked. He'd need time to consider it, if she were really serious. He liked non-tra-ditional families, but did he truly want to become part of one at this time of his life? On the other hand his fears about losing Liz to Lynn would ease if they made room for him, emotionally, in *any* new situation. But they were getting ahead of themselves. "Yes," he concurred, "things are happening too fast. Urge her not to get pregnant until you both feel nicely settled in. There's plenty of time." Brian got up to return to his place. "I'm happy for you, though. Good luck."

"And you, sir, you deserve a break. Don't try to be Timothy, just be yourself. I know how much you're open to love. Just stay alert for it—these days you never know where a new lover might turn up."

Brian jauntily strode upstairs, relieved that this time he had managed to get them to talk a little about Liz's life, too.

17

Just before entering Doug's private room on the fifth floor at Mt. Zion, Brian and Will noticed an exceptionally beautiful bare-chested youth in the adjoining room. Could someone who looked so good have AIDS? Moments later they were jarred into the present by shrill, wild laughter coming from Doug's room. As they entered they saw three men in their thirties, all wearing Burger King crowns, bunched around Doug, who, although stretched out in bed, was holding forth with gusto.

"And remember that Halloween when, dressed as whores in tacky outfits, we got jumped by those Samoans in the alleyway south of Market? We screamed our heads off until they finally ran away. Then, bloodied but still in high spirits, we climbed aboard that Muni bus and sang silly songs to that poor captive audience."

More squeals of laughter. It was Doug's birthday, December 15. Will and Brian joined him, happily occupied with his old friends, and, while Brian grabbed packets of balloons to blow up, Will taped pink and blue crepe paper to the slippery beige hospital walls. Even with IV's sticking out of his arms, Doug was relishing the celebration. "Health is preserving yourself till you're dead," he quipped. Groggy from a massive dose of codeine he had taken to suppress his persistent cough, he accepted a piece of quiche from one friend while trying to balance a container of milk in the other, but the liquid occasionally spilled over onto the sheets. When Brian presented him with a little gift, he waved it off, unable, for the moment to receive it. "I am overburdened by my riches," he slurred. "You know this is a BYOB party–bring your own blood."

Next to Doug a machine sported red digital numbers which slowly descended from 120 to 0 at which time an alarm went off making conversation impossible until a hefty, good-natured nurse, an English woman in a white pants suit, returned, donning rubber gloves, to refill the contraption. Then she took some of Doug's blood, an indignity he no doubt had to endure many times a day. Doug sported a red terry-cloth robe. Brian's eyes were instantly drawn to his white, scarred legs until the patient hastily pulled the robe tightly about himself, repeating the gesture every few minutes when the robe started riding up. From the waist up, however, Doug looked fine, perhaps even better than Will. A huge blonde mustache, which suited his sandy hair and high forehead, overarched his smallish mouth. His pale skin was splotchy. Although already in excellent spirits, Will's entrance had delighted him.

Finished with the crepe paper project, Will made his way through the royal trio, who turned out to be Doug's former roommates, to give him a welcoming kiss. "Doug's much better now," he reported to Brian. "The PCP is gone. A couple of days ago, however, with his fever peaking at 104 degrees, the hospital made a mistake and gave him an antibiotic with sulphur in it. He's allergic to it so his system reacted violently. Then, when he couldn't sleep, they gave him Halcion to sedate him, but he only hallucinated. So that's why I haven't had much sleep lately—I've been spending every night over here."

Just as Will and Brian were pulling up two chairs to sit near the bed, a strange man ducked in, threw two packs of Camels at Doug, waved at everyone and promptly disappeared.

The incident reminded Brian of his smoky ride over to the hospital with Will when, after a quick welcoming kiss, he had inundated him with new information. "I guess I've told you that Doug's from Oklahoma, he's thirty-five, works as a word-processor downtown. That's all well and good. But I saw these marks on his legs and had grave doubts because I have a personal rule never to associate again with anyone who used hard drugs. I had some bad experiences in the Army."

Brian was shocked. Was Will such a fool not to recognize the signs? Didn't he realize that such a situation would soon collapse around him? But then Will turned a worried countenance to him, and went on.

"Because Doug seemed so full of love, I broke my own rule and I'm glad I did. Some weeks ago, though, I had to take him to the Haight Street Clinic because his legs got infected from shooting up—speed, not heroin. And then two weeks ago he had breathing problems and so I took him here. Finally I had to bring him back here again, PCP. He's still not on AZT because he's been avoiding doctors—they always rant and rave when they see those legs. But thanks to me he hasn't touched the bad stuff in over a month." Will's face had beamed with pride as Brian recalled some more ominous words uttered by Daniel— "the ones on speed are the first to go."

Feeling ashamed of his lack of confidence in Will, Brian switched into his familiar role of well-wisher. "So I take it that your living situation with him has worked out well."

"I'd say so." His apologetic laugh annoyed Brian. "At least I got him away from his old roommates who snarfed drugs all the time. They could care less about him." He had reached over to hold hands with Brian who had been taken in by the boyish sweetness of his tone. "Besides, since we're both positive, the doctor told us there's not much more to worry about. I do enjoy having wild sex once again."

Brian's anger began to simmer. He and Will hadn't had anything like "wild sex" for a long time, but once again he stifled his resentment. "So you've pretty much fallen in love with him?"

Will's brow had furrowed. "It hasn't been that long, but, yes, I think I love him. I must be in love. He's almost always late and even that doesn't bother me." That laugh again.

Then, driving on Castro Street, Will had spotted a grocery store. "Could you pull over so I can jump out and buy some cigarettes for Doug?"

Will had been chain-smoking in the car, so an already annoyed Brian, with watering eyes and raspy throat, had blurted out, "The irony of bringing cigarettes to someone with PCP."

Will had left the car without commenting, but Brian was becoming depressed. Will's smoking seemed to be sending the message, "There's nothing to do. I'm going to die anyway. Might as well keep smoking, one of my last little pleasures." As if to prove him right, Will had waited only the three minutes until they had arrived at the hospital's parking lot, and then had managed to light one up while walking to the lobby.

In the hospital room, Brian was jarred out of his thoughts by Doug's delight at being the birthday boy. "This place does have its diversions. Look at that apartment complex over across the street. Perfect for window-whacking. Not that I have to beat off, mind you. I have my own alternative lover here." He embraced the IV machine, then intensified his Okie twang. "Time for dancin', Willy. I wanna dance all night even though I usually don't care diddily squat about dancin'," and he kicked up his legs, letting the red robe fall aside.

"Don't worry honey, we will." Will clasped Doug's hand, then turned to Brian. "Doug's going to be okay. He's on a sedative because he has so much manic energy."

"Yes," panted Doug, pretending to be even more hyper. "I need a sedative for my nerves. Correction—for my nerve. I only have one left."

"Doug's going home in two days," added Will, obviously proud of his progress. "And his boss, this great woman, told him yesterday he'll always have a job waiting for him. That's San Francisco."

After Doug's former roommates left, he quieted down and soon started dozing. Will and Brian continued to chat. Brian was curious about what had happened to Nevin. "Oh, he's playing house with his new boyfriend, haven't seen him lately. But Jacky visited. I told her Nevin should get health insurance, but she just replied, 'Nevin's an adult. He's got to take responsibility for himself.' I was so proud of her." Will beamed once more.

Doug revived for a moment. "I guess I'm checking out for

awhile. I never realized the power of sleep in a social situation," he muttered. Taking the cue, they got up to leave. "Coming back later, honey?"

"Maybe." Will's voice sounded weary. "Probably."

"Why are you so pooped?" Doug sounded a bit petulant.

"You forget. I haven't slept much for a few days."

"You mean those couple of nights you were here with me?"

"More like four nights." That nervous laugh again.

"Oh, do come back later. I love you."

As they left, Brian advised Will, "You need your rest. You shouldn't stay here every night." He had, however, no illusion that Will had even heard him.

18

After their trip to Santa Cruz, Edmund had adjusted well to a life confined to the city by developing a passion for discovering new breakfast places. Brian had particularly taken to the Mel's on Geary, an out-sized, self-conscious tribute to the fifties. The first item he saw on the menu: TURKEY SPECIAL $6.95 WITH LUMPY MASH POTATOES. The first song he heard on the juke box: "Earth Angel," the national anthem of his seventh grade dance club. All the waitresses, including one who was conspicuous by sheer age—she had to be in her late seventies—wore sneakers, bobby-sox and pom-pom sweaters. Edmund picked up on Brian's fascination with her and explained, "It's sad. After the first time no one ever goes back to her table. She's so slow." But Brian found her to be so outrageously cute in those socks that he insisted on her trade, determined to reward her with a big tip for her pluck, for her power, like Edmund, to keep life surging forward.

"She reminds me of Tom O'Malley, you know the eighty year-old guy who manages to limp down to the nude beach and display that cancerous skin. Why does he make us look at him?" Brian couldn't blame Edmund for his resentment. At eighty, Tom was a role-model of longevity for Brian, but to Edmund he represented the years of mellow retirement he would not get a chance to live.

After they ordered, the usually optimistic Edmund faltered a bit. "It's been a rough spring. Two more friends lost to the plague—and then more pounds off my waist. Thank God my friend Ted took in my pants. And then there was the morning I came here to order pancakes—Mel's are quite fine, you know. And this waitress told me, 'No pancakes after 11 AM.' What do you mean? I asked. It's only 9. 'Yeah, it's 9 all right,' she said. '9 PM!'"

"I can't complain, though," and, looking across the booth that morning at Brian, he gave him a big smile. "Six months ago I told myself I'd be content if I could have six more *weeks* of normal living. Six months! The ddI has done it. So what if I blew the money on the black market stuff–I gained back those ten pounds the first two weeks." Brian smiled too, remembering how, last Thanksgiving, a sudden attack of weakness had forced Edmund to flee to his bedroom right in the middle of dinner. Back then Brian didn't think he'd make it into the new year.

"Yeah, so then I started enjoying three square meals every day and also going out to Land's End. I'd meet this guy who looked just like Fred Mertz. He'd always grab the best bench, the one in the morning sun with the great view of everything going on. We started getting friendly, but then I felt this coolness–so I decided I'd leave him to his own devices. A couple of weeks ago, after chatting with him, what do I notice but this Samoan in the bushes who, after I patiently waited around for a bit, signals for me to join him. He had high heels on, all ready for a little action."

That Edmund's sex life had continued, despite all, was not a great surprise to Brian. "That neighborhood of yours, how about that?" he had pursued. "Anything around to hold your interest when Land's End is too cold or foggy?" Brian had second thoughts about his question, remembering his own complaints to Liz about how un-gay North Beach had become. After camping out (somewhat more elegantly than Brian) for twenty-seven years in his old place on Northpoint, Edmund had finally moved into a first-floor apartment off Stockton, near the North Beach Playground. His choice haunted Brian. Edmund had plenty of money to indulge himself on a luxurious final pad, but, as a loner, he somehow didn't give the project the energy it deserved. Brian felt vague guilt that he hadn't helped him search out a warmer, larger place. Why hadn't he chosen a southern exposure for more winter sun? The place was like a goddam wind tunnel. Maybe he had just wanted to be close to his old friend, Bob.

"The neighborhood has been just fine, quiet but interesting. You've seen that sourpuss boxer who looks out his window all day—we call him the Colonel. And all those twelve year old kids play soccer every day after school. Just one incident, this heavy, elderly woman who asked me, 'What's wrong with your face?' What could I say? I could proudly boast of three operations for skin cancer, but what a question. I'd never admit to K. S. And forget all my straight friends with little kids—I've never heard from them—I'm a leper."

Brian didn't know how to respond, but luckily Edmund just went on. "That handsome kid across the street—I don't know if it's such a good idea to be a fabulous looking man these days. All these Chinese girls come around and just camp under his window, giggling. His father finally had to poke his head out and shoo them all away the other night, the same night I saw the German guy who lives above them talking on the phone, his shade down, but he didn't realize that shade had become a movie screen." Edmund switched into his tattle-tale little girl voice. "I saw what he was doing while talking to his girlfriend!"

As usual, Edmund's naughty perspective, his liberating candor about voyeurism and fetishes amused Brian. "Oh, remember that sweatshirt you found out in the street when we came back from San Gregorio? Wasn't it that German's? Did you return it?"

"Yes, that black one," he responded enthusiastically. "Made in Hong Kong. Pure cotton. I smelled the pits. Kept it."

"You didn't give it back?"

"Hell, no. He has plenty of them. Why, I have an old sweatshirt from twelve years back which I *still* sometimes smell while I beat off."

On the drive back to Edmund's, Brian recalled how the morning had begun. Edmund had claimed that his car had been stolen, but Brian had found it parked a couple of blocks away. Some of Edmund's friends had been trying to keep him from driving, but Brian figured that, despite the dementia, St. Francis and other local guardian angels would protect him if he stayed in the city.

He had welcomed Brian with a goofy grin on his face. "I had a great dream last night. Woody Allen and Bette Midler had opened up a candy store a little further up the street. So I got out of bed and went looking for it."

Brian had just smiled and opened the door with a key from Bob, that friend who lived a block away, because Edmund had locked himself out, apparently a common occurrence.

"Last week I went for my treatment at San Francisco General, but couldn't figure out why it was so dark and quiet when I got there. What was going on? And then the guard tells me that there's no one there, that it's nine o'clock at night. I thought it was nine in the morning, like it is now."

Once back in Edmund's flat, Brian had decided that no one need warn him about the dangers of dementia at this stage. He loved this daffy ex-businessman. Goofiness became him—he seemed just fine with the loss of control. Here in the flat, though, probably in his bedroom, must be where he had his moments of terror. "Everything okay with the place?" Brian inquired.

"The new space heater in the bedroom did the trick. Now I'm always warm. The place just doesn't get any sun. It's been so cold this spring. Thirty years out here, the first time we've had so much ocean fog. And wind, too. It's always so windy whenever it's sunny."

Edmund had a finely furnished living room. For the first time Brian wondered how this stuff would look in his place—from one old bachelor's to another. While waiting for Edmund to finish up in the bathroom, Brian had a peek at a bankbook from a Florida account on the coffee table—a $300,000 balance! Probably inherited from his friend down there, the one who got on ddI, did really well, then suddenly dropped dead. Not a bad way to go.

Still the ironies in Edmund's life must hurt. Both parents, having lived deep into their eighties and needing all kinds of special nursing home care for their final years, had just died. Numerous times Edmund had flown east to arrange the details. Now, even with their sizable inheritance already in hand and his own pension kicking in, he couldn't hang around.

It turned out that Brian couldn't help much with Edmund's problems with a lost ATM card that morning. He had tried to call a couple of numbers, but Edmund simply didn't have enough information. What did it matter? Brian had left him, tucked in for the rest of the day in the bedroom, having made a date to return a few days later for breakfast at a new place in the Tenderloin.

19

As Brian began climbing the short staircase in front of Jorge's house, he heard a loud voice coming from inside. At the landing he recognized Robin's annoyed, peevish tone and deliberately held off ringing the bell to sample what was going on. "You have such a roving eye. Your head's on a swivel, spinning around to check out anything attractive. I *know* you play around—I've got crabs from you to prove it." Delighted by hearing that juicy morsel, Brian rang the bell.

"I hope you're not overwhelmingly hungry," Robin answering the door, blurted out an apology. "Daniel's still finishing up his taxes, due at midnight tonight, of course. I'm cooking. Maybe you could help a little. I've put my foot down. We eat at nine no matter what." Robin had cut his jet-black hair short so it closely resembled Daniel's. "Then he'll have to work after dinner so he can make the midnight deadline at the postal annex on Evans Street."

"What a scene that'll be." Brian threw off his blue, hooded sweatshirt and tucked in his flannel shirt. "Postal clerks on every corner, bumper-to-bumper traffic, the whole tribe of world–class procrastinators out in force."

"What nonsense. I filed in February so I could get my refund early."

Brian took in what used to be the chaotic main floor of Chad and Jorge's house. Daniel had knocked out some walls so that the newly enlarged living room opened up right into the bright, modern kitchen, a major transformation since Brian was last here some months ago. He had seen Daniel only a couple of times since then, once for a film, another time for an opera. "Hey, he's a very busy guy," he deadpanned to Robin, trying to incite more than soothe.

"He's always busy." Robin led Brian into the refurbished living room. "Never has any time for me. He even forgot my birthday."

"What about those dozen red roses I sent you?" Daniel shouted from his cluttered home office, which faced out onto Kansas Street.

"Two days late. You only sent them on account of guilt."

Brian wandered in to greet Daniel who was once again typing commands to his Mac at a breathtaking speed. "Sorry, Brian. The company's in such dire straits I've had almost no time for personal business. Why don't you get a drink and I'll join you both in a couple of minutes?"

Brian perched himself on a newly refinished stool in the kitchen, looking for ways to help Robin who, unlike Daniel, had things firmly under control, a huge salad already set on the table and a casserole bubbling in the oven. Still playing a possible devil's advocate, Brian goaded him a bit more. "I envy you guys, getting to enjoy the romance of constantly making up."

"I've been pushed to my limits," Robin countered immediately, while setting out some inherited crockery on the large oak table. Then, lowering his voice and leaning over so only Brian could hear, "He always makes some excuse why we can't spend the whole night together. There's always some crisis at work or some sick person to see. Occasionally, just occasionally, I'd like to linger and talk softly, stretch out and fall asleep together, with no alarm clock at the other end. Just have more lazy times together, more emotional interchange."

"I understand." And Brian *did* understand, recognizing his own complaint about his situation with Will. Now, however, he wished that he could return to those imperfect rendezvous. Already they struck him as the good old days.

Daniel, true to his word, joined them a few moments later to settle into a fine vegetarian meal. While they ate Daniel began complaining about his family—both parents drank too much, his overweight father, a therapist, had resorted to bulimia, his daredevil brother had injured himself in a reckless dive and was now a paraplegic, and his youngest brother, gay but in the closet, still lived at home at twenty-seven.

"I thought *my* family was bad," Robin reacted, half in jest.

Daniel, perhaps a little short from working so hard on his taxes, did not let it pass. "You're even more wounded than I and you feel even more insecure because you haven't had any therapy. What about your own messed up parents? You get occasional glimpses of what's wrong, but you just haven't dealt with it."

"Not that you're any help." Robin whirled about to face Brian. "Whenever I *do* complain about my parents or my brother or my job, all he says is, 'You don't have to feel you're a bad person.' What bullcrap. Yes, I'll admit I'm a talkative person but that doesn't mean he has to completely tune me out."

His dignity ruffled, Robin went on the offensive. "He puts me down. He just doesn't listen. He only pretends he wants to work stuff out—he dragged me to this therapy, it's a farce. When all is said and done, all he really wants to do is cruise." Suddenly Robin, remembering Daniel's presence, turned to confront him. "*You're* the destructive one. The other day you almost got beat up."

"What happened?"

"Go ahead. Tell Brian what happened."

"It was no big deal, for God sakes. I gave this guy a ride on Polk Street. I figured he was probably bisexual, with the usual ambivalences. But when I let him off—I had just flirted with him a little—he walked around the back of my car, opened my door and, well, sort of slugged me."

"I tell you, Daniel, you better watch out or you're going to get into a lot of trouble."

Daniel stuck out his tongue at his lover. "Robin, you're such a prissy old lady—pinching pennies, never forgetting your umbrella, never driving over the speed limit." Brian, staring at Daniel's strong, sharp profile, suddenly found himself swimming in those dark eyes as Daniel abruptly turned to face him. "And he's insulated himself from the plague, too, hardly knows anyone

who has it, doesn't ever do any volunteer work. He got jealous
of the time I spent with Jorge and now he's jealous of my time
with other sick friends. He's so sexually uptight, too. He has
this powerful sexual energy, but not a clue about how to use
it—he's so afraid of being out of control, of being used by
someone physically."

"I'm not buying that for a moment." Flabbergasted, Robin
turned to Brian for support. "Daniel doesn't think sex exists
beyond the sexual act. I'm sticking to my guns—we are *not*
automatically going to have sex every time we get together. For
weeks I'd wake up depressed because he'd leave every time right
after his orgasm. But I was too weak, always reneged and had
sex with him, then ended up with a nervous stomach, hardly
being able to function the next day. I haven't been this depressed
since I was a kid." Then back to the direct attack on Daniel. "I
really wonder about your hidden animosities. They've really
come out in our therapy. But when it got too close to home for
you, you quit." Robin was emphatic.

"I didn't quit. I just realized we could do much better than
this particular therapist." There was an uncharacteristic meekness
in his defensively downcast eyes. "We weren't getting anywhere.
There's this other guy—he's much more understanding of where
we're coming from. All you have to do to is commit yourself to
the process."

"Don't you dare use the word 'commitment' in my presence."
Robin's tone was one of comic outrage. He was beginning to
enjoy performing in front of Brian. "We ended up having a few
sessions with this woman. I liked her, but Daniel decided she
wasn't bringing up the issues *he* wanted to talk about. When she
confronted him and charged him with having an agenda, he blew
his top and quit."

"We both need to get out of this city. It's stressing us both
out." Daniel had strategically retreated to another familiar theme.
"I'm going to sell this place and buy that house in Oregon. We'd
get along a lot better if we'd settle up there."

"No way. No way I'm going to vegetate up in Oregon. I'd be bored out of my mind. I love it here."

Silence. An impasse. He looked up and saw it was after 10:30–he knew Daniel had to finish his taxes. Besides he had had enough–it was starting to get boring, not to mention uncomfortable. "I should get going so you can prepare for your pre-midnight journey, Daniel."

"Thanks for coming, Brian."

He hugged them both, then slipped out into the night, a sudden resentment growing even as he strode towards his car. "Shit or get off the pot" he wanted to scream at them. "Commit yourselves to having a good relationship–or don't bother." What was going on, anyway? Two handsome, intelligent men who were attracted to each other. What was so difficult about it?

As he unlocked his car, however, he heard a much more detached inner voice reminding him that contemporary relationships weren't all that easy, weren't all that clear cut. To be a good sport about the situation he had to be patient with them and let them take as long as they wanted to thrash it out. Why not? They weren't doing anything wrong. If nothing else, they had certainly put on a dandy show.

As for himself, besides feeling a bit Machiavellian, he had found out what he wanted to know. He promptly put in his request to the universe to send him someone from an entirely different mold, and fast. He was ready for something new.

20

Whenever Brian had a free morning and Richard could be convinced that he would not aggravate his back—which was not that often—Brian chauffeured his friend to Greco's, their favorite coffee house in North Beach, a pleasant hangout owned by an Arab and staffed by handsome young Slavs who always delighted Richard. Facing out onto Columbus Avenue, Greco's was often crowded, so they were happy about finding a free table next to the front windows on a windy May morning where they could enjoy the immense variety of *homo sapiens* passing by. Brian rounded up their cappuccinos and biscotti and brought their treats to the table. Richard, who had started chatting to the lady next to him, swiveled back to Brian, momentarily hooking his trench coat on his knee.

"Did you manage to get out yesterday, Brian? Such a lovely day."

"Had a fine time at the beach. It was especially wild near the bridge."

"Bravo. I envy you that, you're being able to reveal your undraped body so enthusiastically. You're lucky you're still so fit, so trim." Brian broke their biscotti in half and gave Richard his share. "You certainly look fine this morning—that green shirt certainly brings out the green in your eyes—I never realized how green they were before."

As usual, Brian was annoyed by the compliment. He was already obsessing on the extra folds that age was bringing to his eyelids. "My physical vehicle is a far cry from perfection." Brian winced, comparing himself in vain to Timothy's corporeal glory at forty.

"I wasn't as lucky as you. When I finally wanted to become sexually active, I was already gray and balding, too. I had to content myself with cruising bathrooms in Cambridge. So much secrecy, so much sense of imminent disaster if one got entrapped, as I once did, by a plainclothesman. I must say, by the way, I like your hair a bit shorter–the better to see more of your face and the shape of your head–I love the shape of men's heads. And your hair is still so full, so shaggy, not yet that much gray, really."

Brian fidgeted awkwardly, never having accustomed himself to Richard's praise. Compared to him he had had it easy. "What was it like growing up sexually in Salt Lake anyway?" he asked, suddenly curious. "Did you get to go on camping trips with your boyfriends? Did you fit in at all or were you totally isolated?"

"More the latter, although you've released a powerful memory. Once right in class in high school, I locked eyes with this particularly handsome boy for many, many seconds, burning with intensity, yet neither one of us ever dared act on it, not then and not even on a camping trip during which we slept–or tried to sleep–trembling beside each other, responding to–and repressing–a power we didn't understand." He paused to regain his composure. "People's sexual awakenings, their first stirrings, fascinate me."

"What was that like for you?" Brian, trying to sip the much-needed caffeine as slowly as possible, was determined to keep the focus on Richard.

"The male figure, so different from the soft female skin around my house, began beckoning, as it probably did to you, at an early age." Richard smiled wryly, noting Brian's amusement at the expression, "male figure," but continued. "My eyes became erotic, probing penises. One of my luckiest breaks came in the form of my mother's demanding I join a gym at about eight or nine, not far from my school. I thought I was grotesque. The instructor, macho Mr. Welch, who badgered us quiet, shy ones, would taunt me in front of all the others. I just wasn't very good–I was scared of the water, of the boys, of being naked."

"So you got to be around other naked boys?"

"Yes, and every day around four, when the little ones left the pool, the older boys arrived. Sheer wonder. I would go up to the balcony the minute I saw them filing in. I'd dress as fast as I could and sit alone up there, watching the wondrous display. The first time I saw them I nearly fainted; I'd never seen such gorgeous bodies, magnificent, beautiful. I never felt like one of them. It seemed impossible that I could ever look like one of them, inexpressibly glorious as they were. It never occurred to me that they exercised, lifted weights. I just knew I was fated to be puny."

"But you grew up to be tall, trim, with a solid, hairy chest. Even now, despite your back, you're fit, trim."

"Back then, though, how I stared at those gods, standing on the edge of the pool, cocks bouncing about, or up on the diving board, utterly indifferent to their bobbing dongs. Had they been lit in neon, had they been electrified, they could not have mesmerized me more. In the showers when they soaped their cocks and balls with luxurious ease, it drove me wild. I always lurked behind to observe as much as I could. They all looked at each others' cocks in those showers with fascination. How some of them must have wanted to touch, to brush against each other."

"Yes, I remember our shower room in high school. We all just stared and stared, often stretching out that time together with long, inane conversations."

"If the balcony were closed," Richard went on, relishing his true confessions, "in desperation I'd seek out this closet with a low grid and peek through, only being able to see from the chest down—those gloriously hairy legs. I just had to have an expanse of male flesh three or four times a week to get myself going again, to hop up my nervous system, to get the blood flowing through my veins."

Brian smiled again. "Sounds normal, healthy even. Either that or become a complete hypocrite."

"Still, it never occurred to me that these young men were the same gender as I, their puny little worshipper from afar. Psychologically I had separated myself as another species, identifying with my mother as I did."

"Yuck. There we're different. I also empathized with dear mater, but tried to become as different as I could as I grew up." Was it insensitive to contrast himself to Richard?

Richard took a slow sip of his latte before continuing. "Meanwhile my mother reinforced my sense of puniness by dragging me to doctors. 'I can't seem to put any fat on him. I feed him, feed him, force-feed him. I've tried cod liver oil, castor oil, it just does not seem to do any good.' And the doctor would say at least once a month, 'He seems okay.'"

"Amazing. There we were exactly alike. My mother spoke the very same words to me. I started drinking eggnogs for breakfast because any kind of cooked eggs would make me gag."

Richard seemed unwilling to accept bonding through common childhoods–true misery must be unique. "Because I had a slight curvature of the spine, a bent back, I thought I was deformed. Such a pigeon-chested kid, too, and, like many gay boys, the last one chosen for a team. I was a basement creature, growling and somewhat vengeful, spiteful. No point in rising to the light of day. Established in my domain, I wanted to operate there as a skulking, nightmare power, like Richard the Third or Quasimodo."

Sad but yet with a funny side, Brian thought.

"Then, at about twelve I started following boys, never daring to approach them, never daring to feel deserving of being around them with all their grace. When I foolishly stopped going to the gym, I just could not see enough male skin–there were no shorts, no shirtless men on the streets of Salt Lake. Just an occasional hairy calf, that little miracle of flesh between socks and pants. Is any of this familiar to you?"

"Don't ask *me* anything about the onset of puberty–somehow I didn't notice."

Richard laughed with a bit of disdain. "And psychiatrists theorize about going 'beyond the pleasure principle.' My goodness, we haven't even reached it yet. I've always thought it strange in regard to cruising that in our denial of emotion it's as if we gays create an even stronger one."

"All that pent-up energy, all that testosterone."

"Yes," Richard stared straight out across Columbus Avenue. "What to do with that energy. You never see women jiggling their legs the way men do—all that enormous pressure, those hormones which demand, 'Spurt! Give it to the world.' Oh, if they'd only show us men hugging and kissing, tenderly and delicately, lying together, cheeks side by side, just enjoying their closeness."

"Oh, you mean like the women lovers in *Desert Hearts*?"

"Exactly. I guess men just cannot do it—they get impatient. But if a director *were* to do it, we'd be bawling all the way through the scene out of sheer delight."

"Oh thanks, Velimir. We're finished with everything." Brian greeted the handsome young man who was bussing the tables in their area.

"Velimir," Richard's eyes widened in enthusiastic interest, "are things okay in your homeland? Are all your relatives safe?"

"Oh yes, no problem." Velimir paused, stood up straight and looked directly at us, his blue eyes set off magnificently by his pale Balkan skin. "We go in August—my father, brother and me—to Zagreb. My father owns an apartment there—we'll check on things—but we also get to see Paris, Amsterdam, Berlin, Prague." He flashed a big smile and indicated he had to keep moving on.

"That's wonderful." Richard's eyes trailed him as he walked away and then glazed over with a faraway look, transported back into the past once again. "In Cambridge I became a hunter, not a gatherer, because of those fears of being touched. I'd cruise the parks at night—dangerous, though less so than today. I'd come home feeling as if I had had satisfying experiences, although it had been frustrating in the extreme. If the other man made the move, I'd become terrified, impotent. As the servant I'd only want to please the other. Today I glory in my role as cock-sucker; then, I'd never use the word. Like Raskolnikov I walked the streets and did foolish things, half hoping to be found out and punished, delighted by the terrible intensity of my kicks. Then the next day I'd share stories about being skulking night-creatures with my one compatriot."

"Was it *all* frustration?"

"One day I met a beautiful youth in the subway, in the men's room. He came back with me to Harvard–a magnificent Irish beauty who would never reprieve that first visit: too much Catholicism. Afterwards I'd always be tempted back to collegiate men's rooms. One colleague's shoes became famous–he practically lived in there. Unlike you we all led secret, double lives."

"Just think, Richard, Harvard–there must have been so many sensitive gay and bisexual men there. All those lost possibilities." Old regret crept back into Brian's voice. "I wonder if we will ever get beyond our sense of wasted youth. Visiting Princeton last fall brought it all back to me." It was Brian's turn to reminisce. "I had three gay roommates, but none of us talked about it then. I was walking the campus on a lovely day when I spied a poster announcing a Saturday night meeting for gay and lesbian students. There it was–right on the main bulletin board next to the largest lecture hall. Something welled up in me and I cried uncontrollably as I wandered around the campus."

"Yes, you saw yourself among them. How wonderful, still enough alive to react that way."

It was Brian's turn for confession. "Sometimes, though, alone at home, I keep obsessing on what I thought I missed in my youth, even back in high school. Images of Patrick Grant doing chin-ups naked in the shower room. Or Dennis Usher doing push-ups so as to show off his dangling cock which, on each downward plunge, caressed those cool, white tiles."

"But now you have your beach life. You're the cunning snake, lying on the rock in the sun, fangs at the ready, waiting for just the right moment to carry off the hesitant bisexual!"

"But it's always only for the moment–still very frustrating.

For instance, yesterday. I saw this Chinese guy, sitting naked, legs dangling off a short cliff, about a hundred yards from the bridge. So I dove into the ocean just in front of him. He noticed and approached. It was too public so we slipped off to a cove. A sweet beautiful young man with a lithe, lean body, so alive to the touch. We both came—looking into each other's eyes. Then we embraced, holding on for at least a couple of minutes, my nose dug into that jet-black hair. Oh, the exquisite smell of that hair. Then he told me he's a physical therapist, that he had, in fact, to rush off to work, after mentioning that 'you made my day.' But I was left feeling sad. Something about us clicked and yet we'll probably never see each other again."

"How can the young know they have had a unique experience, met a loving person?" Richard once again adopted a wistful tone. "The occasion is almost always wasted." He had become the modern-day Solomon in a maroon sweat suit and an old trench coat.

"I know, I know." But Brian was elated by just how well Richard understood his feelings. "At least school will be starting in a couple of weeks. A few crumbs there. I'll get to bump into all those beautiful men in those crowded corridors."

Once again Richard responded in just the right spirit. "Oh, you frotteur. It's lovely. That cunning serpent, once again, zig-zagging down the hallways, negotiating U-turns, taking an hour to get to his office." The unprofessional image amused Brian.

"Oh, I almost forgot—one of your favorites also came to the beach yesterday—so handsome, but so tough—The Animal!"

"That magnificent creature. What was he up to?"

"After he rappelled down the cliffs, he hustled over to that huge retaining wall under the bridge, stripped down to a very small pair of Speedos with a big tear in the rear, and proceeded to perform some violent calisthenics, something out of the martial arts, fists uppercutting in a scary, pounding motion. And then off swimming for half an hour in that frigid water. When he got out of the water, he shook himself off as vigorously as a golden retriever, then yanked down his Speedos and pulled out what looked like a semi-hard cock, pissing in a long, high arc. Then he put on his long, black pants right over those wet, clammy tights and disappeared straight up the cliff, a magnificent performance, as usual."

Richard silently applauded. "Oh yes, that splendid beast—such massive vitality, pure physical being—the Life-Force!"

"The Life Force! Sounds like you're becoming a bit of a believer." Richard had always defined himself as a staunch atheist.

"Only for one paltry lifetime, I'm afraid." Richard returned, momentarily, to the authoritarian tone of the classics professor. Topic not up for discussion. But then he put down his cup and immediately relaxed. "You, Brian, so much Life Force in you at the beach—your whole self's involved—that amazing ability to get hard at a moment's notice—the sea, the surf, the breeze—it makes up for a lot of injustices—it works on a magic primitive level—it's very basic, very primal."

Richard was clearly sincere, but in Brian such comments produced guilt along with pleasure. It was better to switch themes.

"The Life Force—I see it so much in Will, even now with all his powers waning."

"And don't forget Edmund—he, too, had it in his own way." Richard began to button up his trench coat. "And Timothy—all that writing and painting and those endless boy friends." Richard was astute at seeing qualities in others, even people he had met only once.

"Yes, Richard. You're right, although I begrudge it to Timothy. Valuing loyalty as I do, I wonder about all his relationships which never last more than a few months. But I guess it's okay if both parties agree, on some level, that that's all they want. Maybe I tend to be moralistic about it because a part of me is envious." Suddenly it seemed important that Richard be recognized, too. "But don't *you* forget how much of the Life Force you still display yourself. You're the Animal of your own salon, drawing to you so many friends with your vigorous intellect and your vibrant, loving presence."

"Time to go." Richard smiled. "This Animal has a date with another Primal Being—Cleo will viciously attack me if I don't get back soon for our morning petting session." And with that the two friends waved good-bye to Velimir and set out on their way down Columbus Avenue to Brian's waiting car.

21

"Either way, downstairs or up, I think you'd agree that I belong here." Edmund, his lucidity once again established, lay stretched out in bed. His face had changed radically within the last two weeks, so skull-like as to be a stage beyond emaciation. His understanding doctor had prescribed no further treatment, nothing but morphine. "I could have stayed downstairs with the old people, but up here it's all men with AIDS, although most of them are a good deal younger."

Garden-Sullivan, an old nursing home on Geary Boulevard, looking more like an office building than a hospice, had been pressed into service as a place people went to die. Brian was reassured that Edmund was content to be here with his gay brothers, as long as he could not be alone in his apartment. "In a funny way it reminds me of the old dorms at St. Jerome's, the Catholic boarding school in Virginia where I had the best sex of my life, orgies practically every night." Even on his death bed Edmund had the power to rouse Brian's sexual envy, at least momentarily, although he soon began chuckling to himself at the big picture, the huge number of exploits experienced by this solitary creature.

Moments later the brief period of lucidity ended when Edmund drifted off. Opening his eyes a few minutes later, he smiled and issued an invitation, "Brian, let's go out to breakfast at Mel's."

"Not a bad idea," Brian humored him, remembering their last trip there. After the meal, as they were driving down Geary, Edmund had pointed out Garden-Sullivan as the place he and his doctor had chosen. And now here he was—the very last phase. It was possible that he might not even awake from his next nap.

As Edmund drifted off once more, Brian recalled their final breakfast date just a few days earlier at a Mandarin place in the Tenderloin owned by a captivating Chinese woman and her hunky son. "She makes the world's best bacon," Edmund had claimed and Brian had to admit it did look fine, so lean and crisp, reminding him of the breakfasts of his youth. The place had become a haven for the grizzled old specimens of every race. Their charming hostess encouraged every one of them to talk about himself.

They had settled in on a pair of red-vinyl stools at the classic soda-fountain counter. He had checked out Edmund closely that morning. He had missed a lot of spots shaving, especially under the chin. Just one sideburn. Two purplish spots blotched his nose. At that moment he had suddenly recognized the full extent of Edmund's apotheosis. No longer a fastidious business man, he had become a street person—the bare essence of a man—and it somehow became him.

When Brian had dropped Edmund off that morning in early June, it had seemed that the end was near. Edmund had been exhausted, complaining first about a lack of sympathy from Al, the guy who had insulted him about his not spending money. "So I tell him the ddI's not working any more and he just says, 'Too bad. Seems like there's more of the plague stuff out here than in the east.' That's all he said. Not an ounce of feeling in the man." A justified reaction, probably. But then Edmund attacked his friend, Bob, whom he had made executor. "I think he still resents my moving into his territory without asking him first."

Such sad words to Brian's way of thinking. Two tough ol' queens who had made much of life's journey together as pioneers in the sub-culture. He hoped some love for each other would come through before the end. Keeping his promise by making a quick exit that morning, Brian had once again let Edmund crawl back into that drafty bedroom like a wild dog who wanted to curl up at the back of a cave and die—no fuss, no muss.

That night, only a few days ago, Brian could not resist checking in with him by phone. After a dozen rings a snarling Edmund answered with, "Why are you all bothering me? Leave me alone."

"What's wrong, Edmund?"

"It's not only you. It's Bob, it's my brother, it's my landlord. Can't you all just leave me alone?" Later that night Brian had found himself utterly exhilarated. Edmund had maintained his independence, destroyed every urge for others to worry about him. Not everyone's way, though. Good old American stoicism. Dying with dignity meant dying alone.

Edmund awoke once more. He reached out a hand which Brian clasped, an easy, natural thing to do, before the aged gentleman returned to his nap. After another half hour, with Edmund apparently deep in sleep, Brian decided to end his visit, probably his final one, at Garden-Sullivan. As he stood to go, Edmund opened his eyes and smiled, holding out his hand again. Brian held it for a minute or so and then, as Edmund once again closed his eyes, gave him a silly little wave good-bye and hastened out into the night.

22

Will opened the door of his flat very slowly and cautiously. "Watch out for the vicious guard dog."

Brian slipped inside, cringing at the incessant yapping. When his eyes adjusted to the dark hallway, he managed to discern a tiny dog, running hysterically up and down the length of the place.

"His name is Spike." Doug had joined them. "He's six months old, but won't grow much more at all. He is, however, just about the cutest creature in the whole world."

Annoyed at first, Brian took a step or two towards the living frankfurter, right into a pile of dog shit effectively camouflaged on the dark carpet.

"Don't worry. We'll have things cleaned up in a moment," Doug volunteered, rushing off.

"I don't mind Doug's indulging Spike's every whim, but at least he could house-train him," Will complained, but his tone of voice remained upbeat. Brian made a futile attempt to wrest away Spike's rawhide bone as the surprisingly strong creature growled viciously.

Doug, looking hearty and having gained at least twenty pounds, returned to clean up the mess. "Did you tell Brian the naughty thing Spike did?"

"He's done many naughty things, but the worse was his slurping up six capsules of AZT which fell out of a container with a loose cap that he knocked over."

"What happened? He obviously survived, strength intact." Brian was still trying to yank away the rawhide bone.

"The vet said he'd get sick, throw up and that'd be it. And that's exactly what happened. A little chemo-therapy ain't about to slow down my Spike-ums," Doug drawled, beaming with pride. "You know, Will, we need to go out to one of those thrift stores and buy a leather cock strap—it'd make a perfect collar for

Spike."

"While we're there," Will put in, "remind me to grab one of those deluxe leather jackets—maybe Goodwill has one."

After he cleaned up his befouled running shoe, Brian followed the trio to the kitchen. In the improved light he could see that both Will and Doug looked hale and hearty, a far cry from the way they seemed barely three months ago. Curious as always, when he opened up the refrigerator and the cabinets, he discovered a jam-packed larder, filled with many high-caloric foodstuffs.

"The food bank's been really coming through lately." Doug patted his belly.

"So that's why you have barbecued-flavored Beer Nuts—the food bank. But what's this?" Brian had come across a small, blue rectangular package that looked as if it belonged more properly in their medicine cabinet.

Observing his curiosity about it, Doug rushed up, grabbed it away and bitterly complained, with great outrage, "Imagine that Food Bank giving us Jenny Craig omelets. Now that's not the kind of vittles gay boys like us need right now," and he once again distended his sizable belly with pride.

"Well, I have to say both you guys look great. Just keep up whatever you're doing."

"We will," boasted Will, radiating a cherubic quality with his beard shaved off. "Like every Wednesday we hit the buffet at the Hyatt Regency—all you can eat for ten bucks. And what a view of the whole Bay Area from the top!"

"None of my pants fit any more," Doug confessed. "Last time at the Hyatt I popped the button above my fly when we got up to go. Too much lobster and quiche lorraine. I'm beginning to look like some of my uncles back in Arkansas, and Will, Will looks like a miniature Minnesota Viking."

The extra weight did look damn good on Will. "You're lucky all those calories go to those huge shoulders, that massive chest," Brian teased, but he meant it. It was his bad luck that extra weight on him went straight to his gut.

As Brian settled on the couch with his drink, letting the domestic partners rustle up a snack, he was struck by how far Will had come since he had received that ominous phone call from him barely three months ago, back in March. He recalled his exact words. "I've got good news and bad news today."

His heart had sunk. He had tried to stall for time. "The good news?"

"The bad news—they did a brain scan and I tested positive for dementia."

"That *is* bad news."

"The good news—now I can explain those terrifying memory lapses I had in the classroom. Now I know what's going on." Brian had remained silent. He didn't know what to say. "How about coming over tomorrow night? Doug will be out so we can have some time together."

In the good old days, Brian would have jumped at that invitation, would have revelled in their having a whole night together, but at that time he had dreaded it. When he first arrived, the evening had started well enough, with Will's cooking them a fine dinner, but afterwards time had drastically slowed down. 9:22—the red digital numbers of their VCR kept drawing Brian's attention. Silence. 9:24, finally 9:25. Will had slouched down and Brian kept looking over at him, with nothing to say.

Brian had wondered how Will managed to keep going at all. He and Doug were dying, Edmund lay close to death, as did Brian's mother. A shudder of fear shot through him and his whole body started shaking. He wasn't that many years away from being like Richard, old and living alone, hoping a few of his friends could "look in" on him occasionally. More silence. It was *still* 9:25.

In desperation, he had slid in an old porn tape from Falcon where Doug used to work. The adventures of an exuberant hunk who claimed he got a hard-on every time he took off his underwear. But after just a minute or two, Will had become obviously annoyed. "At this point porn does nothing for me. I'm not at all interested in sex. My doctor said the drugs have lowered my libido. And I get totally exhausted at school, not enjoying it at all." Brian had immediately shut off the tape. "I come home from school exhausted, take my AZT and sleep for four hours. I'm like one of those bald, old men sitting all alone in his dingy room with white, hairless legs sticking out, putting acid on his warts every night, teeth lying next to him in a jar."

Brian had laughed politely, but could not say anything. Needing diversion, he had reached down to grab a book from the coffee table. *The Joys of Stress*, a title he'd find much funnier in another setting. "It's pretty interesting," observed Will. "I lose eighty points for smoking cigarettes, forty each for caffeine and alcohol."

But *The Joys of Stress* had provided them with only a few seconds of diversion. Finally after another interminable silence—it was 9:27, Brian remembered, Will had broken down and started crying. "I guess I'm on the edge. Everything seems to be collapsing lately. The assistant superintendent has broken her promise three times to put me on the tenure track. I'm not going to quit, though. I'm going to hang in there, if only for the health insurance."

"Why not go on disability? At least for a few months."

"That's what my doctor recommended, but I'm not sure I can get it. I'm only in my second year in the district. The insurance company might claim 'previous condition' since I tested positive and stayed on the job."

"Don't worry about that now." Sadness had welled up inside of Brian. Will had struggled all his life and here he was, not far from the end, still plagued by fears of poverty.

Suddenly Will had blurted out, "Is it okay if I borrow $500 for a little while? I need help to pay next month's rent. Sometimes I wish I could get a loan to put all my debts into one big bill which I could pay off at a certain amount each month."

"Of course it's okay." Will already owed Brian a substantial amount, but at this point it was all for the "cause." It was the least he could do—another way of sharing loyalty, solidarity. Brian had started feeling anger, outrage even, that someone on the brink of death should have to use up his precious energy in fighting bureaucracies. What was even worse—Will had no strong urge to enjoy what time he had left, unlike others who had used up their credit limit on a whole bunch of plastic cards without a second thought, knowing they wouldn't be around very long. So what was wrong with Will? It couldn't be just his fear of dying a pauper's death.

"To tell you the truth, I have been depressed lately, very depressed." And he had lapsed once more into a self-involved gloom so thick it made Brian, his neck still tight with anger, shudder once more.

"Will, where's that feisty, irascible side of you, the side that doesn't give a fuck about insurance companies and government agencies? I know you aren't afraid to die." And Brian wasn't just bullshitting—anyone who could forgive his attacker on the operating table had to be a cut above the average Joe.

"No, it's not that. It's these other things."

"Maybe it's too many toxic drugs. Maybe you should check out a healthier diet, even meditate more." Brian had been somewhat disappointed by both Will's ready acceptance of what the medical establishment had to prescribe and his refusal to apply any of his spiritual practices. "You know, I bet you're clinically depressed from the side effects of AZT. A chemical imbalance or something. You're just not yourself—you're losing your personality, your zest for life."

"My doctor says I'm depressed, my therapist says I'm depressed, but, of course, they think there are good reasons for me to be depressed."

Brian had laughed to break the tension that day, but Will's response, in its understatement, seemed more like his old self. "You're right. It may all be too much AIDS-dementia and poverty would depress anyone, but you're too formidable a spirit to fall so completely into this black hole of despair. Demand that your therapist give you a *strong* anti-depressant. You know I don't usually like these medications, but you need one chemical to offset another. Please do it. What's to lose?" Brian was on his high horse again. "Remember I was right about your dyslexia. And start right away because they take a few weeks to kick in."

"Okay, I'll ask him. Doug and I are visiting my family next month in Minnesota and I've been dreading having to face my stepfather's hostility, but my therapist has been telling me it'd be a good time to stand up to him. In this mood, I'd just give in to him."

"Good. That's a good motivation." But, in the ensuing silence, the more Brian thought about it, the more he realized he hadn't said enough. "Ever since I've known you, you've been running around like a chicken with his head cut off. All that gastritis you've been having—you know it comes from nerves and stress. It's time to relax, enjoy life. You've even done your bit nursing Doug. Now it's your turn. Go on disability. Make the most of the time you have left. The more you relax, the longer you'll be around."

That had been his harangue that night. In the months that followed they had stayed in touch, but it wasn't the same. Will wasn't really there for him any more. He was dealing admirably with his final days, but Brian had at most a minor role in them. Doug was his principal personal support.

Tonight he could hear laughter coming from the kitchen. Doug came out munching on some cheese and then disappeared down the hall to their bedroom. Moments later Will appeared. "Did I ever tell you about what happened when I confronted my step-father on our trip?" Will was carrying trays filled with cheese, crackers, dip and vegetables meticulously cut up and handsomely arranged. "Luckily, the anti-depressants had picked me up. I girded my loins by remembering the time when I graduated from high school and my step-father wanted to take me out to a cheap Chinese restaurant, but I defied him, blurted out, 'I won't have it. We're going to a good place.' And we did."

Squeezing in next to Brian, Will's hesitant little laugh sounded anything but annoying. "So on this trip, after a few days of being reinforced by my grandma's total acceptance of us, I did stand up to him and he respected me, although he still didn't look me in the eye. But I did notice some tears when he said, 'I like you but can't accept your life-style.' So I told him, 'Men are the ones I love.' But here's the best thing. On the last day he kind of casually stated, 'I hope you guys are doing okay.' 'You guys.' He's never talked that way before—he acknowledged Doug and me—a big step for him."

Brian thought it all a bit pathetic, Will still trying to please that bastard of a step-father, but he realized that protocol called for him to remain upbeat.

"That's great. But, most of all, it's so fine seeing you guys so happy. Retirement seems to agree with you."

"It's just so good to wake up in the morning without being totally depressed," Will smiled. "You were right. That prescription didn't help for the first month, but then, what a difference. My therapist thinks I might go back to teaching, just part-time, in six months or so, although my union's lawyer is against it from a legal point of view. But I just told him, 'Sam, I'm going to live with the thing and not be obsessed by death.' Besides," he added with a naughty gleam in his eye, "I still want to get rid of that racist assistant principle, the one I called 'incompetent' at that meeting. Afterwards, Sam told me to be more careful when I asked him about my legal right to criticize her."

It was good to see Will's feisty, political side back again, although Brian was still a little taken aback by all this domestic tranquillity.

Suddenly Spike's yaps broke the peace, heralding Doug's entrance. "Well it's early to bed, early to rise for me. Maybe that's why we're so compatible—Will loves to stay up late and sleep in. We're enjoying life as best we can—they tell me you don't usually recover from this condition."

"Yes," Will agreed, "and even becoming a bit more independent from each other. Doug agrees with me that I need more time to myself, don't you Doug?"

"Oh, I know I can be a pest just like Spike. I'm spoiled—you know you're very good company, baby." Doug reached over and squeezed Will's hand. Then, looking at Brian, "Thanks to those anti-depressants we even have a bit of a sex life lately." Squeezing Will's hand once more, he exited with, "God, I hope I'm not becoming possessive, like Jacky."

Left alone with Brian, Will got up to play one of his favorite ambient tapes and then collapsed in Brian's arms on the couch where they held each other for a long time.

23

"I've had it with this town. I'm out of here—as soon as this arm heals. There's no reason to hang around. It's all over with Robin. Thunder-Ware is going out of business. I've put Chad and Jorge's house on the market. I've been accepted to grad school—to the University of Minnesota for the Fall term. It's a good, liberal area, not so obsessed with the plague."

Daniel, twenty pounds heavier, with a cast on his arm and a brace on his neck, grimaced as he put down his cup of tea. Brian hadn't seen much of him the last few months and when he had, it was in the usual frantic context of his business and romantic crises. Discharged after a short stay in the hospital after his accident a couple of days ago, Daniel had accepted Brian's suggestion to stay over, having taken a cab from BART, after a "short" first day back on the job. Typically, he had worked late and had not arrived until a few minutes after ten. "You have a beautiful place here. I wish I had had time to visit more often."

"So tell me about the accident. All I know is what Robin told me, that you were injured by a hit-and-run driver in front of your house while washing your car."

"This hood let his fifteen-year old girl friend drive." Daniel was up, pacing about the room, seemingly admiring the summer view of the Bay. "She just careened around the corner and drove right at me as if I weren't there. Just kept going, too. I was able to track them down only because of some witnesses. Lucky for my aikido lessons. I was able to dive out of the way, knew how to tuck in my body to protect myself. Still, she got my arm. And my neck's all messed up. Whiplash. My insurance company's lawyer has let me know I'll get a least a few thousand out of it for 'pain and suffering' as they call it."

Brian grimaced inwardly at the complications of some people's lives. Daniel seemed almost hysterical—couldn't he keep it simple? "Just put it in the bank and use it as a nest egg for school."

"Actually I've pretty much made up my mind to buy that house up in Oregon. Property values are increasing there and, if I buy it, my friends with AIDS won't be evicted."

"That's really thoughtful of you, but do you want to complicate your life that much just when you're off on a brand new venture?" Brian shuddered at the very thought of how much economic entanglement Daniel was willing to take on, but he knew he could not change his mind.

"I saw an ad last week, a job at a computer company in San Rafael," Daniel continued to pace, unable to contain his energy. "They'd start me at only *half* my current pay. It's a dead end here for my career. And the gay scene has become totally depressing—sex clubs without any of the saving amenities of the baths—simulated glory-holes, pretty much. Lots of unsafe sex. Why not? Probably three-quarters of the guys are positive. So depressing."

"At least you'll still do okay—selling Jorge's house?" Brian, still seated, turned his response into a question at the final moment, just in case.

"The house has lost value recently, but I'll do okay. That neighborhood's overrun with crime. My car's been broken into twice this month. I know it's their frustration for not being able to get any crack cocaine lately. Armed muggings almost every night, teenagers with guns, as soon as it gets dark."

Brian had to bite his lip to stop himself from wondering aloud why Daniel had ever wanted to leave his quiet haven in Noe Valley. "And the doctor across the street—who happens to be gay—he tracked down his stolen convertible—found it in the projects—and then phoned the police. He got his car back okay, but yesterday morning his whole porch and living room were destroyed by a fire bomb."

"Egad. Get out while the getting is good."

Daniel preferred to worry about the future. "I'm very

scared—interrupting my career, I mean. Giving up my big salary, all my achievements, all those perks like the trips to Europe."

"But your life was so frantic."

"Yes, that's it. I want to be like you someday—I want my life—my weekends, my holidays."

"I think you'd make a great teacher, although grad school at your age will be a long, tough haul." Daniel had finally sat down again, bracing his injured arm on Brian's favorite armchair. "And you must help me set up the modem on my computer before you leave. We can stay in touch through E-mail."

"Gay computer dating." Daniel had the same cynical edge to his voice as when describing the sex clubs. "It can be bizarre. The other night about midnight I'm communicating with this interesting guy who said he was in North Carolina—it's 3 AM there, remember. After a while I figure out who it is—one of our most prominent local authors." Daniel raised his eyebrows and just stared dead into Brian's eyes, as if to say "So there you are, that's how it is these days."

Daniel's pessimism about the local scene was beginning to get to Brian who turned his eyes away to fix them on the massive, silver structure of the bridge. There was no hope. Will had just checked into Mt. Zion with PCP, Edmund was gone, his mother was on the brink. A wave of nauseating fear passed through him. Daniel was leaving, Liz was not available—there was only Richard with his precarious health. He looked over at Daniel who had curled up into a fetal position in the armchair.

Many minutes passed, neither speaking. Both had their own fears, but both of them wanted to keep to themselves. Words would only trivialize, only ruin something, Brian figured. Frozen with fear, he had no appropriate persona to engage, but had the sense from Daniel that he need not worry about it, need not protect or sympathize or warn or chastise. Somehow they were accepting each other; some kind of intimacy was developing. Perhaps this was their most touching, most fragile moment together, a kind of baptism for their friendship. Why could not affection have played a part?

After a very long half hour or so, Daniel got up for a glass of water. Brian sensed tensions easing and suggested moving to the bedroom where they could stretch out and relax. In bed they hugged and fell asleep side by side, still barely having spoken to each other. At about 4 AM, how-ever, Brian woke up to a frightening sound, Daniel gasping for breath. "What's wrong?"

"It feels like an asthma attack, the worse one since adolescence, but I think I've got some stuff for it." He got up, shuffled through his brief case, pulled out an inhaler and took it to the bathroom. Minutes later he returned looking pale, but breathing more easily. "The most horrible dreams, too—all about hanging onto a rope above this pile of broken glass and falling down on it and becoming all bloody. And being stabbed all over with hypodermic needles."

"Horrible."

"Yes, I survived, though. Thick skin, I guess. Bloody, but unbowed."

"But what about the needles? Maybe your overexerting yourself trying to help those friends in Oregon? Maybe you're stretched beyond your limits. You need to try to avoid getting so tied up with financial schemes—that's not the real you." Brian, set to recruit another humanist, was spewing out advice against his better judgment. "If you stay this way do you think that you and I—you and anyone—could ever become *true* friends?" The words blurted out against Brian's will. He wanted them back.

"We *are* friends. We'll only get to be better friends," Daniel stayed upbeat.

"Well," allowed Brian, "I *can* imagine a solid friendship once you've finished school."

Although he put his arm around Daniel in as reassuring a manner as possible, his own mood turned morbid. Daniel had been a source of some significant benefits—their intellectual rapport, their easy physical familiarity, for example. As he started to fall asleep once again, he tried to be more realistic about his life. His philosophy had been to take what crumbs he could get, but life now offered fewer and fewer of them, with little hope on the horizon for discovering brave, new crumb-granters. He supposed he could make do with less if he had to, but he was determined to be more, much more, than a mere survivor. As for the immediate future, at least he'd get to see Lena at the U. S. Restaurant down on Columbus for breakfast in the morning.

24

"What if I stir up a pitcher of margaritas?"

"Why not?" Timothy and Brian were making a night of it. Theoretically, there were a lot of reasons not to go for this pitcher of potent potables, but Brian, still shaky about Will's and his mother's condition and still adjusting to Daniel's emigration to Minnesota, had, so far, found the evening to be pretty much what he needed.

He had arrived at his colleague's flat at that time when the late afternoon July sun, flooding through several skylights, had bathed the long entryway and attractive living room in bright, white light. Large house plants were everywhere throughout the large, airy flat, set so conveniently in the heart of the Castro. Almost new Danish furniture set the tone: sleek, functional, comfortable. Timothy himself seemed more outgoing than usual, still with that super-short haircut, those gorgeous lips as magnetically riveting as ever, that infectious smile radiating outward a little less self-consciously. Physically, he had moved about assuredly as he served them some snacks and a cocktail.

"I envy you this neighborhood, but I guess I'm just too attached to my perch looking down at the bay," Brian had mused. And then, with irony which had surprised even himself, he had blurted out, "You're certainly conveniently located to spend much free time with the sophisticated young gentlemen who frequent the Cafe Flore. All you have to do is cross the street."

"I'll take you over there as a prelude to this tapas bar in the Mission, if that's what you want," Timothy had responded amicably.

"Are you in a stage where you love it or hate it? The Cafe Flore, I mean."

"I hate the place. I hardly ever go there." Brian hadn't been surprised. Timothy was always making arbitrary pronouncements about it. What about the thousands of hours he had already logged there, the hypocrite?

They ended up going there for a glass of wine. Brian considered it great luck to score an outside table on this warm evening, without the usual frigid gale sweeping down Market Street from Twin Peaks. "It's so nice to have such an establishment so literate folk like us can sit about chatting and well, just once in a blue moon, of course, meet that fascinating stranger at the next table." Timothy's silence had allowed Brian to sink more deeply into this most ambivalent of atmospheres. Could one find a new romance here? Maybe it was better to regard it merely as a place for sociological observation. Only with Timothy could he be so comfortable here, and it seemed that Timothy had been making a special effort to be soothing for him tonight, just when he had needed it the most.

"Have *you*, my friend, had any intriguing romantic adventures here recently?" he had asked, powerless to hold his curiosity in check.

"To tell you the truth, I've had to avoid this place recently because of one of those previous romances." Timothy's twang tended to become even more nasal when he talked about his sex life. "Downright bizarre, actually. We dated a couple of weeks, then I broke it off. But that wasn't the end of it. If I went out on a date with someone new, he'd tried to befriend the guy. He even slept with one of them."

"What's he look like?"

"Your typical Euro-fag. His hair's long on top, slicked down short in the back, like something out of GQ. Blondish-brown hair—usually. But he dyes it to fit his outfit, wears glasses only with certain kinds of clothes—it's all-consuming to him, that certain look. How he sits, how he looks, all poses worthy of photographs."

"Admit it, Timothy. You find that type appealing."

He had smiled, that charming boyish grin. "Yes, I'll admit it."

"But why the gothic twist? Why can't he let go?"

"It's not that he really wants me, personally. He wants his idea of a certain kind of relationship."

"How do you deal with it?" Brian stifled the start of a smug grin. The perfect karma of Timothy being stalked by someone even more image-conscious than he!

"I don't. If I am sitting here at the Cafe Flore having breakfast and this guy, David, comes in, I get up and leave. Once I fled with another guy I was dating and two hours later, when we had finished at another restaurant, there was David, waiting outside on the sidewalk."

"*Another* guy you were dating?"

"Basically the people I've met recently are not affecting me very much. They're not the relationship material I want, not well-developed as individuals." Brian had sat there silent, a part of him still envious of such an active, even if unsuc-cessful, romantic life.

After the Cafe Flore they had had a fine dinner, snacking on many kinds of tapas, washing it all down with a couple of margaritas. Good shop talk. Timothy's "shocking" exhibits at the university art gallery. Their new courses with gay themes.

Invincible allies, they had made the long, refreshing walk back along 18th Street from the Mission as the evening cooled down deliciously. At one point Timothy had even slipped his arm around Brian; a strong current had passed between them.

Now, back at Timothy's, the conversation continued to flow as easily as the margaritas into their frosted glasses. Brian knew that he should try to slow them down. Timothy, if not checked, was capable of a second pitcher. But even as he warned himself that he had to drive home, he let himself be seduced into inebriation by their camaraderie.

At about 2 AM, both of them very drunk, Timothy issued an invitation. "No reason you should drive home. Why not stay over here?"

"You mean out here on the couch?"

"That's not nearly long enough for you. My bed's really

wide. Just sleep next to me in the bedroom?"

"Only if we can have breakfast back at the Cafe Flore?"

"It's a deal."

Was it really happening? Were they really becoming closer, more comfortable friends after all these years? As they stripped down in Timothy's bedroom, Brian found himself intimidated by Timothy's biceps, his muscular arms, his nearly flawless body. It made him feel so inferior that it turned off any sexual attraction that might still be lurking somewhere inside of him. But affection, that was something else. Yes, those gorgeous lips, those dark Irish eyes, but also the warmth of their walk back and their whole evening together had won Brian over. Still in his underwear, he moved over next to Timothy and, full of thanks, impulsively gave him a long, intense hug.

Immediately he knew he had made a major mistake. The atmosphere radically changed; Timothy's awkward smile could not hide his discomfiture. At a loss as to how to respond, the younger man even looked a bit pathetic, definitely much more middle-aged. Brian felt like a fool.

When Timothy disappeared into his bathroom, Brian mulled over his options. He suspected, upset as he was, he wouldn't sleep much on the uncomfortable couch. He then heard a scraping sound in the hallway. Around the corner came Timothy dragging a mattress into the bedroom. He looked up apologetically and explained, "I'm coming down with a cold. My throat's all scratchy from using spray paint earlier today. I just know I'm contagious—I don't want to give it to you. You can have the bed and I'll sleep on the mattress."

"Absolutely not. I'm going home. That's all there is to it. I *can* drive. I've done it much more shit-faced than this." Brian hoped his bluster hid his fear of a DUI, but it was a risk he *had* to take. He had to get out of here, now.

After some more polite resistance from Timothy who, ironically, gave Brian a parting hug, the more conventional, less intense pat-pat-pat kind of hug, Brian pulled away. "I'm off. If you're getting sick, you need your rest."

"This has been fun." If only Timothy hadn't said that, making Brian feel as if he were one of Timothy's adoring students who he was shunting out of his office because he was so drained.

Out on the sidewalk he thought of his options. A cab. A long, sobering walk. No, he'd take the chance.

But the drive lasted forever. Every red light glowed for an infinity. He avoided Van Ness and Franklin, trying to slip home quietly, unobtrusively, along Leavenworth until he had to go on to Union the last few blocks. No police in sight. Pure luck. He vowed never to do this again.

At home, back in the womb, he sipped a cup of herb tea, trying to calm himself down and convince himself that their friendship, after an awkward period of readjustment, would go on about roughly as before. But he felt like such a fool—so gauche, so gullible, so stupid for having tried to grab one crumb too many. Then he caught himself suddenly. Give yourself a break, he thought. Timothy simply has a hard time handling intimacy. He would remember that.

25

The next morning the fog had rolled in. Like a wounded animal Brian stuck to his lair, even when North Beach became sunny towards noon. By about two, however, he noticed the fog had cleared out at the coast. Twenty minutes later he was negotiating the steep trail that led to All-American Boy Beach, not its official designation, of course, but as good a name as any, given the fact that no one seemed to know what to call it. Edmund claimed his cronies had called it Marshall's Beach back in the 1950s.

Almost to the beach, he arrived at the Oasis, a tree-lined area where one could always find protection from the sometimes fiercely cold afternoon winds. Today the Oasis basked eerily quiet in the sunlight, no one around, the vast majority of its frequenters not yet having noted the late break. He slipped down the final section of the cliff to the beach and breathed a sigh of relief, enjoying the friendly, temperate sun once he had deposited his towel in a sheltered spot.

Looking down the beach towards the Golden Gate Bridge, he saw no one in sight. He walked toward the magnificent orange-rust span. Since the tide was low, it was a breeze to cross the rocks to a spot that was simultaneously one of the most public and most private anywhere. There was all the motor traffic above, on the bridge, and the Channel itself was a super-highway for both commercial and pleasure craft. It was easy to climb to an upper level and lie against the immense concrete retaining wall, under the south end of the bridge.

Brian stripped and jogged naked along the upper beach, past historic Fort Point with its windows boarded up and on the final stone pathway to a perch that afforded a view of the surfers who dared the swift tidal currents of the Channel. And there they were, just fifty feet away. Not surfers but three brown-skinned naked men were standing around joking, the one in the middle, the most handsome one, batting his cock back and forth from one thigh to the other. Brian waved them a friendly greeting.

As Brian watched, the trio moved forward to the lower level and into the water's edge, grabbing their genitals in mock-agony each time the frigid surf slapped against them. Sensing no reason to inhibit himself, Brian let himself get hard and looked on as the young men in the surf did likewise. Brian, too, ran into the surf, still about fifty feet away from the boys, and started playing with himself after each strike of the surf. Could he approach them? He'd be content just to be near their smooth willowy, brown bodies. Yet he did sidle through the surf over to the closest one, the cutest one. "God, the water's cold."

"Great beach, though. I've got to bring my girlfriend here." Brian smiled, then, taking the hint, withdrew towards a nearby cove, not wanting to disrupt the chemistry. The short thin one, very comfortable showing off his erection to his friends, got laughs every time he, without using his hands, jerked his hard cock up and down. The third guy, more hunky, with a mat of straight black hair on his chest and stomach, reached down and grabbed one of his socks, slid it over his dick, a la the Red Hot Chili Peppers, and danced about.

Even though all four of them continued stroking themselves occasionally, the uncertainty of what was going to happen next started bothering Brian. This window of opportunity would soon close. They would not all remain alone here very much longer.

The handsome one broke the stalemate. He trotted off to the opening of the cove, played with himself a few seconds, then disappeared from sight. Brian joined his two friends in laughing at his antics, then motioned for them all to go towards the cove. The two friends, after some more laughs, however, walked back to the water and dove in. Brian followed them, needing the salt water's cold sobriety. After he rode a small wave back to the shore, he trotted over to the cove where he could drink in that sleek brown figure at the base of the cliff.

It was an electric moment. As he stared at the young man's

face, he could swear it was yet another, altogether different young man, this one a clean-cut preppy who might have gone to Harvard. But, no, that was actually him—the guy just had this incredible, classically beautiful face.

Once in the cove Brian took about twenty suspense-filled steps towards the young man. How would the guy react? Yes, he had been beating his meat, but now he turned partially away as Brian approached, causing the older man to panic, to retreat to the other end of the cove to allow for the possibility of the thing fizzling out. When Brian turned around again to face him, however, his brown Adonis had resumed beating off, this time looking up at Brian and smiling.

Once again Brian approached and stood side by side with the young man, both of them facing out toward the ocean, toward the warm sun. Eighteen or nineteen, Brian guessed. Probably rarely shaved. Downy fuzz on his cheeks. Brian pressed in closer, thigh against thigh, then playfully caressed his tiny bit of baby fat. Picking up on the kid's affinity for touch, Brian put one arm around his shoulder as they started playing with each other.

Almost climaxing but not yet willing, Brian broke away from the guy's stroke and bent over to suck. He obviously loved it, allowed Brian to continue for awhile, then pulled him down onto the hard, damp sand where they both sucked. The circle was complete.

Minutes later, jumping up, they resume beating each other off, slowly, playfully, Brian using his other hand to massage that brown chest. They heard voices above them on the cliff. This must end soon. Nothing to do but throw themselves into it. Holding each other tightly, pumping each other furiously, they continued with abandon, Brian relieved that he had so much staying power. Hold off, hold off, he commanded himself. Another precious minute of pleasure brought them to the very brink. And then, the explosions, both of them, together.

After a moment they rushed to the surf, diving in to wash up. The friends were busy chatting, pants back on, but in no great hurry to move on.

As they emerged from the surf, Brian, as he usually did, asked for a name.

"Jésus."

"Where are you from?"

"El Sobrante. Good to see you, my friend. But it is late. We must go back." Jésus walked over to his friends and got dressed.

Jésus of El Sobrante! Seeing him clothed, Brian felt a warm glow. No one would ever guess how outrageously Jésus had behaved, with such total abandon. Only he would know how soft the touch of Jésus's cheek against his own. How wonderful that Jésus had been able to seize the moment and then return, fully accepted by his buddies.

Jésus heals, at least for a while. Bless the brown-skinned trio for letting him briefly feel that he belonged with them, was one of them.

He had had this strange run of good luck at the beach for several months, from about the time his sex life with Will had ended. Uncanny how he would show up for a visit at Will's already satisfied at the beach, as if that saintly man had interceded with the heavens to send along divine substitutes.

As he trudged back to his towel, he felt the whole episode with Timothy from the previous night falling into perspective. It was no big deal. Yes, Jésus saves. He waved good-bye to the boys and retrieved a book from his pack. The afternoon was young.

26

Huffing and puffing up Telegraph Hill, his day pack filled with choice treats from Molinari's Delicatessen, Brian didn't even bother to take the booty up to his place when he saw Liz on her deck. Instead, he rushed over to say hello, hoping to have some time to chat before Lynn's inevitable arrival. "Hi. How're you doing? You got off a little early tonight?"

"Yes. I'm trying to catch up on things around here before Stacy and Lynn come over." Liz, already out of her business attire and into her red sweat suit, smiled warmly as she put down her watering can. "Let's have a quick cup of tea—that's all we seem to have time for these days. This whole fall just seems to have flown by."

"I know." Brian dumped his crammed day pack on the floor and collapsed on the couch next to her. "I suppose it'll only get worse when Lynn moves in."

"Maybe not. At least there won't be all this comin' and goin'." Liz disappeared for a few moments, then popped out with their tea. "So how are you? Such a rough period. Your mother? Will? Both pretty much the same?"

It might be helpful to talk to Liz about recent events. "I may have seen my mother alive for the last time, but it was a good trip—definitely some healing. It might be the next phone call—who knows? Much to talk about there—when we have the time. As for Will, it's about the same. It's a matter of days—I don't think he'll ever leave the hospital." Brian hesitated, then scowled. "His lungs are shot. He's pretty much given up, accepted his fate. I don't think he'll make it to Christmas."

"I guess it's like that for a lot of us in San Francisco these days. Seems like you just finished taking care of things for Edmund. I must say his furniture looks fine in your place." Liz gave him what he thought was an it's-about-time smile. She had always been on his case about not sprucing up his place.

Right now, though, he couldn't have cared less about how his place looked. "Yes, don't forget the TV, VCR, microwave—I swore I'd never get one—the futon and enough Nordstrom button-down shirts to keep me supplied for school until the day I retire. Yesterday, there I was, down on Columbus Avenue, chatting with Lena at breakfast. I might just as well have been Edmund. I was wearing his red, pin-striped, all-cotton Nordstrom Classic, size 16 - 35, my exact size, in fact, and a pair of his loafers. I don't find it morbid at all. I even feel this tangible connection with him whenever I watch his TV set or use his microwave."

"At least you could use the stuff. Me, I don't know how I'm going to survive with all of Lynn's junk—I can't believe how much she has. It's already obvious that I'll have to give her complete command of the kitchen." Liz smiled, however, after her complaint, evidently ready to make any necessary sacrifices for her new domestic situation. "What about Edmund's family? None of them ever came out?"

"Nope. They're just happy with all that moola." His simmering anger at the non-grieving family showed in his face. Again he wished he had known Edmund longer, had been able to approach him about leaving some of his money for, say, gay scholarships at his University. "It's being split about a dozen ways among nephews, nieces and other younger relatives—a family man to the end, in his own peculiar way. The body was flown back to Connecticut for burial in the family plot. I sure hope they all appreciate their old faggot Uncle Edmund now."

A knock from the front of the house announced the arrival of Stacy in her usual all-black regalia. "Hi Mom. Hi Brian. Mom, I hope it's okay that Shauna's going to meet me here."

"It's not okay. Lynn's due any minute and Brian and I have barely had a chance to say hello."

"You and Brian could go up to his place if you want to be alone."

"I hope you don't get too involved with that Shauna." Brian
was always amused—probably Stacy was, too—whenever Liz went
into her parental mode. "It's not healthy, the way she follows
you around everywhere. She even follows you to the bathroom."
"A potential stalker here?" Brian's attempt to break up the
obvious tension with a little humor. "Or just a candidate for a
leash?"

It failed. Liz was still pissed. "Really, sometimes I think
you choose women who you know will get my goat. She hasn't
shown up with her U-haul yet, has she?"

"Any day now, Mom." Stacy did seem rather elated that Liz
disapproved so strongly. "You wouldn't do so badly to listen to
my advice. I was right about Sean, wasn't I?"

"That was an aberration." Liz was obviously befuddled.
"Just a little fling—out of curiosity—for old time's sake. So I
admit I was wrong." Liz flashed an ironic smile. "I hope that's
all it is with you and Shauna."

Stacy planted her hands on her hips, ready to defy her
Mother. "Shauna may be a little shy, but she's cute, she's
charming. Anyway, I told you I like free-spirited women, not
domineering, control-freaks like Lynn."

"That's enough about that for now. She's due any minute.
You just don't understand what's involved in a mature
relationship."

"Mature as in 'dysfunctional.' I'll bet you an all-expense
weekend at Orr Hot Springs that Shauna and I will last longer
than you and Lynn. Brian's our witness." Her youthful
arrogance was appalling, Brian thought, but Liz shook her
daughter's hand rather reluctantly on the bet. "Did you know
she's moving in this weekend?" Stacy added excitedly for Brian's
sake.

"Get out of here *now*, and let Brian and me talk a little."

"See you, Brian. Good news for you, buddy. That cousin of
mine, Jeremy, he's definitely coming out here this spring. Did
you tell him, mother?"

"That's one of the things I was about to tell Brian, if I ever had the chance." Already less peeved, Liz heaved a pillow at Stacy who disappeared into the kitchen.

Brian found himself questioning his own maturity. Still envious of Timothy's short-lived romances, he could only shudder at the idea of living with someone whose presence was as strong as Lynn's.

Another knock. "Honey, I'm home." It was Lynn still in her business duds—a handsome green suit which made her look a good deal more trim. She plopped on the single chair across from the couch on the porch and began to relieve herself of the many frustrations of her day downtown.

"Mother?"

"Stacy, I'm busy."

"I just need you for a minute. I'm going to take away some of the stuff I've stored here, but I don't know where it all is."

"That's good news." Liz got up. "You two amuse yourself for a few minutes. I'll be right back."

Brian felt awkward trying to chat with Lynn. No matter what subject he brought up—literature, film, music, art—she would shoot down anything for which he showed the least bit of fondness. She had piercing dark brown eyes and the kind of no-frills approach he usually found refreshing, but tonight he was just too fragile. He started searching for his exit line, wanting to retreat to his own sanctuary now that Liz was no longer available. "Liz told me you're moving in. That's fine with me. I want to wish you both the best of luck."

"Thanks, Brian." A worried scowl came over Lynn's face, as she swept her sandy-gray hair back off her forehead. "There is something I wanted to mention to you, something which I know is hard for Liz to talk about."

"What's that?"

"Well, perhaps she's mentioned that we're interested in bringing up a child together."

"Yes. She told me that you might want your former husband

to be the father."

"Exactly. He and I, it turns out, get along much better when not living together. And he's interested in becoming at least a part-time parent. Or at least he says he is." Lynn paused awkwardly at this point. "I think it's only fair to prepare you now, knowing how close you and Liz have been."

"You mean for all the crying in the middle of the night—I think I can handle it."

"Brian, I've looked over this place and it's fine, it's beautiful, in fact, and I'm looking forward to living here for awhile." Brian suddenly suspected what was coming; it was something about the way she called him by name. "But we've decided it's too small—for the baby, I mean. We'll have to move out. We want to find a place that's more country, one that's still not too long a commute for Liz, of course."

Stunned, Brian found it hard to put on his usual amiable face. "Whatever. I guess it would be cramped. See how you like it. I guess you'll both have at least a few months here?" Lynn nodded and they fell silent. Suddenly fatigued, Brian got up, muttered a polite good-bye, and searched out Liz to give her a quick kiss before going upstairs.

He entered his place totally depressed. Why hadn't Liz told him about their decision to move? Were Liz and Lynn about to become the lesbian version of all the heterosexual breeders he knew who totally ducked out of his life once they had a kid? Unbelievable—that Liz could make so many changes, sacrifices even, for the sake of the relationship. He concluded, from her previous silence, that he had no say in the matter. All he could do was call Richard and kvetch.

27

"Will was not a saint. We will not make him into one." George's opening comments jolted Brian out of his reverie. Comfortably ensconced with another hundred or so of Will's friends and associates in the chapel at Duggins Funeral Home in the heart of the Mission, Brian felt initially reassured to see Nevin's father, George, an unemployed Presbyterian minister, presiding. As the traditional Protestant service progressed, however, Brian began to resent the proceedings as inappropriate for Will, a lapsed Catholic with decidedly mystic leanings.

Sure Will was human, had flaws like everyone else, Brian grudgingly agreed as tears welled up. Certainly his mortality was all too apparent during his last days. No mystic visions near the end. Admitted for the final three weeks of his life to Mt. Zion in early December, to the same room, in fact, which Doug had occupied a year earlier, Will had not been able to shake the lung problems discovered by a cat scan when first admitted. Doug, healthy and chipper, had remained optimistic at first, convinced Will would recover as he had. Brian, however, noting the new note of authority in Will's tone as he voiced his needs to the extremely courteous, competent staff, figured only the proximity of death could motivate his friend to throw off, finally, his sometimes annoying self-effacement.

Sure enough, on December 15, a lung had collapsed. The highly toxic binding substance used to seal the newly inflated lung had caused Will excruciating pain and Brian, looking back, saw that pain as the agent which helped bring about his fairly quick, merciful end. It had so incensed Brian when Will, writhing in pain, had to beg for more morphine because he'd be "locked out" after a certain amount per hour. He wanted to yell at the staff that the guy was going to die anyway—what did it matter? "I'm a brawny guy," Doug had asserted ironically, "but I turned around and grabbed the window when they started pumping that goop in him."

A few days later they had all managed to throw Will a half-way decent Christmas party right there in the hospital. Jacky had organized the food and another close friend, Pat, a former colleague now pregnant and living in Philadelphia, had flown out and volunteered to take charge of all the decorating. Fortunately for Brian, he had arrived early, while Pat had gone out for a moment and no one else was around. Will hadn't looked all that bad. As he had helped him to the bathroom, Brian had noted he still had that naturally beautiful physique and that solid belly. Even his penis looked exactly the same.

"It all worked out so well—you and Doug," he had affirmed. "I was happily surprised. At first, you know, I thought you might come to live with me."

Will had reached out and clasped Brian's hand, mouthing each word slowly. "I knew you were willing, but it wouldn't have been right. You're too much a free spirit—too many others need your energy." And he had fallen asleep still holding Brian's hand, tactful to the end, telling Brian what he knew he wanted to hear.

In due course, Jacky, George, and Nevin, Will's whole surrogate family, had arrived. He could tell Jacky was worried about Nevin. Nevin himself had pretty much avoided Will, preferring to stay out in the outer lobby chatting with other family members and guests.

At about four, Brian had found himself alone, looking out the window in the direction of the ocean. Another golden California day. As the sun slipped behind the building across the street, Brian decided to duck back in to say good-bye to Will. "I'm so glad you came early. It was so good to spend time together," and he had looked up at him with those sad, sweet blue eyes.

Meeting a forlorn Doug out by the elevator, Brian had decided not to try to be comforting. "Only a matter of time, I guess."

"His doctor has made it official. His system's shot— maybe

a day, maybe a week or two." And then with a slight whimper, "I didn't think he'd be the first to go. He's been awfully good company."

Brian had tried to call Will the following night, but had been told "that patient isn't taking any calls." He had run over, hysterically, to the hospital, needing that physical release, and had bolted out of the fifth floor elevator down the long corridor only to find an empty bed. "Where is he?" he had demanded of one of Will's nurses, an extremely compassionate gay man who had anticipated Will's every need.

"Let me check for you."

Doug, not the nurse, had entered a few minutes later. "He's gone, about two hours ago. They had taken him downstairs for another silly test. Afterwards, rolling him back to the elevator, he uttered his last words, 'Oops, I made a mess.' Then he slipped into a coma and that was it. Enough is enough—he had a good doctor who knew what was going on."

Three weeks in the hospital; it could have been worse, Brian philosophized, as George's elegy intruded again into his consciousness. "Let's take the opportunity now to share some of the wonderful things about Will." First Will's sister from Minnesota, then Doug, his lover, and finally Jacky, his surrogate mother and executor. Brian felt a bitterness, a petty bitterness, perhaps, that he had no specific role to play at Will's memorial. Had anyone loved Will more than he? Even in San Francisco it would not be cool for him to come out with, "I was Will's secondary lover for six years." Nevertheless, he felt eager to contribute and was the next one to speak. He lauded Will's work with disadvantaged urban kids and recounted how he had used his own money to purchase new software for them, how he had overcome chronic dyslexia to become an effective teacher, had become so big a person as to let eight-year olds correct his spelling. "A tragic loss to our community," he had concluded as many of the audience shook their heads in grief, murmuring their agreement.

Brian sat down, happy about what he had said, but resentful about what he could not say. Will, his beautiful, sensual, lover had given him the gift of believing someone could find him attractive, especially after the trauma of Marco's sudden departure. Thank goodness for that one, final happy time together back at Will's place the weekend after Thanksgiving, just before he had to enter the hospital.

Will, who so loved the spirit of Christmas, had, as if by intuition, thrown himself into a premature celebration of the season. The big tree, already fully decorated, glistened fully lit. Teddy Ruxpin, wearing a Santa's cap, directed a choir of at least twenty stuffed animals. After Doug had retired, they lit dozens of candles and, listening to Will's holiday tapes, embraced on that small couch in the soothing light.

Later they had gone outside to the garden because, typical of the vagaries of Bay Area weather, a warm storm from the south had fizzled out, leaving in its wake one of the warmest nights of the year. Will, who hated the fierce cold winds which typically blew up Bernal Heights, blew out the candles, eager to take up Brian's suggestion of a stroll in the garden.

What a gorgeous night it had been. The garden had glowed resplendent under a full moon. They had sat speechless on a bench in the evening quiet until Will had whispered, "You are such a beautiful man."

Brian, at a loss of how to respond, had playfully grabbed at Will's crotch, recalling happier times together.

"This warm night," Will continued, "it reminds me of those summer nights in Germany when I was in the army."

"How old were you?"

"Just twenty-one. One weekend I took off with a friend to Paris. We went to a gay bar where I was the only young blond guy. I got pinched, groped, mauled—all eyes were on me, oohs and aahs all over the place."

"Sounds like fun. Young, cute and stationed in Europe—with no war going on."

"Funny, though, I couldn't handle it. I was frightened, totally intimidated by all those strange hands on me. I had to rush out of the back door, crying." Staring up at the moon, Will's face shone, poignantly youthful. "Most weekends we'd leave the base by taxi—my boy friend and I and a bunch of our friends. We'd go to small German villages where we'd have picnics on the hillsides, washing down our bread and cheese with delicious local white wines while we looked at the picturesque little towns in the valleys below. Then we'd commandeer a cab to another town, one with a gay pub, then finish off the evening making love at a gay inn."

Charmed by the story, happy that Will's youth had had its moments of joy, Brian had kissed him long and hard, their last passionate kiss. Then he had noticed Will shudder as the night began to cool suddenly, so they had gone inside where Will, pleading exhaustion, had retired for the night.

As he once again became conscious of George's voice wrapping up the mercifully brief ceremony, Brian found himself arguing with George's original assessment—the guy *was* a saint. Helpful, generous and loyal, Will had never uttered anything approaching a mean word in Brian's presence. A true emotional grown-up, so good, so unselfish, he had made a heroic, courageous response to the shoddiness of his past. And maybe, just maybe, he had died finally sensing his worth as a person—Brian couldn't recall a single instance of that annoying, pardon-me-for-living laugh of his during his final months. Don't forget, George, he concluded his silent rebuttal, this was a great human being who *forgave* his assailant.

The service was over. People were milling around, chatting softly. Doug, who had relapsed on a drug binge right after Will's death, looked only somewhat distraught. Already worried about meeting the next month's rent, he had to confront the eerie task Brian had faced in cleaning out Edmund's apartment—what to keep, what to give away. How strange it had seemed, piling all the stuff out on the sidewalk which he himself couldn't salvage from Edmund's place, and then walking away, only to discover six hours later every last bit of it gone.

Wondering if he had gotten too good at insulating himself from death, Brian braced himself for the Barbra and Judy songs he'd be hearing at the piss-elegant Hayes Street flat where some of Doug's friends would host the reception. He recalled East Coast funerals from his adolescence—Italian, Irish, Polish—mountains of food to fortify the grieving friends and relatives. Indeed, right now Brian was famished and food was all that mattered.

28

"Merry Christmas, Richard."

"Merry Christmas, Brian. So fine to see you on such a gloomy day. So sorry about Will."

"It hasn't hit me yet. Probably will in the next few days. I'll be spending a lot of time by myself during the holiday break. And I'm still pretty much just waiting for the phone to ring—about my mother, I mean." Brian tugged off his heavy sweater and arranged it on the couch so that Cleo could sleep on it. "Oh well, at least there was good news about that big earthquake up north. No one dead or badly hurt, despite all that damage."

"Yes, but consider the terror, consider how many families lost their homes, their entire fortunes."

Richard's dark take on things struck Brian as perfect for this particular Christmas. He plunked down their dinner from Little City Antipasto on the kitchen table and immediately opened a bottle of fine, red wine. He regarded the holidays as the most treacherous time of the year—he and Richard agreed on that. He had gone into hiding as usual on Christmas Eve, trying to open up to the quiet joy of the season by listening to Bach's Christmas Oratorio, emerging only late this afternoon to slip up Russian Hill to be with Richard.

As he sat down on "his" couch, the demonic Cleo, perhaps herself plagued by the holiday blahs, promptly attacked him, retreating immediately to safety atop her master's chest. "Do you think she's too fat?" Richard wondered. "This woman friend chided me mercilessly for her plumpness. She's a Catholic, and that may just be the spartan-and-nun side of Catholicism."

"Nonsense. Plump, sleepy little creatures are so fine by the fire on a winter's night, especially during this plague."

"I recently poisoned her—an overdose of flea stuff. She had to de-tox at the vet for a couple of days."

Cleo opened one blue eye, but only for a moment.

"But here she is back again, still with many lives ahead of her. Let's start a fire. It's almost dark out already—rain's on the way." Brian ignited a Dur-a-flame which soon glowed an eerie, un-Christmassy blue-green. Outside holiday lights twinkled on Coit Tower and the two luxury liners currently berthed near the Embarcadero. "I have my own theory about families and holidays. Let's face it. The name 'Christmas' should be dropped and changed to 'Family Day' when all decent folk unite with their kin to be ritualistically evaluated."

"Oh, you mean Judgment Day."

"Exactly. The day when people like us must see ourselves through our families' eyes—and find ourselves wanting, of course. As for Mr. Jesus the Christ, since no one knows his true birthday, let's celebrate it in August and see if anyone makes a big deal out of it then." Raindrops struck the roof as the storm moved in off the Pacific. "What can beat good company, fine food, the rain and a fire?" Brian was determined to enjoy the day with Richard. "So much better to be here than with our families."

"Yes, the soothing rain." Richard sat up for a sip of wine, then eased back down again to the couch. "Yes, as it is, we're outsiders if we visit someone else's family, melancholy and depressed if we don't." Brian got up to play a tape of his favorite European carols. "Christmas was very unpredictable back in Salt Lake," Richard continued, "especially during the depression with all its attendant insecurity. But I must be so careful thinking about that gloomy family of mine—it can make my back worse. No 'poor Richards' allowed during this holiday season. One must fight off all fatal tendencies towards self-pity. In your case, you must still be shaking off the consequences of yet another trip back east."

"One more trip to go. I'll see her alive, maybe, once more, if all goes well. Then it's just a question of 'putting things in order.' Materially first."

"Yes, psychologically it'll take much longer."

"The good news is that this last trip was one of the best, a marked contrast from those treks when I had to leave my genitals back in San Francisco to become the eunuch, her ideal son, while she endlessly rehashed the past, justifying and distorting all events to fit the mythology she was creating for her life, crushing my own perspective whenever it didn't suit her. And then concluding her narrative by bitterly regretting that she hadn't been more expressive, more aggressive, this coming from one of the world's most volatile people."

Even as he ranted on, Brian set the table and brought out Christmas dinner, a potpourri of half a dozen scrumptious antipasti from Little City. "Luckily I saw through her self-absorption after talking to my cousin a year or so ago. She pointed out how my mother loved only the image of me she needed to see, sometimes condemning, usually ignoring all the rest."

"That was astute of your cousin. Sometimes we cannot accept the most obvious things about our parents until someone with some objectivity shows us the light."

"Yes, that's one thing a lover could do," Brian murmured regretfully. "Anyway, ever since that insight from my cousin, I noticed that my mother showed me love only to the extent I fit into her idea of the 'perfect son.'" Brian paused, appreciating anew how perfect an audience Richard was for these crucial disclosures. "So then I started regarding her much more critically, more objectively, seeing her as someone in the 'wrong', not so much as a victim, as someone tragically damaged by life who had sacrificed so much for me. Of course there's some guilt about this 'cold' detachment, but it's there, it's real."

Brian offered to refill Richard's wine glass after gulping down his own. "But this time," he continued, "well, maybe it's the proximity of death, but she seemed to like me more. Just before leaving I kidded her and suggested, after a typical complaint, 'Oh, you've got to have *something* to worry about,' and she just let it go. Very atypical. Sarcasm and irony always fanned the flames. And then on our last night together she bowled me over with, 'Brian, it's so wonderful talking with you. You've become such a friend, my best friend.'"

Richard perked up. "Friend? That's hopeful. A friend. Yes, I'd be happy about that."

"And then there was one final gift, although you might not think it such at first. She looked me right in the eyes and said, 'I've suffered so much for you kids.'"

"Brian, that old theme—it's horrible."

"Wait, there's more. 'I believe there's meaning for all my pain—I've suffered so you don't have to.' So I've decided to take her at her word, probably because I've lived long enough to feel deserving of such a gift. Our bond, the mother-son bond, it's so strong. Why not accept her blessing? Why not give her suffering some meaning? We've got all sorts of psychic and intuitive connections—I've tried to open that side of myself up. If nothing else, whenever she says, 'Don't worry about me,' I don't! I detach myself without feeling a lot of guilt, although I'm still very scared about how I'll feel after her death."

Richard appeared more pale than usual. "Yes, when these strong, feisty survivors succumb, they leave us feeling so mortal, so vulnerable."

"Did things improve with your mother in her later years? She died at ninety, didn't she?" Again, Brian kept talking as he zipped out to the fridge to get the crushed garlic.

"Somewhat. Sexuality remained the big barrier between us. And so I, too, detached myself from her life." There was some relief for Brian in Richard's confession, but also inevitable, residual guilt. "She thrived quite nicely in her seventies and early eighties after my father died, living in Southern California with relatively few worries. Such a stony love. I still envy you your crying. It's so difficult for me. I'm so attracted to intensity, but so scared of it. That father of mine, such an embarrassing man. And yet I must not use that as an excuse any more to run away from intensity. If only he had become a teacher, but that was too unmasculine for her. I wonder if she suspected something?"

Brian wanted to follow that up, but Richard pressed on. "She did the same to me. That's why I first studied math and science at Harvard. Can you believe it? When you talk about Faery Gatherings I still shudder with fear. To someone like me from the thirties and forties, 'fairy' was the ultimate put-down." He seemed to require sympathy, but Brian wanted him to continue on this fascinating new theme.

"It sounds as if you are suspicious of your father's sexuality."

"Strangely enough, he always warned me to beware of 'loose women,' but never said anything against men. And then he'd just love to take me to Temple on Wednesday nights, revelling in the all-male environment as if it were a liberation, saying things like 'Isn't it wonderful to be surrounded by nothing but men?'"

"That's interesting."

"And, you know, there were two men who actually fell in love with him."

"Really?"

"Yes. One actually confessed it in front of my mother."

"What did she do?" he pressed incredulously.

"She just froze."

"Amazing. How did your father take it, how did he react?"

"Oh, he just chuckled a bit and then dismissed it, pretending it was just silly and had no significance."

"And the other man?"

"Reverend Applegate, of all people. A very sweet man in his sixties. To my mother's horror, he began writing love poems to my father regularly. For months he'd send a new poem every week and a dozen roses. Yes, it's true."

Brian bounced up once more to clear off the dinner dishes. He could hear the south wind whistling through the eaves, the storm now raging full force. "Let's face it, Richard. The evidence is in. Your father was, at the least, bisexual."

"That may be. What's interesting is that, after years of thinking of him as a demon, I'm now seeing his good side. His family was much less cold than my mother's. Your magnificent mother, she never holds anything back."

"And at least we both seem to have put the 'emotional incest' of our youth behind us." Brian smiled gratefully at his friend.

"It's been fascinating watching the same process in a 'healthy' family." Richard leaned forward conspiratorially with a bit of gossip. "My former neighbor, Bob, came by with his young son, my godson, Richard, whom he named for me. You know I've always been struck by what it must be like for a mother to watch her son become a sexual being. Bob said that mothers just take to their sons because suddenly it's as if *they* have a penis—in the sense they have created a being with one. The energy there is so intense that Bob, the father, mind you, says he feels he must step aside for a bit!"

"That's fascinating. I totally believe it. Remember last month when we dug up *Suddenly Last Summer* and could laugh at Katharine Hepburn's outrageous pronouncements about how intimate, how meaningful a relationship she had had with her son, Sebastian."

"Yes, I now unabashedly love films and books with incest as a theme."

"Oh, you sicko," Brian laughed, but then raised his finger, the professor about to make a telling point.

"Richard, listen to this tale of an all-American family from All-American Boy Beach."

"I'd love to."

"Remember that really warm day, last Saturday? A group of five people—two young men and a young women in their early twenties and an older man and woman. The three younger ones take off all their clothes and are soon joined in their nakedness by the older man, but not by the older woman whose domineering presence strikes sensitive me as so controlling that I recoil a bit from her. Then suddenly another bystander lying on the beach nearby questions them, 'Are you all a family?' 'Yes, yes, two sons and a daughter, a mother and an uncle,' answered the young woman."

"Goodness."

"I'm flabbergasted, especially when the two guys, both immensely attractive, let their members stiffen up as they enjoy enthusiastically conversing with each other. All this right in front of their uptight mother who won't even take off her top. When even the uncle goes naked, I'm emboldened to seize onto this therapeutic occasion. I, too, get hard right in front of Mom!"

"I can't imagine."

"But, as always, it's all too short. Everyone, me included (but not Mom), takes a plunge together. But once out of the water, she rounds them all up with, 'We have to go. We have to meet Leonard so we can be at the Glaser's in time for dinner.'"

"Delightful, Brian. Some people have all the luck. And I envy your being able to show off your body like that—I never could." Richard took a sip of wine without looking up.

They polished off the rest of the wine after their Christmas rum cake, then lapsed into a drowsy silence, Brian even dropping off for a bit. He awoke with a start, needing a moment to figure out where he was, until Cleo scampered off his chest as he sat up.

"Aren't those cat naps soothing?"

"Indeed." Brian felt the best he had all day, as if Richard had irradiated him with his loving presence while he dozed. "Thanks, thanks for being so warm, so giving on this accursed holiday, you Salon Animal, you."

"And thank you, kind sir, for all you've given me. Your tapes and CD's—such a gift of love. Now I listen to some of Schubert's haunting melodies, letting the tears come, and then I move on, almost always to a better place. I'm functioning so well that I may be concluding my therapy sometime soon."

"That's great news." Brian rose, a rush of happiness surfacing from having spent Christmas with someone with whom he could be his most honest self. Besides, it was after seven. Christmas was over—things would be back to normal out on the streets, once again crowded with cars and pedestrians. A lull in the storm, too. Maybe he'd check out that concert at the Old

First Church on Van Ness.

"One final word, Brian. My old boy friend from the late forties, David, we've been back in touch for years now, thank goodness. He's coming out for a visit soon. We had an absolutely passionate affair that first summer—Paris, Rome, London. But after a year or so, he became sick and his parents insisted he go into therapy." Richard's eyes dropped and he once again invoked a resonant, ominous tone of tragedy. "Soon he met a very, very good (but fat) woman whom he married. I'll tell you more about him later. Time for my ice in the bedroom."

The two men embraced, then Brian zipped down the long staircase, feeling good about himself, but surprised at how much, even in his fifties, he still needed an older man to love and understand him.

29

On New Year's Eve, Brian slowly climbed the steps between Julius's Castle and the Shadows up to Coit Tower. After a week of storms marching across the city, one after the other, the overcast had cleared off at sunset leaving a spectacular twilight. He had no trouble finding a bench to himself since it was too early for serious revellers. As the darkness closed in, the full moon rose slowly from behind the East Bay hills. Only the vaguest of breezes stirred. Breathing in deeply, Brian tried to relax. He didn't resist his tears, but, like most of the past week, he still felt too tight, too petty to deal with the immensity of Will's passing.

The time had finally come for his own ritual, his own ceremony for Will. He felt apologetic to Nevin's father. No doubt he had taken his comment out of context, lost as he had been in his own mind. But after a week of painful grieving, he felt more than ever that Will had been as much of a saint as our culture would permit, so generous without quite being self-sacrificing, principled without being puritanical, except for being too hard on himself. Brian felt in awe of his goodness, his unselfishness. He himself was, by comparison, so selfish, so judgmental.

The day after Christmas, Doug had called him with the news that he (and Spike) were moving to Hot Springs, Arkansas to enjoy his remaining days in a simple, natural setting. Would he take care of Will's gray cat, Ingrid? Brian agreed, but it was more desire than duty because there was something about Ingrid he had always loved. He could also try to soften her losing Will by indulging her with treats and affection. Then, too, he had to admit, she might help fill the same vacuum in his life.

But he couldn't have anticipated the torrents of tears Ingrid's presence released in him, stripping away any facade of normality, as he imagined her waiting for Will's return in vain. First he would feel his throat tense up, then his whole body shuddered. Defenses down, the sadness hit full force, like the worst of flus. Instead of his usual vigorous appetite ther was nausea, a wrenching sensation in the empty pit of his gut that no amount of tears could banish. He wanted Will back. When his body stopped heaving, he would remember precious little details of their times together, but memories were just that—a bit consoling, but altogether inadequate in helping him feel connected to Will in any way whatsoever. He had blamed that on his own tenacious agnosticism which granted him only the meager hope that eventually time would somewhat relieve the pain.

Sobbing, however, was preferable to the hysteria and the depression. His hysteria about AIDS, as irrational as that was. He knew this phenomenon to be a common occurrence. Daniel, for example, had just gotten tested a third time, totally unnecessarily, after yet another friend had tested positive. He, himself, had refused his straight doctor's request to be tested during his last check-up. "We recommend all our gay clients be tested." How he had fumed at those words. He had written him an angry letter saying that the policy should be, "We recommend all our clients be tested who have engaged in behavior that might have put them at risk." Maybe he should get a gay doctor—or did it really matter if one was healthy? A therapist—that was different. How Richard was thriving with his *gay* therapist.

All during the week he had been vulnerable to minor annoyances and worries, often victimized by his "loose end syndrome" when he'd go crazy looking for the one item, no matter how unimportant, which he couldn't find. Or he'd lapse into his poverty consciousness, trying to account for all the cash he had spent since last visiting an ATM. He was high-strung, restless, and bored, resorting much too often to using TV as a mindless distraction. What scared him most was the sense that the worst had not yet hit.

Panicky, he rose from the bench to get a better look at the last of the red twilight on the horizon. How old did one have to be before one gave up the illusion that the great romance of one's life might still be ahead? Did life demand the illusion that romance was still possible just to keep us going? Depression smacked him every time he concluded that Will had been his last, his best shot at it. Neither of them had ever thrown up barriers to communicating as equals, and both of them had made themselves available for sexual intimacy whenever they could. Still, it had only been a part-time thing.

Perhaps it was too soon to figure out any strategy for the future, for a gay man in his fifties who perhaps should simply accept the model of Richard as an older man who had survived, emotionally, deep into his seventies, through his many fine friendships and his great love of the arts. Marco had fled so long ago it seemed like another lifetime. And Will–already it sometimes seemed as if those six years had never happened. But he had found he couldn't give up–not yet at least. Why not a romance with someone roughly his own age, roughly on his wave-length? Or perhaps he might search overseas in a culture where younger men often harbored erotic urges for fatherly figures. Join organizations, perhaps. Or use his computer for long-distance communication, now that Daniel had set him up with a modem.

Perhaps older people should not expect either hot sex or true romance. Those ancient caves in France, he had found out on National Geographic, had become too fragile to handle any more hordes of tourists. So now there were facsimile caves in which local artists had copied the ancient drawings. Was that "substitute" cave almost as good? Or Glenn Gould, refusing to play before live audiences later on in his life–was listening to his recordings almost as good as hearing him in person?

Maybe, but on some level Brian felt separated from "real" experience. As sexual opportunities had dropped to new lows, he felt this period of relying on books and film for his happiness to be a glum, gray time. He even had a hard time fantasizing about sex without some kind of authority figure intruding. Maybe he needed to channel his desire, get himself in gear that way, write something, but so far sublimation had only thrust him further into the doldrums of non-participation. He probably wasn't yet ready to be creative, but he still kept torturing himself about needing to work, to write, to accomplish something. Here he was on the brink of the unique freedom of an upcoming sabbatical and all he could feel was a sense of dread, a terror about how to fill up the time. He would travel some by himself, but after that, what? Nothing to do. Nothing to look forward to.

He had learned one thing from Will who had submitted to the American way of death—AZT, the medical establishment, and an unwillingness to talk about his impending death: we must make our gains in life before we get either too sick or too old.

The worst self-image that tortured him was that of the aging actress who willfully refused to adapt to new roles. Should he somehow re-design himself, take on a new persona to fit his age? Did he try to be too youthful? He *was* an eccentric, but maybe he needed to become a different sort of an eccentric, a little less frivolous, more dignified somehow?

The twilight was gone. Coit Tower rose up massively in the moonlight. Just yesterday, realizing how precious Ingrid had already become to him, he had made the connection that his grief for Will was so surprisingly strong because his death cut Brian off from qualities he felt his lover had in abundance, compared to himself. Now, though, as he started aimlessly circling the giant, phallic tower, he had a slight ray of hope that Will might bequeath him something of those noble qualities. He shifted into something of a internalized chanting mode. "Let Will go. Let Will in."

Brian returned to his bench, uttering his prayer a bit longer until he felt its power dissipate. He sat silently in the moonlight for another half hour. Then, annoyed that Liz was gone for the holidays, returned to his house to sit out the rest of the old year by himself.

30

Friday night and picking through the used tapes and CD's at Recycled Records on Grant Avenue—hardly anything new in the bins, but anything to get out of the house. At least the young proprietor was open to easygoing conversation, plying Brian, as usual, with his questions about the parrots. It was yet another evening of trying to fill up the time, of fleeing from the edge of desperation that his solitary domestic life had become.

This was *not* how he had envisioned his sabbatical, now that he had enough money to be a world traveller. The trip to Asia had gone well, but six weeks was about his limit away from home when he travelled by himself. Since he had come back, however, he had fallen into a severe depression which his involuntary loneliness had intensified. Gone was his usual take on life, his jauntiness, his swagger. He felt inconsequential—who could ever be attracted to him? Even his vicarious life of good films and books had failed—or, rather, he wasn't giving it a chance, no longer stockpiling recent films on tape. He had taken to throwing down book after book in disgust, none of them able to hold his interest. How could they, given his restlessness, the black pessimism that had somehow taken him over? The absence of anything remotely interesting in the music bins seemed to confirm the point.

His intuition about the Liz/Lynn coupling had proven all too true. Liz was still genuinely friendly and they still invited him to dinner every now and then, but gone was the easy informality of their rapport. He remembered fondly her first months in the house when they'd have long conversations on the phone every night until first he, then she, wondered aloud whether they should baby sit for each other to quite that extent. After that they had relied on daytime rituals, particularly having tea on one of the decks.

He knew his mother had her agoraphobic tendencies, but he never thought *he'd* ever have such a home-bound siege. Life had become drudgery at best; a stiff back discouraged exercise, causing him to feel old and fat. On the occasional night, like this one, when he felt he had to get out to preserve his sanity, his back had acted like a reluctant lover. "Not tonight. Let's just go to bed early." Now he understood Edmund's crack that the older you get, the more arguments you have with your body. And what was the point in getting out tonight? (Bach, Beethoven, Mozart–the same old stuff.)

The bad spring weather hadn't helped his disposition, but, even so, he had never before been so grouchy, so irritable. Just this morning, he had let his whole day be gobbled up by his "loose-end syndrome." Remembering that KKHI was going to play a rarely-heard Schubert sonata, he had spent three hours in a frenzy searching for their monthly program guide which had mysteriously disappeared. He kept telling himself to call the station and find out from them when the damn thing was going to be played. Maybe they could have sent him an extra guide they had lying around or at least given him the names of nearby stores that might have copies for sale. But, using the excuse that he had to make a tape for Richard, he chose the misery of trying to find that loose end. Then, suddenly remembering that he couldn't find a twenty dollar bill he had mislaid, he became paranoid about the guy whom he had recently hired to clean his house, mentally charging him with robbery for about the sixth time until, as usual, he found the money under some mail on the kitchen counter. (Wouldn't you know it–that expensive Schubert sonata he bought recently was now marked down to $9.95.)

His worst moods encouraged self-pity. He couldn't stop ruminating about his lonely adolescent summers, and he became haunted by a walk he took along his old paper route on his last visit to see his mother. How lonely he had been. When strolling along familiar streets he wondered why he hadn't made more friends? Why hadn't he tried to be more sexually aggressive in those days?

That deep, gnawing emptiness inside had opened up and he would start drinking, even in the morning. Luckily, just as trashy television worked as his baby sitter, the phone remained a lifeline. There was always Richard, of course, but especially Timothy who, thank goodness, had always encouraged them to disclose their alcoholic excesses to each other.

Just then, Timothy walked into the shop. "How are you doing, Brian? I decided I needed a break from the Castro. I like the atmosphere here at night—it's been so long since I've been to good ol' Grant Avenue. Kind of nice, all these handsome young guys strolling about and probably not one of them thinks he's gay."

"You've got it." Brian immediately left the bins and walked over to his friend, wanting to hug him in relief, wanting to tell him that he was a sight for sore eyes. He didn't, of course, remembering his previous embarrassment. But there was something different about Timothy tonight that disarmed him. "I was so depressed," he confessed. "I just had to get out of the house. How about a glass of wine at Mario's?"

"Perfect. What's our limit? Two or three glasses? Imagine imposing any restrictions on wine in the old days."

Once outside on Grant Avenue Timothy had taken charge and put his arm around Brian's shoulder for the first few steps. North Beach was starting to come alive. It *did* feel different at night, especially when one had a companion. They turned left at Union and walked the final block in silence until they reached Columbus Avenue, but Brian's mind was very busy. He was recalling how he usually got competitive with Timothy, always wanting to justify himself, his work and his life. For some reason it was very important tonight to promise himself to let go of that insecure side of himself, even though he felt unusually defensive. To hell with his ego—let Timothy know the worst, if that's what he feared.

Cramped into a tiny, triangular corner, Mario's Bohemian

Cigar Store was crowded as usual, but luck was with them as a couple was just leaving a tiny table in the darkest corner. The place exuded old-world Italian ambience and Brian sensed it would provide him with the temporary womb he needed on this terror-stricken flight from his own usually reassuring nest.

He wasted no time in thanking Timothy for their talks about booze. "You know about a month ago this fatalism hit me, that I was going to be just like my other male relatives and drink myself to death. I was losing all faith that I could remain a 'social drinker,' especially since just about my only social interaction lately has involved my cat, Ingrid."

Timothy smiled with that charming, playful, almost silly look on his face which, for years, Brian had observed him give to so many others, but never to him. "My pal, we must always be there for each other and we must never, ever go to AA. You have been helpful; at least you don't binge the way I do–but I haven't much lately, since we've been having our 'sessions.'"

"It helps so much to confess to you, especially when I get shitfaced during the day." Brian unselfconsciously slipped his arm around Timothy's waist for a moment. "You always give me the sense that I can easily change the pattern the very next day. So, following our plan, I'm sticking pretty much to good-for-your-heart red wine before dinner and one very stiff shot of the hard stuff later on." Years ago Brian had laughed at his mother for her insistence that all drinks be measured, but as his drinking had subtly, insidiously increased over the years, he had come to acknowledge the wisdom of her ways. And of Timothy's. Together they kept their drinking out in the light, away from the powerful shadow of secrecy. The temptation to overindulge was still there, but he could still rationalize that drinking worked, providing pleasure and needed relaxation.

So far Brian had resisted, had not seen a doctor, despite his troublesome back and stomach which were, more than likely, symptoms of his depression. For some reason he found it easier to talk to Timothy about depression than about loneliness.

Despite all their calls during the last few weeks, another kind of fatalism had kept him from ever inviting Timothy over. No doubt his insecurity made him feel like their previous debacle was *his* fault, that *he* had been rejected and therefore needed to wait for an invitation from Timothy which, of course, had not been forthcoming.

"You've helped me too, dude," Timothy gave him that smile again. "If I stay in our limits, there's no nausea later, none of that unfocussed sleepiness when you can't get anything done, can't even do anything interesting."

"Not to mention, in my case, at least, becoming over-whelmingly oral-needy and eating too much, causing more nausea and gas." And then, almost miraculously, Brian felt himself backing down from his, from their success story. Taking a long sip of wine, he let himself feel good about not having to prove himself, but he also admitted to himself that he still needed to censor, that he could not yet confess the extent of either his neurotic condition or his loneliness.

More time passed in pleasant conversation. It struck Brian that his holding back from the usual verbal traps with Timothy had somehow cleared the air. Timothy was smiling that silly grin which seemed to say, "Well, here we are in it together and it's not that bad." His bearing gave Brian the sense of a permanent truce between them. Were they admitting they needed each other? Liked each other? That they somehow were going to manage to be kind to each other almost all of the time? Timothy's sharp tongue, when no longer aimed at Brian, that hard-edged anger which fueled his political activism, might even show him the way to possible new outlets for his own frustrated energy.

"What a horrible period." That good urge to confess had come back strong. "Sometimes I think I'm precocious, that I'm already the archetypal lonely, old gay man. I wish I could go back to being the dirty old man. But there's no lust left in me anymore. Even porn doesn't work—it's lifeless and empty."

Timothy had already figured that out and distilled it into one of his theories about contemporary urban life. "It's part of the zeitgeist, the post-plague epoch when a cock doesn't automatically cause the salivary glands to flood the mouth."

"I suppose the plague is making us grow up a little," Brian admitted begrudgingly. "I am less desperate, less greedy, for sex, the commodity, and don't want to settle for anything that doesn't involve some kind of satisfying interaction, romantically. On the other hand, it seems, for me at least, as if it's nowhere to be had these days." Brian stopped–and caught himself just before entering the old turf of self-justification, curious as to how Timothy would react.

"I'm finding it stimulating to not be involved with someone, to let the energy build."

Was this bullshit, Brian wondered? Should he be enticed to believe it? He reacted as honestly as possible. "Yes, except if one goes too long without expressing it, when there's no good place to channel desire–well, Marco and I used to call it 'the screaming red eagle.' And then the energy somehow becomes counter-productive, turns back in on itself."

"I know what you mean, when you have powerful fantasies of loving someone, but can't do anything with your energy. Part of life, I guess." This was Timothy's most impressive disclosure so far. "How about a snack, one of their foccaccia treats?"

"No way. I'd get a gas attack just when I was about to fall asleep." Brian paused and took a deep breath, protecting his still delicate constitution. "How about a compromise, like something from across the street at Ben and Jerry's?"

They ambled down Columbus Avenue to what used to be his favorite Chinese grocery store and purchased their treats. Back outside, while eating his non-fat strawberry yogurt cone, Brian worried that he and Timothy would slip back into their old ways. Timothy, however, was continuing to clown around in a way that nicely maintained the new place they had reached. They hugged good-night unselfconsciously.

Then Brian ambled up Union Street, his back still stiff, but with perhaps just a bit of his old jauntiness. It was a reprieve which was to be extremely short-lived. The light was blinking on his message phone. His cousin. His mother had finally passed on. He was numb. Another major challenge to his sanity. Nothing to do but take things one day at a time. Tomorrow he would fly east.

31

The phone, damn it, at seven in the morning, probably from the east coast, after one of the worst nights Brian had ever spent. He had hardly been asleep at all. Painful gas attacks (and numerous Mylantas) had been followed at around 4 AM by diarrhea (and Imodium), then finally nightmares which left him gasping for breath, pillow and sheets clammy with cold sweat. "Hello. How are you, Charles? Oh no, a quadruple bypass? By all means—I've got a pen. Give me his number at the hospital." His friend, Dwight from New Haven, a massive heart attack. Only sixty years old. "Yes, I'll wait a couple of days before calling."

Horrible. Dwight was only a few years older than he. The fragility of life, the proximity of death—that was all he could think of since his mother's death. He got up and fed Ingrid who might, he suddenly realized, outlive him.

Two weeks back from having buried his mother, Brian found himself miserable. His back was even worse, his stomach a mess, and his depression all-consuming. Never had he been aware of so much fear within himself. His mother had also had these gas attacks. She hated them—the loss of control had made her very nervous, very fearful, fearful of death.

He had, at least, made a kind of tentative peace with his only sibling, his younger brother who ran a small business in Arizona. Apparently Larry's homophobia had diminished enough so that he could now invite Brian to stay with his family. They had agreed that with the loss of their mother they needed to be closer, and decided to see each other at least once a year. At least that was the agreement.

He had expected some fear to hit him after his mother's death, but he had never spent such endlessly long, terror-stricken days in his entire life. He gave himself tacit permission to cry as much as possible, but when he heard his own sobbing, it sounded phony, as if he were an inexperienced actor. Mere pathetic whimpers about the inherent cruelty of life. Only by constant phone calls to Timothy had he been able to control his intake of booze. Still avoiding the medical profession, he had cheated by scoring occasional tranquillizers and pain killers from Richard.

If only Dante the parakeet hadn't disappeared that first morning back—that had seemed the cruelest twist of fate. Still no sign of him. And then, as if life wished to mock him on the most banal of levels, his once dependable Toyota was itself constantly breaking down. Just after he got back, his radiator sprung a leak and he just about blew out the engine, being too distracted to notice how badly it was overheating. Next the timing belt and this time the damage was extensive. Then he got sideswiped by a delivery truck and the company showed no inclination towards wanting to pay damages without a messy legal battle.

Worse than the money and trouble involved with the car had been his emotional regression to a neurotic self of twenty years ago when the temporary loss of his vehicle symbolized a grounding, an imprisonment of his new, mobile California self. He tried in vain to accept the rightness of it. After all, given the state he was in, he was barely able to leave the house anyway.

His car troubles suddenly evoked the memory of one of last night's dreams. He was driving around a new area on the East Coast until he came upon the Pinecrest Parkway, a hilly, affluent area of his home town. First soaring up a hill, then cruising down, but then suddenly his passenger grabbed the wheel from him. It was Tommy, the son of Richard's downstairs neighbor, Rose. Tommy had Down's Syndrome and had survived into his late forties only with his mother's help. Brian had managed to wrest back the wheel from him, but his effort suddenly thrust him back into everyday consciousness. He had awakened with more diarrhea, more gas pains.

Still he'd willingly put up with these nagging back and stomach problems if only the late night anxiety attacks would

stop plaguing him. Even before the call about Dwight, he had
sensed a pain in his own chest and had become convinced he was
going to have a heart attack. His blood pressure readings had
been so abnormally high that he refused to change the batteries
in his machine when they gave out. Worse, the anxiety triggered
a haunting sense of emptiness. Frozen with fear, he wouldn't
move for hours. He'd fixate on his fear of Richard's death,
feeling incapable of going on without him. Or he'd indulge in
more self-pity, as the miserably lonely old gay man who had no
younger man to come by and be there for him, as he tried to be
there for Richard.

He thought about visiting Richard that morning, but it was
still too early. He tried to evade the anxiety by keeping busy
with mindless chores, then attempted to nap around ten. But as
soon as his head hit the pillow, anxiety overwhelmed him. He
feared he might be losing his mind. He bolted upright, threw on
his shoes and socks and, still restricted by his back, walked down
Telegraph Hill and up Russian Hill as fast as his ailing body
would permit.

He rang Richard's bell—two quick thrusts, his code. He used
his keys and hustled himself up the stairs to find his friend on his
couch reading *The New York Times*. "Sit down, Brian. You look
distraught."

Brian blurted it out: "I don't know how you do it,
Richard—I'm such a mess myself. Depression. Anxiety. Here I
am on my sabbatical—all this free time—and I can barely function.
All these deaths—my mother, Will, Edmund. It all seems so
bleak, so meaningless, so pointless to go on."

"Well, Brian, it looks like this is your dark night of the soul."
Richard talked haltingly as he put down the paper, but there was
something in his tone Brian very much needed. "Most
middle-aged men, you know, take depression for granted."

"But why? Why?"

"One doesn't need a reason. It's part of life. It's in our
genes that we worry more, fear more, become more depressed as

we draw closer to death."

Normally Brian would have disagreed vehemently but this morning he said nothing.

"It's all catching up to you now, a little later than most."

"The whole planet's become a rotten place. Dante the parakeet disappeared. Yesterday, such a gloomy day, I never should have gone to the ocean, but I had to get out. First I saw this turkey vulture pecking away at a baby seal washed up at the water's edge. Then, after I managed to accept that as a 'natural' occurrence, I was walking along and came upon this twelve year old boy throwing rocks at a wounded sea gull. That said it all."

"Soon you'll realize it's time to move forward. It *has* been a rough year. And you don't have that rock-solid base—your work—to fall back on." In the quiet of the early morning, they could hear the barking of the sea lions from Pier 39. "It's been painful to watch the joy seep out of you this year with all its darkness. But some of it is your doing, your needlessly invoking the paranoia of the past. Fighting those tickets in court, arguing with chairman and dean about funding at school—didn't you tell me you couldn't even fantasize about sex these days without having to confront a policeman or some other authority figure?" Richard was locking Brian into his logic.

"Yes."

"We need to keep fighting, but we need to choose, to pick our battles carefully. If you want to get back something of your *joie de vivre*, you'll need to surrender more to life, to whatever it brings, including death. Not let little things freak you out. You say you're bothered by gas attacks—it's GAS all right—Gay Aging Syndrome."

Brian chuckled briefly. "That's me, I'm afraid." He tossed off his shoes and leaned back against a pillow, beginning to relax. "You know, I smelled Rose's cooking this morning coming up here—it reminded me of a dream I had last night where Tommy tried to grab control of my vehicle—I was terrified, totally unable to believe he knew what he was doing."

"Tommy, your deeper, wiser self perhaps. Let him have some say in your life. None of us is perfect. You've done such a good job of cruising through life this past decade or so—healthy, productive, sexy. But don't discount your wounds from the past. You apparently adjusted nicely by avoiding them, but they do catch up with us from time to time."

Brian felt himself start to mellow. Cleo jumped up on his lap and started purring, the sound a perfect complement to Richard's soothing tones. "Don't try to be perfect—otherwise you'll waste too much energy trying to prove that you're 'right.' Or maybe it's better to say that being wounded we have a strong tendency to feel 'wrong,' and that's when the paranoia starts." His therapist had done wonders for Richard's assertiveness.

"You mean too much self-justification. I've had much too much of it lately. I am sick of it. It's so boring."

"Yes, we expend too much energy trying to justify ourselves and forget about simply engaging life, enjoying things a bit. Both our mighty mothers fell into that trap, but remember, too, that both of them rebounded and reached their happiest periods late in life, even though friends and relatives were dropping like flies around them."

Richard swept back his hair and sat up, his gaze fixed on the Bay. "You have just received the sum total of wisdom from my therapy. It's over. The good doc approves of my desire to set out on my own."

"Congratulations. I think I get the point." Brian rose and peered down into the gardens below—lots of green for a crowded city; magnolia and plum trees, princess flowers with bright purple blooms all year long, even bird feeders where the parrots occasionally dropped in for a cameo appearance. He could hear a more confident quality return to his voice.

"It's time for me to return to life—a time to live."

Brian began cautiously to pet Cleo who continued her atypical purring. "Two days ago, lonely and miserable, I decided to go to Traffic School, after that damn judge found me guilty of running that stop sign. So I chose a gay one, the Pink Triangle Traffic School. The men there were nicer than those in any gay bar, all ages, so human, so intelligent, attractive in so many ways." Traffic school—a strange but perfect catalyst for his new active phase. "And the instructor was so fine—anti-authority, like so many of us, but so non-destructive, genuinely concerned that we avoid the trauma of a drug bust or a DUI, for example. The camaraderie was so reassuring—it made me feel so proud to be gay. I didn't get any phone numbers or anything, but I want to meet more men like that, I want to get back into life again."

"That sounds better." Richard looked weary as he paused, drained of therapeutic fuel, but then he resumed with a radical shift of tone. "By the way, I should tell you that my old boyfriend David just got here yesterday for a brief visit. He's down in North beach exploring the cafes, but should be back soon."

"How's it been going?"

"So good, so healing. Over the years I often regretted not staying more in touch, but that's been remedied recently—many letters and calls. Slowly I've been overcoming that initial loss of him—a sense of abandonment lingering and deep." His faint smile disappeared, replaced by a sadness in his eyes. "But with the help of my good doc, I've started to take some responsibility, too. The crucial memory was a moment many years after our affair, David standing next to me in his kitchen, begging to be hugged, but I was in such a state of disarray, still, after all those years, that I responded in no way at all. I pretended I did not see his pain, his need. But that dear, wonderful man had made an opening for something new to happen." Cleo jumped off Brian's lap to assume her usual perch atop Richard's chest. "I have wept over that sin of omission, of which I have committed many, many more than of commission. But now he's here and it's already been very healing, thank goodness."

"That's wonderful, after so many years. There's the bell—that must be him now." Brian jumped up and pushed the buzzers that released the outer and inner doors. Up the stairs came a slim man in his early seventies, with considerably more white hair than Richard. As he settled into the arm chair across from his host, his brown eyes struck Brian as full of kindness.

"Richard, you should have come with me."

"We'll do it soon." He was evasive.

"It's fascinating down in North Beach, people from all over Europe. My son's going to enjoy his trip out here."

"Did you say when he was coming, David?" Richard lifted himself up to be at eye level with his former lover.

"In a couple of months, no definite plans yet." I think you'd like to meet him, Brian, maybe help him get to know the gay side of the city. Richard figures he's only a few years younger than you. He's quit his job in New York City, just got fed up with the routine. I think he's been working like crazy since his divorce because he couldn't quite figure out what to do next."

"Switching careers?"

"No, no hurry about that. He's saved plenty of money." David paused. The silence was intense. "No, how to be gay. Funny, I never put any pressure on him to marry. Maybe it was his mother, maybe society itself, but he's such a hard worker, always has wanted to be a success—and that meant not only material success, but marriage with children."

"He has kids?"

"Two of them, both in college. Are you into E-mail, Brian? You and Chris could communicate by computer. If you do, urge him to come out here. He needs a change of pace, a supportive community where no one knows of his past."

Coaxed a step out of his depression by this new possibility, Brian noted to himself how David's son fit his latest profile for a possible lover—a contemporary to whom mature responsibility was second nature.

Thinking it best to leave the two old friends alone, Brian got up to say good-bye. As he hugged Richard, he felt his new, larger back brace needed for his worsening condition. "Is that contraption helping your back?"

"I think so, but my body's been acting up lately—I've been going to the doctor's practically every day. The diarrhea's returned. Some prostate trouble—I need to take more tests. Blood pressure problems, and an old mouth infection flaring up. . . . Cheers, Brian."

Brian realized, slowly descending the stairs, that Richard, despite graduating *summa cum laude* from his therapy, still had a body that insisted on constant melodrama. Once again he was awed by Richard's capacity to charge forward into life despite it all. He was ashamed of his own inability to cope with life's changes while still physically vital. It was time to stop babying himself, time to get on with it.

32

"Finally, you're beginning to look like your old self, Brian-boy. You've had a tough few weeks." Timothy snared another of the strawberry tarts which he had picked up at Victoria Pastry. "The day is yours, partner. Maybe a little walk—you could probably handle a movie."

"Yes, life as I have known it is returning. I have travelled much in my poor humble bed during this siege." The smell of Timothy's coffee still made Brian a bit nauseous, but if he leaned away from it, he could breathe in the sweet morning air out on his deck.

"It was such fun feeding the parrots. I love that pair of blue-crown conures, so sweet and gentle. Sometime this summer, when we're both around, we ought to trade places for a week."

"Sure, anytime." Brian still wasn't feeling spunky enough to look forward to cruising around the Castro for a week, but he was so grateful to Timothy for his help during his illness that he'd agree to almost anything he suggested.

Once Timothy left, however, all Brian desired was to stay out on his warm deck that May morning and stare out at the bay. The surprises life held for us. Just when he thought he might be coming out of his depression after his mother's death, especially after he had been inspired by Richard's advice to re-engage life, he developed a high fever and a severe sore throat. His stomach remained a problem, his sore back worsened and his whole body had ached from head to toe. After he had confessed his symptoms to Timothy over the phone (his friend became suspicious when Brian mentioned he hadn't had any alcohol for three days), he had let Timothy come over and drag him to his own doctor, a gay man, who confirmed, to his great relief, after only a few questions about his sexual history, that he had a rough case of the flu. The flu in May? What kind of flu? "'Flu' is as good a term as any," the doc had explained. "These kinds of episodes are not unfamiliar in these parts. Just hang in there. You'll be fine."

Brian had been surprised that a M. D. would be willing to ascribe his condition to primarily an emotional cause (he suspected Timothy had briefed him about Will's and his mother's deaths), but his relief had nevertheless been great. After the diagnosis he no longer felt that suicidal despair, that uncharacteristic pessimism which welcomed death. He had settled into the womb of his bed much more relaxed, sleeping through great portions of each day. Liz and Lynn faithfully checked in on him, but it was Timothy's visits which most perked him up.

Brian was still wary about their old tensions and ambivalences re-surfacing. One morning, when he had just started feeling a little better, he was pursuing the mindless copying over of his old address book, dropping the names of those who had died or disappeared from his life. Timothy had ridiculed him, playfully, for wasting his time and had whipped out his Wizard. Further conversation revealed how heavily his colleague had indulged in searching for potential romantic partners on the Internet and, even though Brian himself used his computer for quick communication with David's son, Chris, he found himself almost depressed by envy of his friend's new expertise in the world of technology.

But when he had chided his friend about having become so obsessed with his new toy, Timothy had seemed to enjoy confessing such excesses. "I'm still a victim of my obsessions—physical and aesthetic as well as technical."

Most of the time, however, Brian had only his own thoughts for company. But as the spring days grew warmer, he had begun a vegetable garden behind his house and discovered he enjoyed the feel of the earth. Even if upset, he found he could gradually empty his mind of anxieties while working in the garden. As his black moods slowly dissipated, became more infrequent, he remained self-critical but in a more constructive way. He surprised himself by how much to heart he had taken Richard's perceptions about his slipping into a self-indulgent paranoia. Slowly, as the days passed and he harvested his first carrots, he zeroed in on bad habits he wanted to break. He had not lost his momentum about alcohol and a healthy diet. Pizza, fried chicken, barbecued tortilla chips—all well and good for the young—would not enter into the sanctuary of his house.

He soon discovered he had the power to stop his paranoia about the law, to stop putting himself on trial. He would try to catch himself before he launched into one of his vehement pre-judgment condemnations of somebody, like one of those obnoxious cruisers at the beach, for example. The image of the new, improved Timothy helped greatly here. Brian was most inclined to attack his friend mentally out of habit, but upon recalling his recent kindness he could easily curb the urge.

He also started monitoring his own inner dialogues, becoming embarrassed upon realizing how much the adult but puritan work-ethic and the child, the hedonist, still competed so brazenly for his soul. Sometimes when he observed the vituperative arguments of both sides pushing towards preposterous conclusions, he'd laugh. He supposed these inner voices were trying to work out some kind of balance for him, some kind of dialectic between work and play, but, really, he was a professional educator in his fifties. Did these inner voices still have to be so crude?

If the puritan could be easily faulted for his unrelenting work ethic, the hedonist's compulsiveness was at least equally unattractive. (Perhaps one was no longer a hedonist when compulsivity took over?) While weeding his garden he would think back to some times at All-American Boy beach when, because it was all anonymous, he himself engaged in what could be considered obnoxious behavior with relatively little embarrassment. Sometimes he had rivalled Pepe le Pew in his ability to *not* accept his quarry's lack of interest in him, dreaming up all sorts of rationalizations for perversely continuing the hunt.

Or he would try too hard to get turned on to situations which weren't really arousing to him, attempting desperately to sexualize anything and everything.

More resolutions about the beach followed from his musings from under his down comforter. At the first sign of negative body language, someone turning away from him, for example, he decided that he would give up. More important, if he got the least bit bored, he'd move on, return to an interesting book, for example. If there was the slightest opening to be personable, he'd try to start a conversation—he knew that would be a rough one to implement, knowing the chronic unwillingness of cruisers to supply any opening if one didn't pass muster physically. So many of them were so unrelentingly cold to their fellow seekers that it wasn't hard to imagine how one might start feeling like a leper while amongst them.

Then one Sunday morning, after reading the comics, he stumbled onto his most important reform. He'd invoke Zippy the Pinhead's "Are we having fun yet?" Too many times he persisted while not having fun at all. Once, after the frustrating pursuit of a physically attractive but totally closed-off young guy, he discovered, upon returning home, that his blood pressure had soared. Such futile persistence was more than frustrating—it wasn't good for the system. No, if a hidden camera followed him on any given day, he'd want that imaginary audience to agree that his behavior had been sensual, not creepy. He must not regress just because there were so many other creeps about, many of whom played the role of party-pooping, body-language policemen as a result of their own obnoxious desperation. That's why it was so hard not to judge them—they reminded him, painfully, of himself.

All this was irrespective of age. Sure, he could keep on cruising, sure, his age would be a negative factor, but at the beach he'd be outside, in the fresh air, still able to gather all sorts of crumbs. He had claimed to Richard on several occasions that he wouldn't cruise any more if he had an ongoing romance, but who was he kidding? He now admitted to himself that he probably wouldn't stop cruising, that his sensuality at the beach had become an important part of his happiness. That was something he could control. And he promised himself to keep reappraising what he would do as he got older to keep on expressing his sexuality. In the continued absence of a lover, he might want to change his mind in five or ten years about sex clubs, gay theaters, magazine ads, computer dating and even, gulp, paying–or giving gifts–for sex.

These kinds of insights prompted Brian to want to talk to Richard. With a surge of delight, he reminded himself that he was finally feeling well enough to enjoy visiting him. Even though the morning was warm, he knotted a jacket around his waist, still fearful of a relapse. Then a warning call to Richard, a quick petting session with Ingrid, and he was out the door.

As he walked down the hill, he recalled some new ideas about sex he had conjured up while still bedridden, following that long stretch of depression and illness during which he had had almost no sexual urges at all. Despite a temporary lack of interest in videos as a stimulant, he recognized the need to stay fit sexually, the conventional "use it or lose it" philosophy.

When he returned to jerking off, he refused to start tugging away in earnest until suffused with some kind of warmth or affectionate turn-on, trying to rely on respons-iveness rather than friction. He was surprised that this somewhat gentler approach resulted in more satisfying releases, his cum sometimes arching high to youthful distances.

Many times Doug's offhand quip about Will's sexuality at the reception encouraged him–"Thank goodness Will wasn't a size queen." Although Doug had been gently making fun of the fact that he, like Brian, wasn't humongous, the point for Brian was Will's sexual health, his ability to love someone sexually who was less than physically ideal and, in his own case, significantly older.

The last block on the walk to Richard's. If you lived on one hill and your friend on another, you always finished with a climb. He'd often get impatient and observe the number of each passing house in this final block. This time, however, a handsome blond man walking down the hill asked him, in a strong German accent, for directions to the Maritime Museum. Brian answered his question and several others, drinking in the energy from the young man's bright blue eyes. He then walked the final stretch up to Richard's feeling better than he had for weeks.

Once settled in with a cup of tea, Brian immediately mentioned his positive reaction to those brief moments with the young German man. "I'm reminded, Richard, of our appreciation of The Animal. Better yet, back before my siege began, I remember this beautiful Japanese man emerging nude from the cold, invigorating surf. How much I enjoyed that tiniest of encounters. Enough just to stretch out in the sand, absorb the sun, and just let my body respond to his beauty, after we briefly smiled at each other. The quiet joy of that particular afternoon. That moment has lingered, has brought much satisfaction."

"Yes, the Japanese have many words for beauty. 'Shibui,' that's the beauty of aging." When Brian glanced at Richard he seemed to take on the aura of the late Zen master, Suzuki. "They probably have one for this too—the deep appreciation of an 'aesthetic moment.'"

"But is it enough? Little crumbs of pleasure. This year the beaches have been so dull, with no one even trying to have fun, no one looking to trade even these wonderful little moments."

"True enough. We've become an anhedonic society, disdainful of all pleasure. Even the Elizabethans had a Lord of Misrule for their celebrations; we need someone to kick us out of our work-a-day selves."

"But where are those Lords these days? It's got to be someone younger than I to get the ball rolling. Out at the beach someone spray painted on one of the rock outcroppings, 'When having fun is outlawed, only outlaws will have fun.'"

Suddenly rattled, Brian knocked his tea over. He signalled

for Richard to stay put and grabbed some paper towels in the kitchen. "I know I'm getting older, but must I drop my expectations so low? These 'aesthetic moments' don't really amount to much, you know, at least in certain moods. Sometimes they strike me as kind of pathetic."

A rare frown of displeasure gave Richard's face an uncharacteristically hard look and momentarily disturbed Brian. "You're viewing this from the arrogant perspective of the young and the healthy." Richard paused, then started petting Cleo with long, sensual strokes. "After a while, though, when one is older or infirm, one doesn't see these moments that way, as a pathetic substitute for life. They *are* life. They celebrate the Life-Force. I was blind, myself, to this way of seeing things until deep into my own middle age. But then my back worsened and I couldn't even have an erection without experiencing pain. Only then did it hit me that, given our shrinking possibilities as we age, the proper appreciation of 'crumbs,' like your joy in the German and Japanese youths, can, given our circumstances, radically increase our sense of being alive."

"Yes, I remember Edmund near his death. How much gusto he had for small pleasures, like those Tenderloin breakfasts, almost to the end. Or my own mother, how much she loved just to 'people watch' in her final years. I guess it's a question of one's recognizing the possibility of pleasure when it comes along and then not holding back, fully indulging any way we can."

"Crumbs *can* explode into incandescent moments. Watch out, Brian. If several lucky breaks come along at the same time, you might find your capacity for pleasure increasing exponentially."

Brian laughed because it seemed so long since he had had any crumbs at all. A sudden unusual sound broke into his thoughts. "What's the horrible sound, Richard, from the kitchen? Cleo isn't throwing up, is she?"

"Every day for the last week. I keep meaning to call the vet. Are you well enough to drive her over to the Marina? I'm worried."

"Sure. I can be back with my car in fifteen minutes." Brian got up and cleaned up the mess to save the strain on Richard's back.

"One other thing, Brian."

"What's that?"

"All your resolutions. Keep in mind the words of David's wife—she may be wide, but she's also wise. 'No one in the history of the world has ever learned a single thing from experience.' An exaggeration, perhaps, but you'll find as I did that you'll regress many, many times. It's in the genes."

"Sage advice, kind sir. Mine to you—get out your leather gloves so I can pack off Cleo in her cage without our becoming bloody messes. You see we do learn something from experience after all."

33

After hiking south for only a few hundred yards from Limantour Beach, Brian found himself almost alone. Barefoot, he walked briskly on the firm, wet white sand at the water's edge. He had timed his visit with the tides so that he might enter the pristine world of Point Reyes' most beautiful seascape, Sculptured Beach, which he calculated to be about three miles from the nearest car and at least a dozen miles from the closest store back in Inverness Park. Although he was all by himself on the kind of day trip he inevitably associated with Marco and their high times together in the seventies, in recent years he had been able to fight off his old nemesis, nostalgia, to enjoy this place by himself every now and then.

His first inclination, of course, would be to find a companion for such a foray. Because of the necessity of choosing a warm day so as not to be chilled to the bone by the usual gale, it had been many years since he had been able to find a compatible spirit who had the free time to spare a whole day off from his or her inevitably busy schedule. But, even alone during a luscious June heat wave, he found the ritual itself sustaining—the drive through quaint Nicasio, the town clock mooing 10 AM as he stopped for a snack in Pt. Reyes Station, the roller coaster twisting of the road to Limantour, and the long, peaceful trek down the beach.

The beach was warm and satisfying, with just a very slight southerly breeze which heralded the "revenge fog." If precedent held, the fog would sweep its way north up the coast from Big Sur tonight, abruptly terminating this place's highly transitory existence as a tropical paradise. After his long period of hiding away at home, it felt good to be walking briskly, stimulating his underutilized body. Three harbor seals playfully followed him along for most of the way, while scores of brown pelicans skimmed the waves as they headed north to their rocky island sanctuaries just beyond the lighthouse. He invoked the memory of Edmund to enhance his sense of gratitude for being alive, for being able to enjoy his mobility unimpeded by injury or illness. Somehow, although he didn't quite believe it, he was still intact.

There, just ahead, was the first subterranean archway. He ducked through it and entered a cave directly under one of the most beautiful sections of the sculpted cliffs. He breathed in the balmy, sweet air deeply, opening himself joyously to it, absorbing it completely, offering no resistance to its cleansing possibilities. As he moved on, the three harbor seals reappeared and continued along with him until he came upon more of the "sculptures," the organ pipe cliffs which, like the seals, announced his imminent entrance into this nether world of arches and caves which the surf had temporarily abandoned.

He continued to weave through the caves and archways until he came to the "cathedral." It too had remained intact, although, like himself, he mused, it wouldn't take too many more years, too many more violent storms, until its arched entrance would erode away and collapse.

He entered into its main room and, throwing down his pack, sat down in the soft sand, allowing his mind to drift–receptive to nature and the sighing surf. After a few minutes of silence, he sensed the presence of his mother and tears began to flow at the remembered sound of her voice. For the first time he felt some understanding of her "gift," her wish that, because she had suffered so much, life wouldn't be so hard on him. After her death, his constant awareness of his own fear had been very painful, threatening to diminish life's possibilities to a petty despair. But slowly her death, its impact now receding, was beginning to liberate him, allowing him to return to the pleasures of life. Out here he found it easier to believe her and let her single-minded, motherly logic take effect.

As his tears ebbed, he left the cathedral to set up head-quarters at his favorite little sandy beach where a stream ended its journey to the ocean in a quaint, miniature delta. He stripped naked and jumped into the surf, looking around in vain for his three absent pinniped friends. After a few minutes he returned to the beach, content to doze in the sun for a while, but then sat up abruptly at the sound of voices; a young man and woman sauntered by and spread out their blanket about a hundred yards away.

A few minutes later they began frolicking around the shoreline, and then jumped into the surf. Brian, already toasty warm, followed suit. They ignored him, acting as if he were not there, satisfied with and totally absorbed by each other's company.

One doesn't expect any company out here anyway, he cautioned himself, returning to his towel disappointed by their lack of interest in him. But restlessness had set in and he found himself walking south to find solitude once more.

As he meandered down the immense strand, things began to take on a bit more comic perspective. Like his resolutions.

Richard had been right. He figured he had broken every one of them at some point, yet he still maintained some momentum with most of them. He had tied on a couple of mid-day binges, for example, but was, for the most part, helped by Timothy's reinforcement, drinking less. Last week he had gotten slightly sick eating a whole bag of Sun Chips.

As for his sexual reforms, he had waxed horny from time to time and had a couple of non-touching, jerk-yourself-off sessions at the beach, staring at a couple of hot, closeted bisexuals who did likewise. Absolutely mutual, if nothing else. Although he, in the spirit of Richard's aesthetic moment, had allowed himself to enjoy these episodes immensely, a few days later he had felt flat, asexual, and wanted to condemn them as trivial; he was intensely disap-pointed that it had been years since he had met anyone the least bit interested in starting up something full time with him.

As he walked on, he could see taking shape the cove where he used to go with Marco. Eric's recent visit popped into Brian's mind; Eric, a handsome bisexual in his mid-twenties who, after moving back to New Mexico, only had time to pursue a once-a-year affair with him. As busy as anyone else these days, Eric had called him at a moment's notice with only three or four hours to spare for a visit. Brian had hustled him out to a nearby beach where it was usually possible to get off alone. Not so that day. They probably would have done better near the bridge. A large group of picnickers had settled in close by, obnoxiously staring at them necking through the cracks in the rocks behind which they were trying to hide. Even when they lay low on their blanket, they could hear conversations around them, giggles even. Eric had showed signs of discomfort, obviously missing the absolute privacy they had usually shared. Why bother, Brian thought to himself, it's not worth it. And he had moved away from Eric, had given up without pouting. Once a year. Their only chance was blown and he didn't care.

Brian walked as far as he could, all the way to the cove surrounded by the cliffs which prevented anyone from going over to Kelham Beach. Instead of finding abalone shells in the cove as he had usually done with Marco, he stumbled instead on the bloated body of a dead sea lion. Retreating far enough away so he wouldn't pick up the smell of the rotting carcass, he sat down once more, laughing to himself about what had happened next on that day with Eric.

The obnoxious picnickers had departed and he and Eric had settled into some peaceful lovemaking. Suddenly they had heard squeals of laughter to their right. They sat up to see five young girls, all about twelve or thirteen, laughing and pointing at them about seventy-five yards away. "They snuck up behind and were watching us," Eric had deduced. "Look at that!"

One girl had turned around and dropped her panties, twitching her bare bottom about. Another pulled up her sweatshirt to reveal small, perky breasts. The others followed suit. "They must feel guilty for sneaking those peeks," Eric ventured. "I thought I heard giggles behind us. They're paying us back."

Delighted, Eric stood up to reveal himself half-erect, sending the girls into wild shrieks of delight. Brian dug Eric's role as teenage idol, the insolent stud showing off to his fans. Again the giggles. Brian had jumped up to join in. He encouraged Eric to play with himself to please his fans.

"I just wonder where their parents are," cautioned Eric. "Maybe it'd be a good time to go, right now." They packed up, even while the show continued on both sides, both sexes preserving anonymity by holding their respective ground. Eric's fear of a parental reaction struck a chord of morbid humor with Brian–the irony if he were arrested as a heterosexual molester!

They started walking away from the girls who continued to prance about at a safe distance. One last time he and Eric turned around and dropped their pants, playing with themselves to the girls' delighted squeals. "I trust you're enjoying this, Eric."

"One thing's for sure–they'll never forget this afternoon."

Nor will I, thought Brian as he watched Eric, a naughty gleam in his eyes, performing for the girls.

And, as the days had passed by, he had had no trouble evoking that stance of Eric's, knees slightly bent, jerking off, playing the role of heterosexual stud. Too bad that their lovemaking had been cut short, but this image of Eric persisted, enriching his memory. Funny, he mused, how some mighty pleasurable episodes fade into instant oblivion while others, like this one, manage to persist vividly in the mind's eye. Evocativeness–he wondered what Richard would say about that as a concept.

Bemused at the ironies of fate, he began walking back toward his towel, fantasizing about David's son, Chris, whom he had been courting first by E-mail and then by phone. They had exchanged pictures. Chris looked young for his age, with glasses and plenty of curly brown hair. In another picture he looked trim in a pair of briefs by the pool. On the phone his voice had sounded good-natured and he seemed quite likable. Brian had allowed himself some cautious optimism–he loved Chris's enthusiasm about coming to San Francisco, on the brink, as he was, of that archetypal journey from old to new, from heterosexual to homosexual. Chris also liked the ocean, liked to hike, liked classical music—that was all to the good. If nothing else they should become good friends and Brian looked forward to help orienting him in all kinds of ways.

In preparation for Chris's arrival in San Francisco in just two weeks, Brian had been consciously, at All-American Boy Beach, trying to expand his attraction to men roughly his own age. He discovered that somewhat bulging bellies did not turn him off at all; they helped him feel more relaxed about his own imperfections. Roaming the beach, he had approached several middle-aged men. Not a single one gave him eye contact, but when he spoke to them, every one of them became genuinely friendly. He had ventured into sexual play with a couple of the more appealing ones and things had gone okay, although neither had been on his wave length.

Then he hit a snag with a "younger man," a handsome guy in his early forties with long, dark hair and a lean body. They ended up spending most of an afternoon together, exchanging phone numbers after some good talk and very comfortable sex. This man had approached him in a way that made their respective ages seem irrelevant, had made Brian feel ageless. He had even called Brian "charming." Had anyone else ever called him charming?

It turned out, however, that he had been living with the same man for over twenty years. And his life was breath-takingly busy—this was the first time Brian had ever seen him at the beach. Brian hadn't dared call him and, of course, had received no word from him. The damage, however, had been done. Brian had been reminded how fine life might be with such a companion.

The pain of it hit him hard as he continued to the spot where he had left his stuff at the edge of the stream. How much he wanted such a person, how lonely he was out here all by himself. Recovering, however, by recognizing the tell-tale self-pity, he asserted that the point of being out here by himself was that this, too, was life, sad or happy, and that he wasn't about to give it up while he was still physically capable.

Back at his towel, he noticed the couple had gone and the wind had come up. After a short rest, he'd be ready to begin the long trek back to all the comforts of his flat. At least the wind would be at his back.

At Coast Camp, where Marco and he had spent a couple of weekends, he noticed a fox nosing through the garbage cans. Even the fox was required to settle for something less than optimal. Feeling a bit melancholy, he started dreading the long drive back by himself until he remembered that the weekday traffic would be light and he could listen to some more of the opera he had taped from the Met the previous Saturday.

By the time he crossed the Golden Gate Bridge, the fog had already begun rushing through its towers into the Bay. Let it come. He had made his move and captured an exquisite day, thereby renewing his vision, and all by himself, too. Following Doyle Drive into the Marina, he anticipated returning to his flat with pleasure. He had emerged from his little breakdown, entirely comfortable with his own company. Besides, a perfect evening with a perfect companion would follow—Ingrid would see to that.

34

The 'N Touch, Brian's "neighborhood" bar, filled up early on Sunday nights for the strip shows. Brian had let Christopher drag him there because, if necessary, he knew he could slip away and walk home. (At their first meeting, Chris informed him that his San Francisco name would be "Christopher," not Chris.) Already on his second drink, he grumbled to himself about how silly it was to watch these guys strip down to their g-strings in the light of his having been a habitué of nude beaches for more than a couple of decades. Located further north than the other grungy bars, porno palaces and hustler hangouts of Polk Street, The 'N Touch, long and skinny, painted jet black, gleamed with mirrors and strobe lights everywhere. Beyond the long bar, the back area opened up into an appealing dance floor, with tiny tables ensconced at the edges. As usual, somewhat more than half the clientele were youngish Asians who Brian, during other visits, had found cliquish and unfriendly.

Christopher, on the other hand, brazen as always, had pretty much left him alone at their tiny table to dance up a storm with a Filipino named Eugene to whom he had introduced himself. Christopher had blown into town about a week ago sporting an unexpected beard, neatly trimmed to the point of severity. The mop of curly brown hair had been replaced by an ultra-short brush cut. For the first couple of days, Brian had managed to maintain some sexual interest by stressing to himself Christopher's maturity as an educator and an intelligent, sensitive adult. Through sheer will-power he had remained attracted to this slight but well-toned former teacher whose ambition had trapped him, at a higher salary, of course, in a dead-end bureaucratic position in the New York City college system. Recently divorced, he had taken a year's leave without pay, but had told Brian he had no plans to ever go back.

Seemingly open to almost anything sexual, Christopher had agreed to a rendezvous at Brian's place his second evening in town. At the last moment, fidgety and overwrought, he had backed off from anything physical claiming he wasn't in the mood because of a little miscalculation of a dose of meth. Brian no longer cared anyway. Any lingering sense of attraction had diminished at Christopher's disappointing response to Brian's rap about San Francisco's Weirdo Magnet. "You know, Sutro Tower, the city's TV antenna, we call it that because it attracts all of us weirdos." Christopher, however, did not laugh and appeared slightly offended at being so designated. Thereafter it was easier to accept the reality that they were not meant to be.

The blaring of the dance music jarred on Brian's nerves. Valentino, one of the professional strippers on the circuit, gyrated in a totally predictable manner just inches away from him. If anything he preferred the amateurs from places like Gold's Gym who didn't take themselves so seriously.

Despite himself, Brian fixated on Valentino's dancing, pretending he was a director choosing different camera angles by switching his perspective through first one mirror, then another. In doing so (one could see anyone in the entire bar without appearing to look at them) he accidentally caught a glance from Alfie, a guy about his age whom he had met here previously, accompanied by a youngish, seemingly suicidal hustler-addict. He kept himself turned away from Alfie, not wanting to hear about his exploits.

That same evening of their sexual misadventure, Christopher had demanded that Brian sit down, pen in hand, and list the name and location of every possible way to seek out sex in the city. He had tried them all and liked Club Chaos and Fiend, but Bondage à Go Go, a mixed scene specializing in public spanking, had become his favorite. In the ensuing days, as he had energetically tested out Brian's many suggestions, he had become more effeminate in his mannerisms, as if a side of himself too long suppressed had abruptly broken out. Suddenly he was also raving about Liza Minnelli and Barbara Cook. And so Brian had witnessed the fascinating process of watching this distracted, scattered, ditzy air-head come out of the closet, somehow overwhelming the neatnik control-freak with the upturned, little nose who had worn three-piece suits to work in Manhattan.

Once Christopher had his list of sexual venues, he had pretty much ignored Brian to go out constantly on the prowl. Nor was he open to any advice as to how he could best survive such a lifestyle. It had become apparent that Christopher was only interested in getting involved with men at least fifteen years his junior.

"Eugene and I are taking a cab over to Club Uranus. Don't be the usual old fogey. Come along with us." Maybe it was because he didn't have to worry about driving that, against his better judgment, Brian decided to go along for curiosity's sake.

During the taxi ride, he watched Christopher, with those bleary eyes, watery smile and annoyingly thin lips feverishly chattering away with the round-faced, attractive Eugene who, Brian confessed to himself, he wouldn't mind taking home for the night. "Eugene has been telling me about the scene down in LA, about how even the S & M bars are much more intriguing than up here. I think I'm going to check it out soon."

Club Uranus, despite being gussied up with posters of many varieties of posteriors, turned out to be the End-Up. Supposedly it was *the* Sunday night hang-out for the wild, avant-garde crowd. Christopher and Eugene danced to the savagely unmelodic din which thumped continuously and unmercifully. After fifteen minutes of observing, Brian found himself with an acute case of *déjà vu*, cursing "the same old people," some of whom he had seen in the bars a decade ago. Why did he end up here on an evening when everyone acted utterly conventional, standing around in little closed groups, not a single person willing to give out even a tiny "How're you doing, pal?" look of welcome. Even the hired dancers lacked sex appeal and seem too jaded to go through the motions of trying to turn on the crowd.

Once again, as he had in his last visit here with Will, Brian sought out refuge on the patio. From his perch up the stairs on the terrace, however, he could think only about how much he missed Will—and his Beautiful Buns. Looking out at the stonily foreboding freeway underpass softened by the August fog, he decided to leave immediately.

When he found himself near Christopher during a brief interlude from the blare of the music, he was asked for directions to Blow Buddies—and if he wanted to join Eugene and him there. The club was within walking distance so Brian indicated what he thought to be the safest way, ending with a warning to stay alert. "South of Market late at night can be a dangerous place, you guys."

"If I survived New York, there'll be no problem here," Christopher smirked, giving Eugene a conspiratorial wink, emboldened as they were for further exploits.

"The trouble with living for sex and beauty—you always want a little more," Brian countered with his exit line and then waltzed out, leaving them to their own devices. His words backfired, however, haunting him as he left. Had he ever had enough? When was the last time he had approached anything like deep satisfaction in matters sexual?

Out on Harrison Street, waiting for a cab, Brian recalled their recent outing to San Francisco Jacks. (At least Christopher was getting him to check out some of the more "wholesome" possibilities on his list to see if he had dismissed them too quickly from his life.) Once having paid his $10 to the cheerful volunteers and having taken heart from the DON'T BE SHY sign above the box office, his mood had plummeted because, after quickly checking out the crowd, he had seen no one on the ground floor of the long clubhouse who looked at all interesting. Cock rings, mustaches, pierced nipples, huge muscles—not his scene, really. He and Christopher had stripped and traded in their clothes for the inevitable towel and went their separate ways, Brian heading up to the overhanging balcony.

Okay, he figured, here was another chance *not* to be prejudiced against older men. Occasionally tugging at himself, he let men in their sixties, maybe even their seventies, stroke him from time to time. It couldn't hurt, he'd be like them someday, after all, and maybe they'd bring him good luck.

Then Brian saw a black guy sitting comfortably on a big, long couch, jerking himself off. He stood awkwardly nearby, observing, stalling for courage, and then walked by the couch several times before the DON'T BE SHY injunction worked its magic and he squeezed in next to his lone prospect on the couch. The guy pressed his leg against Brian's as a welcome. Probably about forty, he had sensual lips, thick glasses, a smooth massive chest, a solid gut and a fascinating two-toned cock, very dark at the shaft, but dusky pink at the head.

Knowing Christopher would want to hang around forever, Brian postponed his ejaculation as long as possible, delighted that Donald (his partner's name) had figured out how to keep him excited without coming. Many minutes passed before Donald, finally on the brink of his own eruption, released Brian to finish the job on himself. Brian found himself missing the warmth of his touch so much that he moaned, pleadingly, "Oh, man, I'm coming," and Donald, responding to the cue, did reach over to finish the job.

After he had cleaned up and got dressed, Brian had found Christopher busy in a circle jerk. Tapping him on the shoulder, Brian quickly indicated that he'd be waiting for him in the coffee shop across the street. (He had made sure he had brought along a good book for the occasion.) Upon encountering Donald on the way out, the two men thanked each other. Brian imagined that Donald felt as he did, relieved and ahead of the game to get out of there with one good experience.

But that night, as Brian hailed a cab outside the End Up, he thought about a change he had noticed in Christopher's expression when he had said good-bye to him a couple of minutes ago, a change that suggested to Brian he was somehow making peace with his demons. His face had no longer looked so crimped; his attitude no longer suggested he was in a constant, mild fit of pique.

As the cab bounced along, he wondered what time Christopher would end up creeping into Richard's spare room. Richard still meant so much to him—any threat of losing his friendship terrified Brian. Just two nights ago, knowing Christopher was out, he had panicked, thinking Richard might have fainted or fallen when all he could get was a busy signal the entire evening. Finally, he had let himself in late that night to discover that Richard was fine and the phone was simply out of order.

The cab careened down Taylor Street and then up Union Street towards his house. Brian recalled how little he had seen of Liz recently. Just two days ago her nephew, Jeremy, had finally arrived, determined, according to his aunt, to patch things up with a former boyfriend who had moved to San Francisco from Philadelphia. She seemed annoyed by him, referring to him as a kind of black sheep, mentioning that he had arrived so introverted and depressed as to be a drag to be around. Brian had only caught a quick glimpse of him, a lanky, pale-faced man in his thirties.

He paid the cabbie and climbed the stairs to his place, deciding, once inside, to indulge himself in a nightcap. As he lay on his bed listening to Mozart, managing to convince himself that he didn't want to be out there in the night with Christopher, he remembered an incident at his college a few days previously. One of his good friends from high school, whom he had not seen in many years, had been scheduled to give a guest lecture. This friend had taken a prestigious job as the chief editor of a research project at UCLA. Brian had decided to make a rare visit to school during this "wasted" sabbatical to check him out. Outside in the corridor he had seen a white-haired, corpulent man in a dark suit whom he had not, at first, even recognized. But once seated inside he had made the connection.

His old friend's body language defined the repression that had become his life. Brian had received what he needed from the occasion even before his friend had opened his mouth. But then, as a bonus, he had discovered that his friend's hearty, All-American boy voice of his adolescent years, so eager to laugh at any of Brian's antics, had been replaced by a tinny whine, a voice Brian remembered as being one and the same as his friend's father's. And Brian had once harbored such a strong crush for his tall, handsome classmate!

As Brian turned on his side to sleep, he figured that at least he had battled his repression, at least he still had a life with a physical side, and he could still look forward to his next trip to the beach.

35

A few weeks later, Brian returned to school following his sabbatical with a regular passenger, Liz's nephew, Jeremy. On sunny days they had taken to stopping off, on the way back, at All-American Boy Beach. It was one of Brian's favorite kind of days; a late breaking fog had left them almost alone on a warm but slightly breezy afternoon.

Something had changed for the better in Jeremy after his rocky start a couple of months ago, especially with Liz, and Brian had been enjoying his company at films and concerts. But, at least for Brian, the beach was the acid test of compatibility.

Things had started famously today with the lanky, almost ungainly Jeremy overcoming his shyness and immediately taking off his shorts. Just as he did so, a most attractive heterosexual couple, both very blond, perhaps European tourists in their middle twenties or so, established themselves about fifty feet to their left. Jeremy was carelessly sprawled on his back, his body no longer pasty white; he drank in the newcomers, his deep-set brown eyes wide with appreciation. Brian, sensing a twitch between his legs, searched for the right words to enhance the situation without making them both overly self-conscious.

"So I like to think anything's possible out here, especially with the help of that Greek poet, Anonymous, and other willing folks." Brian gave a quick nod towards the couple. "I mean, it can be a kind of theater out here, a quiet rave, with erotic waves rippling though everyone, each one finding a comfortable place within himself, each one finding a situation which allows for some kind of abandon."

"Yes, I see what you mean. You just let the energy keep building." Jeremy, evidently understanding fully, put on his prescription Ray-bans and checked things out a bit more, allowing himself to become aroused.

The blond guy was also letting himself get hard as he applied sunscreen to his girlfriend. "The ambiguity saves everyone. That guy over there can think what he wants, that we're attracted to his girlfriend—or to him—or each other—or maybe he can get off by showing off."

After that promising start, however, the sensual tension of the afternoon slowly waned. Soon both the man and woman were napping and Jeremy went off for a walk. Brian took a quick dip and stretched out in the soft, white sand, relaxing until he was in a light trance.

Certainly things had improved for the better since Jeremy had first arrived. He had been thrown off at first by Jeremy's complete inability to get along with Liz, who struck Brian as constantly being miffed at him, often describing him as hostile, even truculent. Because of his fierce loyalty to Liz and the credibility she had earned for her shrewd estimates of people, and because Brian had reached the point of being fed up with emotionally immature men—Jeremy, after all, was pushing on towards thirty-five—Brian had more or less written him off. Then, too, Jeremy was supposedly unavailable, pursuing an old heart throb.

Finally there was the issue of a certain generation gap. The ungainly Jeremy had arrived with his head completely shaved. Liz had mentioned that Jeremy had scars where rings used to be—nose, ear, nipple—but that in recent years he had become disillusioned with that particular sub-culture, having had some kind of nervous breakdown in New York. He had fled to Liz's parents, his grandparents, in Philadelphia to recover, but had remained introverted.

Brian had noticed him sitting on Liz's deck several times, his bony knees protruding from his shorts. He was taciturn to those around him, often slouching or cringing in a way that drew attention to some minor scars from teenage zits. When Brian tried to sustain a conversation with him, Jeremy would mutter a response so low that he had to ask him to repeat himself. He would express himself, however, in a very individualized way.

There were no easy agreements, as Jeremy always insisted on projecting his own take on things. Brian had learned quickly never to try to fill in one of those long pauses—he *never* could guess what Jeremy would say next. Yet, despite the guy's torpor, the droopy, half-lost look about him, Brian sensed something pent up, something smoldering, which might erupt into a disturbing rampage.

The day it all started to change began ominously with Brian hearing water running somewhere. He checked everywhere he could think of, upstairs and down, but no taps were turned on. But because his water meter was rotating frantically at an alarming pace, he shut the water completely off. It had to be an outside leak. He called the water department who told him that since it was on his property it was his responsibility and that, with so much water pouring out, it had to be surfacing somewhere. Resigned to spending hundreds of dollars on a union plumber, Brian called the same one he had used last year when he had had trouble with Liz's toilet. No answer—only a message that he was on vacation for two more weeks.

At that point Jeremy entered. Jeremy was calm, curious about Brain's plight, wanting to be helpful. "I bet I can find it. I did a lot of work on my grandparents' place in Philadelphia to make up for not paying much rent." Jeremy's eyes seemed bloodshot, but Brian had to admit that with his goatee shaved off and his hair growing back, his jaw struck him as more prominent, somehow stronger, more attractive. "Show me where the main line comes in. I bet it's connected with the pipe to the outdoor faucet, back near your garden. It slopes enough there so that, especially with gopher holes, the water might run off without ever surfacing." After Brian had detailed how things were set up, Jeremy had set off by himself to investigate.

After a few minutes, Jeremy had found the leak only about fifteen feet in front of that outside faucet. Relieved, Brian had thanked him profusely. Jeremy had smiled, a rare occasion, and what a revelation it had been. Brian liked the fact that Jeremy usually didn't smile very much—neither did he. Neither of them had Timothy's social charm, but when Jeremy did smile, it was worth the wait.

From that point on, Jeremy had found many other ways to be useful, and feeling useful seemed to help him emerge from his shell. On successive days, when Brian had to be at school for meetings, he had made Brian's life much easier by patiently waiting around for new computer equipment to be delivered and for the cablevision company to come in and finish some much needed upgrading. Best of all, Brian had hired him to help stem the chaos of his home by making more bookcases and racks where he could store his hundreds of tapes and CD's. That whole prospect had resulted in Brian's feeling much more upbeat about returning to school after his sabbatical-from-hell.

But the interchange between Jeremy and him had remained severely limited. Most of the time they met at awkward dinners with Liz and Lynn. On one such occasion he had discovered that Jeremy was no longer seeing his old boyfriend who had apparently changed from political activist to Montgomery Street businessman. Liz, who herself worked in the financial district, would sometimes lightly taunt her nephew about that irony. Brian figured that, with Lynn's pregnancy and Liz having to assume the responsibility as the breadwinner for both of them for a while, she probably had some resentment towards her confused but still unattached nephew. Did she resent his spending more and more comfortable time with her old pal, Brian? He had also wondered whether she was at all jealous of the strong bond Jeremy had forged with her own parents, although he knew she would never admit to such a charge.

If Jeremy had been wary, even jumpy around Liz and Lynn up until about a month ago, at least he had gravitated upstairs to Brian more often. Not yet ready to venture out into a nightlife of his own, he had accepted Brian's suggestions to attend various films and concerts. He had a strong inclination toward satire and a lively sense of the ludicrous. It had been he who had encouraged them to attend more live performances in small, neighborhood theaters.

But mostly Jeremy had just hung around, often reading out on Brian's deck. Brian had began worrying that Jeremy was exhibiting too much reliance on him, at least as far as his social life was concerned, so he had become suspicious and had pulled back emotionally to keep a safe distance away.

They had reached a more comfortable place together, however, the morning Jeremy had shown up with a gift, a Chinese clock Brian had admired when in North Beach Hardware. Jeremy had used that occasion to announce he had managed to get accepted at the last minute at Brian's college. "I wasn't capable of work or school when I first arrived here, but at least I learned there's a big difference between having free time and having fun. You know what I mean. Before you and I started going out together, I felt trapped in my own mind–all those books and films. I had become an energetic but voyeuristic intellectual. I was never living in my body."

"You and everyone else in the nineties," Brian had replied. But Jeremy's words had impressed Brian whose appreciation of first his kindness and then his ideas began transforming him in Brian's eyes from a seedy, self-destructive punk to an attractive, mature man.

Meanwhile, after talking through his own re-entry fears with Richard, who, as usual, was most eager to help Brian avoid repeating past errors, Brian had returned to school determined to enjoy the whole process, keeping the intellectual freshness of his new course alive by remembering to enjoy his fascinating students. No longer would he press to reach some intellectual standard about which neither he nor his students cared a whit.

Jeremy apparently sensed something childlike in Brian's strong need to develop a rapport beyond the verbal. He began to relax with him at the beach, at first clinging to him a bit too closely, but then like today, encouraging Brian to go off on his meandering and doing the same himself.

Brian sat up. The blonde couple was still dozing, but they were now ensconced in each other's arms. To his right he could see Jeremy striding back towards him. What a cute guy, thought Brian. So lanky, yet so solid, with that slim, slightly hairy chest; I bet he has no idea how beautiful he is. Almost hard, too. He was surprised Jeremy wasn't being followed by a long line of admirers. But just as Jeremy had settled back in, a solitary beautiful youth in his early twenties, no doubt attracted to the spot by Jeremy, spread his towel just to their right.

Brian and Jeremy shared a long drink of juice, then stretched out, basking in the sun, Brian joining Jeremy in first quivering, then stiffening. Here we are, thought Brian. I think this is cool, Jeremy thinks it's cool, that kid over there's starting to get hard and the blond European's kissing his girlfriend. "Feeling okay?" He felt compelled to check in with Jeremy.

"Just great!"

"Well, I see nothing wrong in getting hard while keeping a discreet distance. The last thing I want to do is intrude." The words were true, in general, but Brian knew he could still break his resolution and regress, make an anonymous ass out of himself. "Of course one is expected to do one's share when one cruises," he went on. "I mean, don't be overly aggressive in situations where the odds are astronomically against you—that's one of the lessons of aging gracefully. One is happy just to be able to take it all in."

"It's awesome." Jeremy sat straight up, unusually enthusiastic. "I see a guy, get hard, he gets hard, we look at each other. I'm so in the moment, so right here that I'd be overwhelmed if he wanted sex. I couldn't do any more than this—at least not yet."

Pangs of affection swept over Brian at this evidence of Jeremy's fragility. "You will," he reassured him. "Just keep the frame of mind you're in right now. I used to think there was something pathetic about this sort of thing, but discussing it with Richard changed all that. Oceanic sex. The ripplings of sexual energy on a beach where everyone feels it's okay to play. Some people would think that getting hard—look, Ma, no hands—and just allowing a total turn-on wasn't much of a sexual act, was just a crumb. But for someone in his fifties it's reassuring that this kind of unpredictable excitement remains available as long as I can get down—and up—that cliff behind us. Coming out here and staying hard for an hour ain't exactly torture."

"I love your attitude." Jeremy flicked off his Ray-bans, ready for a dip. "It's a bit scary what you do, but it's so fine. The seized moment! We need more exhibitionists, more of us willing to cavort and gambol out here."

"Yes, one must act, perform even. Passive spectators need not apply." Brian rose, energized.

"We must throw off the yoke of non-sexual pretense!" Jeremy called out, taking on a revolutionary air as he started a dash for the water.

"While still maintaining proper beach etiquette," Brian reminded himself as he followed Jeremy into the ocean less energetically. As they splashed into the frigid water, both the European couple and the gorgeous young man followed their lead. The lazy surf occasionally concealed their hard-ons, but the spirit of communion persisted for the rest of the October afternoon.

36

"I told you you'd like him." Stacy sipped her margarita, raising her eyebrows as her tongue plowed a path through the salt on the rim of her glass. "I told you that you guys would get along fabulously, didn't I, Mom?"

Liz sat next to Lynn on their couch downstairs, momentarily at a loss for words. Brian observed her as she looked first at Lynn, then across to Jeremy and himself. "Yes, you did, my sweet."

"If I'm not mistaken," Brian hastened into the conversation to avoid its taking an awkward turn, "you two ladies are still neck and neck with your own bet about whose relationship will last longer. Liz and Lynn living in Albany, anticipating a blessed event, and Stacy and Shauna setting up house in Noe Valley." Brian gave out an exaggerated, wistful sigh. "It's strictly 'til death do us part with you lesbians. You're all so good at relationships."

"Well, I must say," rejoined Liz, "that I never thought my nephew would ever take such a domestic turn himself. His living in my old place here—it takes some getting used to, especially with some of my old stuff still around. I loved this place, Brian. I envy him every time I have to get on BART to commute to work." And then, turning directly to her nephew, she assumed that parental tone Brian knew would annoy Jeremy. "So fortunate for you that Brian took you in, the way my parents did."

"I'm the caretaker here, don't forget," Jeremy asserted. "I have to keep Brian's place clean, fix up stuff, garden, even cook sometimes."

"I'm the one who benefits," Brian jumped in again. "He gets a break on his rent so he can work part time and keep going to school and I get relieved of a lot of headaches." Liz's strong ambivalence about leaving the single life for a second round of parenting seemed to surface in her resentment towards Jeremy.

Lynn, who had remained quiet, shifted a bit nervously on the couch, then checked her watch. "Well, kids, we should be off. It takes about twenty minutes to walk to the Gateway—I'm dying to check out that lesbian romance." Two months pregnant, radiating health and enthusiasm, she had seemingly lost that slightly sour quality which had always put Brian off.

"And I've got to meet Shauna for dinner down at that Italian place on Columbus." Stacy rose, too. "The only dyke-owned business in this whole God-forsaken part of town."

It was fall, the season of warm Bay Area days and nights. Brian had begun following Jeremy's lead, wearing shorts more often.

The knocker. It was Timothy. Brian introduced him to the departing women, then sat him down with a cocktail next to Jeremy. "Jeremy will have our dinner ready soon, if you want to stay. Thai food."

Jeremy decided to check on things in the kitchen, still a bit peeved by Liz's remarks.

"Thanks for the invite, but I wouldn't think of intruding." Timothy still teased Brian, but no longer with that competitive undercurrent.

"It's not like that and you know it—except I'm not exactly sure what, if anything, it *is* like. So far at least we're very good company for one another, keeping ourselves out of trouble."

"I'm hanging in there, too. Say, what did you do to your leg?" He was genuinely concerned about the minor bruise.

"Up in my place this morning—I knocked my shin into the coffee table, for about the five-hundredth time. I hate doing it, hate that feeling, but I'm a klutz and some things never change."

Reaching out for some chips and dip, Timothy leaned into a particularly well-illuminated area of the living room. To his surprise, Brian saw a good deal of gray hair which, from this perspective, shone brightly amidst his very short but very dark brush-cut. "I just want to tell you how happy I am for you, whatever situation you're in." Timothy hesitated and then smiled warmly. "You may be interested to know that in a curious way, I used to find you a little intimidating, the honest way you lay everything out on the table all the time. I'm so glad we've made it through everything."

Jeremy rejoined them and the three men chatted over their cocktails for another half hour until Timothy had to leave. Then Brian heard his phone and bolted upstairs. It was Richard calling to check in with them on their plans for the week. Another new development. Jeremy was going to help Richard with cleaning and shopping so that the younger man could continue going to school without having to deal with the stress of his part-time job in the financial district.

Brian decided to relax in his place a bit longer while Jeremy finished preparing dinner. Inevitably his mind took him back to that day a week ago when, following a lead from Liz, he had called and then visited a recluse named Mark in the neighborhood who had, with great patience, induced the parrots to feed from his hand. When he and Jeremy had arrived to witness the daily 4 PM feeding, who should they discover feasting on the parrot leftovers but the long lost Dante!

"The flock had rejected him," the bearded Mark had explained. "I knew he'd never make it through the winter on his own so I adopted him. He hangs around here all day. You can take him if you want–I'm busy enough as it is, nursing a couple of wounded parrots and trying to bring up three of this year's babies who also couldn't have made it on their own." Dante was as friendly as ever with Brian, but considering Ingrid's likely interest in him as a snack and Dante's obvious happiness with Mark, he respectfully declined.

And then, later that night, he and Jeremy had made love up in his place. So far it hadn't happened again and neither of them had mentioned it. Surely Jeremy knew Brian was interested in pursuing it further, so it was just a case of waiting to see what developed. They had had, from Brian's perspective, a fine time together. Brian had fallen back into lovemaking as if he hadn't gone these many months since the good times with Will. Both of them had responded hungrily to each other's touch in a sweet tangle of arms and legs. They had kissed, tenderly at first, then long and hard. At that moment, Brian had realized that kissing had been one of the things most lacking in his life.

Nor had they fallen right off to sleep. Instead, clasped in each other's arms, they had talked, Jeremy revealing some of the blackest moments of his breakdown, Brian recounting his own dark period during the first months of his sabbatical. Only after the first faint light of dawn had managed to filter through the gray overcast had they finally drifted off.

Back in his own private world the next morning, Brian had deliberately dosed himself with an extra cup of coffee to help will himself back into his everyday world.   Maybe Christopher's mother was right and people never learned anything from experience, but *he* wasn't going to make the mistake of developing even the tiniest expectation about this relationship.

A visit during the week to All-American Boy Beach had pretty much squelched the fear that a night of lovemaking might ruin their friendship. On the dunes, in sight of that breathtaking bridge, Jeremy continued to celebrate the significance of the "seized moment."

And so the good times there continued. Sometimes nothing much would happen, sometimes their sense of heightened eroticism would suddenly cut off—and they both would know it and settle in instead for quiet, satisfying talks. "Thanks to your inspiration," Jeremy had told Brian one afternoon, "I want to get back to painting, to writing, maybe even directing films." At such times Brian would begin to fall in love with him, but then he'd catch himself and just try to enjoy the day.

Tonight, with the guests gone and Jeremy in the kitchen, Brian found himself haunted once again by the fragility of their bond. Here was no dramatic victory for his middle-aged ego. They had entered a strange nether-land of a beautiful but precarious friendship. Funny, Brian could deal with the seeming hopelessness of their ever becoming lovers, could even adjust to the idea of Jeremy's bringing in a lover to live downstairs with him, but he could hardly bear to think of an end to their adventures at the beach. He guessed that his life needed those spontaneous moments of brightness, those crumbs which at times seemed nourishing enough to help one get by in reasonably good shape.

During the bleak times, besides missing Will, Brian had unexpectedly yearned for his camaraderie with Daniel, their easy physicality of sharing hot tub and bed. He knew, however, that Daniel had never been deeply attracted to him, and that had taken something away from their friendship—or more to the point, the ambiguity of Jeremy's possible attraction to him definitely added something he did not want to lose.

And he must not forget the convenience of their arrangement. First, he totally trusted Jeremy in all things financial. He could also count on him as a dependable house-sitter for Ingrid and his plants. So timid about travelling alone, he would continue to plug away at it, possibly avoiding freak-outs by resorting to more and more comforts, more pre-planned hosts and itineraries. Maybe he'd even check out tours and cruises when he got older. Already, though, he had asked Jeremy about accompanying him on a forthcoming trip. Jeremy had held out only a vague promise of someday becoming such a companion.

The aroma of another fine Asian dinner wafted up from the kitchen below as the chef zipped up the stairs to rejoin Brian. "Just another ten minutes or so. Grilled salmon, Thai-style. I just need to let the sauce simmer for a moment." He plopped himself next to Brian on the couch, formerly Edmund's, so that their bodies almost touched. Touch—still such a problem for them. When to express it. How to express it. If he let Jeremy initiate, we can avoid any problems with it, thought Brian. But what about Jeremy's chronic passivity? Maybe sometimes he wanted to make a move, but just couldn't.

Away from his steamy kitchen, Jeremy wiped the perspiration from his forehead with the back of his hand. His hair had grown long enough so that he had to brush it out of his eyes occasionally. Such an endearing gesture, thought Brian, who impetuously leaned over and flipped up the offending brunette locks. "You have such lovely hair," he ventured, censoring an impulse to tell him how fine it had smelled that night a week ago.

"*Your* hair flops much more than mine—you have so much more of it than I do," and Jeremy reached over to riffle Brian's own dirty-blond mop.

"Yes, but it's getting gray." Why, why did he feel compelled to say that?

"So what? I like you because you're so willing to be so un-gray, so—I don't know—so naughty."

"And you, you're so, well, so mature," Brian joked, except it wasn't really a joke. "Let's have a toast—to naughty maturity and to mature naughtiness." He raised his glass and Jeremy followed suit, clanking his hard against Brian's.

"Let's have dinner. You're going to love it." His voice was bright. He jumped up and was off to the kitchen.

It seemed it might be an excellent evening for after-dinner naughtiness.

TO ORDER OTHER BOOKS
BY THE AUTHOR

CASEY: THE BI-COASTAL KID   US $ 10.00   _____

"Libidinous pubescents!" "A tasty tidbit of a
novel." "An outrageously wild, raunchy, rowdy
romp of an adolescence."

ISBN 0-941362-01-9

JACK AND JIM   US $ 10.00   _____

*A unique and intense experiment which offers
strength, imagination, self-questioning, and
support to others.*

– Charles A. Reich, Author of
The Greening of America

ISBN 0-941362-00-0

ADD $2.50 FOR EACH BOOK FOR SHIPPING/HANDLING   _____
(US Only)

TOTAL   _____

Send check or money order to:

Equanimity Press
P.O. Box 839
Bolinas, CA 94924

Ship book(s) to:

_____

_____

_____

OTHER GLB FICTION

The Bunny Book   US $11.95   _____
Novel by **John D'Hondt**

A Classic of literature that deals with AIDS...
                                        – Robert Glück

Snapshots For A Serial Killer   US $10.95   _____
Fiction and Play by **Robert Peters**

Beautiful, layered, taut, weird, surprising...
                                        – Dennis Cooper

Zapped: Two Novellas   US $11.95   _____
Two Novellas by **Robert Peters**

Comic book gestalt, as featured in *Atom Mind*.

The Devil In Men's Dreams   US $11.95   _____
Short Stories by **Tom Scott**

Sentiments from ironic humor to painful remorse...
                                     – Lambda Book Report

White Sambo   US $12.95   _____
Novel in stories by **Robert Burdette Sweet**

Powerful and touching vision of gay life...
                                        – Shelby Steele

ADD $2.50 PER BOOK FOR SHIPPING/HANDLING (US)   _____

Check or money order to: **TOTAL**

GLB PUBLISHERS
P.O. Box 78212, San Francisco, CA 94107

Mail to: _____

_____

_____

GAY MEN'S POETRY FROM
GLB PUBLISHERS

A BREVIARY OF TORMENT
Poems by **Thomas Cashet**   US $ 13.95   _____

Erudite, witty and mordant, fascinating in its repulsiveness and ever-so-delicate in its graphic excess.
— Felice Picano

GOOD NIGHT, PAUL
Poems by **Robert Peters**   US $ 8.95   _____

This is some of Peters' most personal and revealing work, and belongs in the library of every poet.
— Dumars Reviews

KINGS AND BEGGARS
Poems by **Paul Genega**   US $ 9.95   _____

Paul Genega is rapidly distinguishing himself as a major voice in contemporary American poetry.
— William Packard

THE WEIGH-IN
Collected Poems of **Winthrop Smith**   US $ 12.95   _____

There is an ecstasy here, and an incantatory voice, wonderully erotic in the way they explore the many locales of male sexual migrations.
— The James White Review

ADD $2.50 FOR EACH BOOK FOR SHIPPING/HANDLING   _____
(US Only)

Send Check or Money Order to: TOTAL   _____

GLB PUBLISHERS
P.O. Box 78212, San Francisco, CA 94107

Mail to:

_____

_____

_____